The Marquess Takes a Misstep

IMPROPER LORDS
BOOK TWO

BY MAGGI ANDERSEN

Dragonblade Publishing, Inc. is an imprint of Kathryn Le Veque Novels, Inc.
P.O. Box 23
Moreno Valley, CA 92556
ceo@dragonbladepublishing.com

Produced in the United States of America

First Edition July 2023
Print Edition

ARE YOU SIGNED UP FOR DRAGONBLADE'S BLOG?

You'll get the latest news and information on exclusive giveaways, exclusive excerpts, coming releases, sales, free books, cover reveals and more.

Check out our complete list of authors, too!

No spam, no junk. That's a promise!

Sign Up Here

www.dragonbladepublishing.com

Dearest Reader;

Thank you for your support of a small press. At Dragonblade Publishing, we strive to bring you the highest quality Historical Romance from some of the best authors in the business. Without your support, there is no 'us', so we sincerely hope you adore these stories and find some new favorite authors along the way.

Happy Reading!

CEO, Dragonblade Publishing

Also from Maggi Andersen

The Marquess Meets His Match

Beth

White Lady Lost

Bright star, would I were stedfast as thou art—
    Not in lone splendour hung aloft the night
    And watching, with eternal lids apart,
    Like nature's patient, sleepless Eremite,
    The moving waters at their priestlike task
Of pure ablution round earth's human shores,
    Or gazing on the new soft-fallen mask
Of snow upon the mountains and the moors—
    No—yet still stedfast, still unchangeable,
    Pillow'd upon my fair love's ripening breast,
    To feel for ever its soft fall and swell,
    Awake for ever in a sweet unrest,
    Still, still to hear her tender-taken breath,
    And so live ever—or else swoon to death.
            Bright Star by John Keats

Prologue

Mrs. Grey's salon in Mayfair, London March, 1817

ON A GILT-LEGGED chair upholstered in satin, Viscount Hartley Montford crossed his arms and stretched out his long legs. Then, with a glance of apology at the elegant lady seated beside him, he settled them into a neater but less comfortable position.

Lady Florence Ainsworth turned her graceful head and raised slender dark eyebrows, which always spoke volumes.

He resisted a defensive shrug. A damnably unsuitable chair for a man of his size and build. It creaked when he moved.

Standing before the audience in the stuffy, overly-perfumed salon, a jeweled hand resting on the pianola, Mrs. Garvey, the famous pigeon-breasted coloratura soprano, was in the throes of a dying aria. Hart could only hope that the end wouldn't be long in coming.

Thankfully, she soon finished with an appropriate flourish to wild clapping around the salon and cries for an encore.

The guests rose and moved toward the supper room.

Hart and Florence stood, and he waited as she gathered her shawl, fan, and reticule.

"Ready to leave?" he asked, eyeing the door which represented their means of escape.

"In the midst of her performance? Mrs. Garvey is to sing again,

Montford." Her gray eyes narrowed. "Surely you won't leave before she has finished her repertoire?"

Hart doubted Mrs. Garvey would miss him in this enthusiastic crowd. He could think of an entirely better way to spend an afternoon. "I intend to do just that. May I escort you home?"

The sensual look in her eyes spoke of possible pleasures awaiting them. "Certainly. After the performance. I have ordered champagne chilled for our return."

The offer of champagne seemed a metaphor for something even more delicious, but Hart was annoyed. Florence was well aware of his distaste for sopranos. He had accepted her invitation, believing it to be the celebrated violin virtuoso, Niccolò Paganini, who it now appeared had not come to London. Something of which Florence failed to advise him. The widow of a much older man who gratified her every whim, she expected the same from Hart. That didn't bother him until now when a battle of wills rose between them. If he agreed and endured another long-winded dose of Mrs. Garvey, he could enjoy Florence with all her flawless beauty. Tempting as that was, he disliked being treated like one of her lap dogs.

"Forgive me." He held her hand in its soft glove and pressed a kiss on the back of it.

She pursed her lips and turned away from him.

Hart headed for his hostess, Mrs. Grey, to apologize. As he left, he imagined another visit to the widow's charming bedchamber would probably not be in the cards. Donning his evening cape and taking up hat, gloves, and cane, he was surprised at how quickly he'd recovered from the disappointment.

When he reached his lodgings, his valet, Leonard, handed him a letter from his father's address, which lacked the marquess's seal.

Hart sat down at his desk and slit the paper with the letter opener. His father's secretary wrote that the doctor attending him advised the marquess was failing.

"Dear God!" Hart had thought it was rheumatism. He did not know things were this serious. He pushed back his chair and called for Leonard, who brewed coffee in the small kitchen.

His valet popped his head through the door. "My lord?"

"Pack a portmanteau, Leonard. I must go immediately to Pembury. My father is ill."

"I am deeply sorry to hear it. Shall I accompany you?" Leonard adopted a hopeful expression which reminded Hart of Rasputin, one of his favorite hounds, sitting at his feet as he dined on steak.

"No. I don't imagine my stay will be of long duration. If I need you, I'll send for you."

"Very well, my lord."

In the late afternoon, Hart drove his curricle out of London into the clean fresh air of the Kentish countryside. While he had loved his mother dearly before she'd passed away, his childhood home held little attraction for him. He and his father did not get on, and rheumatism had not improved his disposition. They argued about Hart's preferred lifestyle, which his parent saw as dissolute, having apparently forgotten his past mistresses while Hart's mother was alive. His father had been a bully. Hart, as a young boy, had tried to protect his mother from him and often got a beating for his pains. Once he settled down, he intended to remain faithful to his wife. Which was why he'd decided not to marry until he was ready.

Hart's reluctance to spend more time at the estate he would one day inherit had been a source of resentment between him and the marquess. *One day?* Hart realized with a chill that day could be near. His dislike of his father no longer seemed to matter. He suffered a heavy dose of guilt at failing to appease him, and it appeared it might be too late. Hart hoped he'd have time to reassure him the estate was in safe hands so he could peacefully go to meet his maker.

Chapter One

Pembury, Near Tunbridge Wells, April

HARTLEY MONTFORD, MARQUESS of Pembury, and the other five pallbearers carried his father's coffin into the dank smelling family vault.

The depth of his loss surprised Hart. He'd thought he had time to right the ship and do what his father demanded of him. He wasn't even sure his father heard Hart's heartfelt promises before he died.

Seated by the library fire in the evening after the mourners departed, he thought back over the day. His steward, Albert Carver, had commented on the impressive array of dishes ladies in the area had brought. Kind of 'em, but Hart expected to be awash with invitations to dinners and dances, and urged to meet the ladies' daughters. If only he could return to London immediately, but that was not to be.

Hart removed a book from the shelf to distract himself and opened a page of Omar Khayyam's poetry and read.

The moving finger writes; and having writ,
Moves on: nor all thy Piety nor Wit
Shall lure it back to cancel half a Line,
Nor all thy Tears wash out a Word of it.

Hart snapped the book shut at the sad truth of the words. He swallowed the last of the whiskey in his glass. It left a sour taste. His father's dissatisfaction with him seemed to linger in the library as if he still sat in his favorite chair.

He and his father had never been close, although he'd tried to be a dutiful son, coming down to see him whenever he was called upon. But that was not enough to satisfy his father. Hart had tried to live with him and take over the reins. But his father, a stubborn man, was not prepared to relinquish them, which resulted in arguments and a tense atmosphere that caused Hart to escape back to his life in London. But why hadn't he noted the signs of neglect when last here? The home farm in need of restocking, fences down, hedges out of control for want of cropping, land lying fallow not yet sown with spring crops. For whatever reason, his father failed to offer an explanation.

Hart was determined to restore the estate by learning the true state of affairs in the morning when he consulted the estate manager. It appeared he would need to extend his stay here for several weeks. He yawned. He'd retire early with a book with no ladies available to warm his bed. Society in the country was stultifying.

The following morning, his estate manager, Ted Hewes, shared his gloomy view of the estate's rundown condition. "It has worried me, my lord. I broached it with your father, but his hopes rested on a shipment from the East. It disturbed him a great deal when the sea claimed it. Lloyd's have been quibbling over the insurance ever since. It will take a considerable amount of money to fix the problems here."

"Then I must find it somewhere," Hart said. He wouldn't become a penny-pincher like his father, but he must be more judicious. He would write to the bank and inquire if any monies were readily available. If so, the money would only stretch so far.

Carter added to the grim news. "There are many unpaid accounts and taxes, which won't wait," the steward said. "Your father sold a few paintings to pay the most pressing of them. The stables are all but empty now, the horses sold at Tattersalls. That pair of Ming vases from the dining room fetched a good price at auction. However, there's not much left you might easily turn into cash. I'd advised him to sell one of his other properties, but he refused. Said he wanted to keep them for you."

"My father said that?" Hart stared at the man, as surprise, despair, and a sense of shame rocked him. Why had he not seen this side of his father? He was a stiff, unbending man, but still he had cared.

The news which came in the post from Hart's banker was of great concern. With the investment in imported silk carpets and goods robbed by pirates who left the ship lying at the bottom of the sea, the coffers were alarmingly low. Enough to run a skeleton staff for a few years, perhaps, while the neglect of the estate continued unchecked. Their biggest investment, a colliery in Newcastle-on-Tyne, could take years to sell. There appeared only one thing to do, and that was to sell the estate. But Hart found this incredibly difficult to accept. Not only would his father bitterly disapprove, as Hart rode over the acres, visiting all those places he knew as a boy, he realized his home was of great importance to his soul. "A man's land is as vital as the blood flowing through his veins," his father had been fond of saying. And it appeared to be true in his own case. Hart wasn't ready to give it up just yet. But how could he hold on to it?

And then a week later, like a bolt out of the blue, Hart received sad news. His Uncle William, his father's brother, had passed away. As his uncle had never married, Hart was the beneficiary of his will. It appeared as if The Lord took a hand on Hart's behalf, despite him hardly deserving it.

A sennight later, he entered his uncle's drawing room in Canterbury along with a few hopeful relatives and staff for the reading of the will. An hour later, he left it, shattered. Had his Uncle William, the Montford second son who grew up at Pembury, been in cahoots with his father? Uncle William had stipulated in his will Hart was to cease his rakish lifestyle and restore his inheritance. He must be seen to have dealt with his obligations, settled down and married, or the inheritance would go to a cousin on his aunt's side of the family.

"Is this condition enforceable?" Hart demanded of his solicitor.

"As there's no entail, your uncle could leave his money to anyone he chose. If it is not to you, to Mr. Frompton, your cousin."

"Frompton! That pious cretin!" Hart expostulated.

"Surely, my lord, a man cannot be both." Mr. Spilsby coughed. "Either pious or er…the other."

"He's a fraud," Hart raged. "He slithered around my uncle like a snake, advising him. It is my bet he listens at the door." Hart turned. "I hope your ears are burning, Willard. I have your measure."

They heard a faint sound of footsteps retreating down the corridor.

"There, I told you," Hart said, folding his arms.

"It won't do a bit of good whatever Mr. Frompton's character might be like. He will inherit if you have not done as requested in your uncle's will by the end of the year." He handed Hart his uncle's letter.

With a deep breath, Hart read the spidery writing. *My dear nephew, I took this action after advice from my friend, the Marquess of Lyle, who has applied the same strictures to his son. Lyle doesn't seem too fond of his heir, Phillip Ormond, but rest assured, I have always had a deep affection for you, and feel that this is for the best.*

Hart turned to the solicitor. "Who decides whether I have brought the estate to a proper standard?"

"Your uncle appointed my firm as the trustees, and we will have to make that decision. Bear in mind that we will remain impartial in the matter. And if you have not met those conditions that your uncle set out, then we will have no alternative but to let the estate pass to Frompton." Spilsby smiled briefly. "I wish you good fortune in your endeavors."

At least his uncle had not made an agreement with Hart's father. Somehow, that would have been the ultimate betrayal. There had been no love lost between his uncle and his father. But that Uncle

William, of whom Hart was extremely fond, felt the need to do this, crushed him. He took several minutes to calm himself. Whenever he visited his well-read uncle, they enjoyed deep discussions on politics and history and all manner of things while playing chess. He had cherished those times, which in the last months had dwindled after his uncle became ill.

"After I've sorted out some urgent matters at Pembury, I'll return posthaste to London and set about finding a wife," Hart said to the solicitor, hating how he'd fallen far short of what his father and his uncle expected of him. He bit back a sense of shame.

He rode back to Pembury from his uncle's estate, deep in thought. Next month he would attend the Season. Go to all the dashed balls and affairs which bored a fellow. Despite his best intentions, he suspected he would make a very indifferent husband. He'd find someone quiet and amenable. Happy to be left to her own endeavors, whatever married ladies did: sewing, running the house, morning teas, that sort of thing. Tending the nursery. His hands tightened on the reins, causing Blaze to sidle. Hart reined him in. A baby? At twenty-seven, he hadn't intended to become a father for years, perhaps never. It unnerved him. He'd rather face a raging rhino in Africa than hold a tiny babe in his arms whose very life depended on him. Losing his mother so suddenly at eight years of age and then being told to keep a stiff upper lip by his father before being sent away to school, where he'd been constantly roughed up and teased, hardened his heart. Although he considered himself a loyal friend, he doubted he could care deeply enough to marry.

He urged Blaze on. Enough of that. First, see what repairs could be put in motion at the estate with the little money available to him. And then London.

LADY MADELINE HOWARD pulled on her leather riding gloves and walked downstairs to go to the stables. Riding had become essential for her sanity. It was almost a year since she came to live with her Uncle Arthur, and she still felt overwhelmed with sadness by the loss of her beloved parents in a carriage accident. She missed their affection and yearned for a little tenderness, but none was forthcoming. Her uncle was a strict disciplinarian. He invited no one to the house and had no wish to visit their neighbors. Nor did he attend the assemblies or house parties in the district where she might have made some friends.

When news had reached them the Prince of Wales planned a stop in Tunbridge Wells while passing through, she begged Uncle Arthur to take her to see him, but received such a cold scolding for her ridiculous demands that afterward, she kept silent. She could ride her gray mare, Pearl, however, brought to her at her uncle's estate, from her parents' stables by her father's groom, Jack Forest. Jack had been put off along with the rest of the servants, except for Henry, their groom, and Jane, Maddy's lady's maid, who was still with her.

"I hid Pearl, Lady Madeline," Jack had told her. "I doubted they'd miss her, and as it turned out, they didn't." Jack grinned. "The fellow who came to take the horses to Tattersalls couldn't count."

"You are remarkable and very brave, Jack," Maddie told him, while hoping her uncle wouldn't discover the mistake and sell Pearl. He hadn't. It was fortunate that he didn't care to ride and had no interest in the stables. "I wish there was something I could do to repay you," she had said to Jack before he left to seek work. "When I have a home of my own, I shall find you. My mother and father would wish it."

Jack had run his hand along the brim of his hat and smiled, apparently having considered it unlikely she could ever help him.

Uncle Arthur made his displeasure obvious at what he saw as Jack's betrayal, but couldn't do anything more to him.

As her father had no heir, her uncle had full control of Green Oaks, and ruthlessly sold off the estate and everything therein, as he had inherited all but her dowry. Her parents' effects, including her father's hunters, were sold with the estate. Maddie's world had crumbled. With tears in her eyes, she'd wished the staff well, furious with her uncle for letting them go without a character. Some had worked for her father since she was small.

Her one contact with the outside world was her cousin, Cathy, who lived with Maddie's Aunt Elizabeth in Bath. Cathy wrote almost daily, keeping Maddie up to date with news: those of importance who visited Bath; the latest fashions and news, and a fascinating view of her life in Bath society, which turned Maddie pea green with envy.

As Maddie entered the hall, she found one of Cathy's letters had arrived in the post. Maddie was up early to search the salver in the hall for a letter addressed to her before her uncle rose from his bed. Hugging it to her, she hurried up to her room to read it.

Have you met the Marquess, Lord Montford yet? Cathy wrote. *For him to live so close must be greatly frustrating. You should endeavor to gain a glimpse of this splendid gentleman. Cannot your miserly uncle invite him to tea? You simply must meet him. A friend of mine danced with him at a ball and said he is enormously good company. If one doesn't wish to pursue him for marriage, that is.* Cathy had underlined the words twice. *When you do meet him, you must write immediately and tell me everything!*

Well, there was nothing to tell. So far, Maddie hadn't spoken to him and doubted she ever would. Apart from that one glimpse of him over the fence, she knew nothing about him beyond what Cathy told her. Maddie read on as her cousin described the handsome rake, phrased in censorious but slightly awestruck terms.

She smiled at her cousin's description of Lord Montford and left her room in a hurry to reach the stables before her uncle was down and might decide to prevent her from riding. He seemed to take delight in making her unhappy.

Anger and frustration at her lot tightened her stomach as she galloped Pearl over the fields. A hedge loomed up, one they often took.

She gave Pearl's neck a pat. "Ready girl?" They sailed over as they often did, but this time, as the horse's hooves cleared the topmost branches, the saddle slipped sideways. Thrown off Pearl, Maddie landed on her bottom on the hard ground. She lay propped on her elbows, stunned, then sat up. She rubbed her sore hip, and pushed back an escaped curl threatening to blind her, seeing her hat atop a bush. Pearl came over and nudged her, and Maddie came up on her knees to run an anxious eye over the horse's fetlocks. "You're not hurt, girl? No? Oh, that's good." She released a relieved breath.

"You're lucky she isn't," came a deep masculine voice from behind her. "What got into your head to take the mare over that high hedge? You, as well as your horse, might have been killed."

Maddie, aware of the unladylike view she presented, quickly rolled back onto her bottom. Her breath whooshed out as he dismounted from a tall, black thoroughbred. With the reins in his hand, he walked over to her with an easy, confident stride. It made her recall Cathy's words. Close up, Lord Montford was indeed immaculate and intimidating. She felt at a great disadvantage. What should she do? Scramble to her feet and curtsey?

"Hardly likely, Lord Montford. Pearl jumps it most days of the week."

His steely blue eyes regarded her as he bent to offer her his free hand. "Are you hurt?"

She made no move to take his hand, instead gave consideration to how she might rise with grace. "I am perfectly all right, thank you."

"Nonsense. Take my hand."

Maddie quickly realized the sense of it and grasped his large hand. How firm his grip was. She rose as elegantly as she could manage, painfully aware of her dishevelment, and quickly released his hand to shake the grass from her skirts. A quick inspection found a smudge of dirt on the back. She ignored it, fearing brushing her bottom might lack grace, and she'd done enough to give him that impression.

Reclaiming her hat from an azalea bush, she arranged it on her head, disregarding the state of her hair, which threatened to escape its pins. One wisp hung before her eyes, and she blew it away. It was difficult to appear confident and argue one's point when one looked like a ragamuffin. But she was prepared to make her point. She disliked how he cast aspersions on her riding, and he was on her uncle's land.

"We have not been introduced, but are you not my neighbor, Lady Madeline? I believe it was you I saw peeking over the wall on my last visit?"

Drat. An impulse she now regretted. Montford came to Pembury so rarely she'd taken advantage of the moment. "I apologize, sir. My maid was curious." She shrugged. "I indulged her." She would never admit to being consumed with curiosity about the rakish marquess of Pembury. Or that Jane held the ladder for Maddie to look over the wall. She had caught sight of him as he strode away along the garden path, and almost slipped off the rung of the ladder when he turned, as if aware he was being watched. He must have spotted her.

He was, as Jane enthusiastically described, a fine-looking man, Maddie had to admit, broad-shouldered and slim-hipped with dark, tousled hair. The slightly ironic smile in his blue eyes annoyed her. As if her riding skills were amateurish and amused him. Maddie refused to be put in her place by someone who did not know she was an accomplished equestrienne. She still kept the cup and ribbons from her childhood. She'd refused to leave them behind, along with other things which meant a lot to her. "Pearl can easily clear that hedge. I take her over it most days. Something must have gone wrong."

He shrugged a shoulder, reminding her of how large he was. "Something can always go wrong. Especially on a sidesaddle. You should keep that in mind."

"I feel I must thank you for your advice." She gave a brisk, discourteous curtsey, her lips pursed.

His blue eyes were warm. "You're welcome. Do you feel all right to ride? Or shall I give you a lift back to your stables? You can send your groom for the horse."

"Thank you, but there is no need, sir," she said firmly. "I have managed perfectly well before and shall do so again."

"You've fallen at the hedge before?"

She flushed. "No, I have not." She frowned at him. "When Pearl cast a shoe."

He tipped his hat and prepared to mount.

"Perhaps you are not aware you are on my uncle's land," she said to his back, unwilling to leave it there.

"I was riding over my land when I saw you make that reckless attempt," he said over his shoulder. He mounted easily, making her aware of his muscled thighs in snug riding breeches. Then, without granting her a chance to reply, he turned his horse and rode away.

Maddie frowned after him. She would have liked to have the last word, but he was firm in his conviction that she was inept, foolish, and reckless, and she could say little in her defense. She hoped for a chance to show him how wrong he was and wondered how long he planned to stay.

When she tried to remount Pearl, she discovered a broken strap on the sidesaddle. "Well, that's what happened," she said, wishing he'd been there to learn of it. Her misjudgment had not caused the fall, and it galled her for him to think it had. With a firm shake of her head, determined not to give the man another thought, she gathered up Pearl's rein and walked the horse back.

By the time she reached the stables, she was hot and thirsty. Henry, her favorite groom, ladled a cup of water from the barrel and handed it to her, then examined the saddle. "This is indeed strange, Lady Madeline. The strap didn't break. It was cut."

Maddie's blood went cold. "Surely not." She hurried over to see. It certainly looked like a cut. "How could that happen?"

Henry scratched his head. "Never seen the like before in all my born days."

"I would like you to examine the saddle carefully before I mount Pearl tomorrow, Henry. For now, please attend to the horse." Maddie wanted to go to her room and shut herself away and think. The strap must have rubbed against something sharp. While she couldn't dismiss it so easily, her thoughts centered more on their neighbor than whether the saddle strap had broken or was cut.

Chapter Two

LADY MADELINE'S LONG, slender legs were the first thing Hart noticed about her, as he approached where she sat examining her horse's fetlock. She was slim and curvy in all the right places. And once he'd helped her to her feet, he discovered she was quite tall, her eyes just below his. But she was not pleased to see him. And that might have been his fault. He had been curt. He didn't like to see a horse suffer in the hands of an inexperienced rider.

The following day, she remained stubbornly on his mind even when he rode to visit their tenant farmer, Wilkins. Hart left Wilkins heavy-hearted after listening to the farmer's litany of problems. He wanted to help the fellow and he would. But when?

Passing the south meadow, Hart bellowed, "Hell and damnation!" When he saw another fence down. A flock of sheep had wandered onto his neighbor Wakeham's land to graze in a field of turnip tops. He wished Rasputin was with him. The dog would do the job in half the time. Hart dismounted, rounded them up, shooing them back through the break in the fence. The obstinate creatures darted out of his reach, and as he uttered every swear word in his vocabulary, he spied Lady Madeline crossing the stream on her mare. The water almost came up to her boots. When she emerged, he saw she rode astride in men's breeches. He gave up his thankless task, allowing more sheep to jump over the broken railing while his gaze fixed on her with wonder at her audacity. If she came across some fellow who wasn't the gentleman Hart was, she'd be in danger. But he had to admire her devil-may-care attitude when she jumped her grey mare over a low fence and rode across the field to him. What a sight! He had to admit she sat well in the saddle, and was obviously a far more competent rider than he'd given her credit for.

She dismounted, jumping down before he could assist her. "Lord Montford. You have some renegades, I see."

He couldn't draw his eyes from her, and feared he was being crass, but good lord, her curves in those pants! "Yes, and they're a rowdy lot." He reluctantly turned to the errant sheep gathered together, happily grazing on the wrong side of the fence, making a mockery of his attempts to move them.

Lady Madeline tied her mare's reins to a fencepost and walked over to him with an elegant swing of her hips. "I'll help to round up the last of the reluctant stragglers," she offered.

Hart swallowed. "Good of you."

He sighed as she bent to give a woolly animal a push. The glimpse of her rounded derriere yesterday had stayed with him. He gave himself a mental shake. He was behaving like a schoolboy.

Half an hour later, they had corralled the sheep on the proper side of the fence.

Hart shoved the broken bit of fencing back into place to form a temporary barrier. Then turned to watch her mount her gray. She did it gracefully, and the effect on him was startling and immediate. "I appreciate the help." He bent to brush the mud from his breeches. "You will need refreshment after all that work. I am happy to offer you some, but you are closer to your home than mine." Dear lord, he could see his stablehands now.

"No, thank you. I appreciate the offer, but I enjoy physical exercise."

He brushed away the thought of what form of exercise she might indulge in and whether he might be involved, and averted his eyes from her slender thighs before all the blood rushed south from his head and he sounded like an idiot. "You prefer to ride astride?" he asked inanely. Too late. His reaction surprised him. He was familiar with many ladies, most of whom flirted and invited his attention. Lady Madeline did not flirt. And he'd never felt so off his game.

"They are more comfortable," she said, fortunately unaware of his difficulty. "I don't expect to wear them again. Today it was necessary. A strap on my sidesaddle broke when I took Pearl over that jump." She raised her eyebrows, a slight rebuke. "This happened the last time we met."

He frowned. "It broke when you jumped that hedge? Dear lord. I'm glad you weren't hurt." He admitted his error and cleared his throat. Eating humble pie wasn't easy for him. "I acted unfairly that day and must apologize. But your stable staff are not up to scratch to allow you to ride with a damaged saddle."

"My groom and stable master are very reliable. The damage would have been difficult to detect. It was half cut through at the back of the strap." She glanced at him and said wryly, "But your apology is accepted."

He stared at her. "The strap was cut?"

"It looks like it." She shrugged, but he saw worry in her eyes. "Must have rubbed against something sharp."

That didn't wash with him and made him profoundly uneasy. "I imagine your groom will be more careful in the future."

She nodded.

"Better cross at the bridge." He pointed downriver. "The water is deep here after the rain. If you should fall in wearing that heavy velvet riding coat you wore yesterday, you'd be in trouble."

Her amused brown eyes met his. "We have had little rain as of late. I am well aware of the risk."

"Good." She did not take advice well, but he'd be damned if it stopped him from expressing his concerns. "You prefer not to have a groom with you?"

Annoyance thinned her lips, usually delightfully full. "I prefer to ride alone." She turned to view the sheep now safely shut in his paddock. "It is my uncle's hope that you will have these fences fixed soon, Lord Montford. There's been trouble before."

"Then I am sorry for it. I shall deal with any problems here as soon as possible."

Lady Madeline nodded, looking down at him from her well-behaved gray. "My uncle will be pleased to hear it." She settled her hat over her abundant locks. "And now, as I can offer no further help, I'll say goodbye."

Did she have any idea how she aroused a man dressed in those breeches? If she could have read his thoughts, he doubted she'd wear them again.

He watched with approval as she jumped her horse over the lower fence. She performed it superbly. But her shoulders were stiff with indignation as she rode down the bank. He chuckled. Unwilling to take his advice, back she went over the stream without hesitation. She was plucky as a tit-mouse in an owl's nest. They were unlikely to become friends, and he was sorry about that. They seemed to have gotten off on the wrong foot. And he remained more than a little intrigued by his enigmatic neighbor.

Lady Madeline stubbornly occupied his mind until he settled at the desk in the study while Rasputin stretched out before the small fire burning in the grate. Hart groaned at the pile of unpaid accounts. "Not getting any smaller, is it, Horace?"

"In my experience, they never tend to, m'lord," his steward said soberly.

The sooner Hart married and improved the estate, the better. Until then, it was possible to get a bank loan to tide him over, which would allow him to show some signs of progress to please his uncle's trustees. Enough to release his inheritance? Recalling Spilsby's sober face and his words of warning, Hart was doubtful. It appeared he must marry, and despite despairing over his dwindling days of freedom, he intended to seek a bride in London.

"Send the carpenter out to fix the fence in the south paddock," he said to Brownly. "Some posts are down, and the sheep get through."

"Yes, milord."

"What do you know about Arthur Wakeham?"

"Not a lot, m'lord." Horace scratched his nose. "Keeps to himself. Though I've seen some questionable visitors come there after dark."

"Questionable?"

"Rough-looking types. Who knows what he wants with them?"

"What indeed." Before he went up to London, Hart would meet Madeline's guardian, Mr. Wakeham. As the fellow hadn't stirred himself, Hart would call on him to invite him and his niece to dinner to discuss the work to be done to the boundary fences. It would be difficult for Wakeham to refuse. Hart intended to invite his sister along to make a four for whist. Diane could charm the very devil himself.

He began a letter to the bank, but after writing the salutation, he replaced the quill on the standish. Lady Madeline still hovered in his mind. She must be about twenty. And unmarried. Had she made her come-out? He doubted it. She'd be married if so. And stuck away here, she was unlikely to meet a suitable man to marry. Surely it was Wakeham's intention to see her married? It would be her father's wish. Hart disliked the man before he even met him. But he shouldn't rush to judgment. He wasn't aware of the fellow's plans for his niece. Wakeham might have introduced her to suitors. Would a tall, independent girl like Lady Madeline put off men who looked for a biddable wife? He doubted it. She was far too fetching and would be pursued if she appeared in a London ballroom. He remembered how she'd stood up to him, and yet, he sensed a vulnerability in her, which, along with that cut strap, left him more than a little unsettled. He shook his head and returned to his letter.

IN HER BEDCHAMBER, Maddie peeled off the breeches Henry had found for her. They were remarkably comfortable. How lucky men were not to have to contend with yards of material while riding, as well as the cursed sidesaddle. Riding astride gave one so much more control. She was careful not to appear before her uncle in this garb. He needed little prompting to censure her, which could mean being shut away in her bedchamber until she groveled sufficiently to satisfy him. She held her tongue, unwilling to apologize, especially when he was so often in the wrong. But she did it to keep the peace. He would be right this time. She'd been bold, but desperate to get away from the house and feel the scented spring air on her face. And she could not ride Pearl until they mended the sidesaddle. Henry had promised to do it today. She grimaced and chewed her lip. She hadn't missed Lord Montford taking her in from head to toe. Her power to move him sent an odd thrill through her body. She hadn't expected to meet him, but seeing him struggling, she couldn't leave him to deal with it alone, could she? Had she shocked him? So sophisticated a man. He must have seen worse, so she refused to worry about it.

She remembered Cathy's words concerning Lord Montford. *A handsome devil, always with a different woman hanging on his arm when he visited Bath. I saw him dancing at a ball, and setting all the women aflutter. Now he is a marquess, he is one of the most desirable bachelors in England, but word has it he doesn't seek a wife, and ignores any matron's attempts to push their daughters his way.*

He obviously preferred city life. Would he stay long here? Long enough to make the improvements to his estate? She hoped he would stay. And they might meet again if he rode near the boundary between the two estates. Maddie welcomed more conversation with him, but that was probably because she was profoundly bored. She had tried again at breakfast to persuade her uncle to allow her to attend the London Season. Cathy wrote of Aunt Libby being well enough now to consider her come-out. She was sure her mother would be delighted to chaperone Maddie, too, and if they decided to go to London, she would write to her Uncle Arthur. But after Maddie mentioned this to her uncle, he remained resolute. He did not trust her aunt to keep the fortune hunters on the lookout for a wife with an excellent dowry at bay. Maddie was to remain here until he could escort her himself.

It was a lie. Her uncle had no intention of taking her to London. But why would he not let her go? she wondered, frustrated and close to screaming point. He appeared to dislike having her underfoot. Although she'd leaned to be careful never to do anything to draw his ire, he still found fault with her. It wasn't her nature to be a meek, bread-and-butter miss. To cajole and appeal to his masculine vanity. She'd choke if she tried. And there was more to worry about. What went on in this house at night after she went to bed? She never ventured from her room when his visitors were there, knowing her appearance would surely anger him. But it gnawed away at her. She doubted his explanation of them meeting to play cards after she stayed up late to watch them through her window, coming furtively down the path. They looked more like highwaymen and not at all the sort of guests a gentleman would welcome into his home to play cards. What did it mean? She swallowed the sense of panic; she didn't know her uncle well at all. Had seen very little of him before her parents died. The last time was when he'd come at her father's bequest, she believed, to discuss the will. It was after her father's heir, his younger brother, Frederick, had died of pneumonia.

Maddie moaned. Her twenty-first birthday was in a little more than a month. Then she hoped to have more control over her life. Otherwise, she could see herself a spinster shut away in her declining years. She wanted to meet someone she could love, who might love and care for her. She'd become so lonely it was all she could do to rise from her bed in the mornings. Only birdsong and her love of riding through the verdant countryside, spying shy deer darting through the trees, eased the grief of losing her beloved parents, her home, and her freedom.

While her maid, Jane, did up the buttons on Maddie's morning gown before she went down to breakfast, Maddie thought again about Lord Montford. His handsome aquamarine-blue eyes changed like the sea at Brighton in summer. Pale in the shallows and darker in the depths. They darkened when she told him about the strap. Why would it concern him? And yet, she felt sure it had. It must have been an accident, for what else could have happened? But it warmed her to think he was concerned, although he must have dismissed it by now.

"Will I return these breeches to the attic?" Jane asked, holding them up as if they might bite her.

"Mm. No. I'll keep them. I might wear them again." A plan was tinkering at the edge of her mind. At this stage, she wasn't sure she was bold enough to carry it out.

Jane giggled. "Lord Montford must have been stunned to see you wearing them."

"If he was, he didn't reveal it," Maddie said, although she had noticed his gaze flicker over her. What did he think of her? That she was shameless? She sighed. It hardly mattered in the scheme of things. She wished she could turn her mind to something else other than Lord Montford. But there was something in his manner which invited confidences. Charm, she supposed. All rakes seemed blessed with it, apparently. How easy it would be to cast herself upon his broad chest and tell him all.

"He wouldn't mention it. 'E's a gentleman, after all," Jane said with a gusty sigh.

"Mm." Maddie bent to put on her house slippers. She had no intention of leaning on anyone and bemoaning the sad state of her life. She would sort it out herself.

Her nights were filled with dreams, some she hoped for and some she feared might become an unhappy reality.

Chapter Three

A FOOTMAN ANNOUNCED Mr. Wakeham and his niece, Lady Madeline Howard, punctually at eight o'clock. Diane, Hart's widowed sister, regal in a lavender gown trimmed with satin at the sleeves and hem, her dark hair smoothly dressed, waited with him to receive them in the hall. Diane had arrived to stay that morning. She instructed the cook how best to prepare the tasty hors d'oeuvres, and set the maids polishing the drawing room furniture, beating the rugs, and cleaning out the grate and still looked as fresh as a daisy when they led their guests into the spotless, refurbished drawing room scented with vases of spring flowers from the overgrown gardens.

Madeline looked different tonight. A lovely English rose in a delicate white gown, which should have been demure, yet wasn't because of the way she moved, that slight swing of the hips, and the enticing glimpse of her full breasts in the scoop-necked gown.

Hart tried to banish such thoughts and stepped forward with a smile to welcome them.

His first impression of Arthur Wakeham was unfavorable. There was something cold and calculating about his expression as his gaze took in the room. A thin man, he had a perpetually pinched expression, as if he found socializing a trial. And it quickly became evident that he did. Hart felt a rush of sympathy for Madeline. Living with Wakeham would not be a bed of roses.

Directly after the introductions, Diane took Madeline upstairs on some pretext to tidy her hair, because the night was uncommonly windy, or some such excuse ladies used when they wished to talk unhindered by gentlemen. He'd give a pony to hear what they talked about and hoped Diane would tell him later.

Left alone, Hart attempted conversation, which Wakeham merely answered in monosyllables. "A glass of wine while we wait for the ladies, sir?" Hart said at last.

Wakeham paused from his study of the gracious room to settle small hazel eyes on him. "Red. Thank you."

Wakeham continued to study the room as if judging Hart's wealth. He revealed a lack of interest in any subject Hart raised, beyond the work to be done to the boundaries. It only made Hart dislike the fellow more.

Hart directed Wakeham to a chair and went to the drinks table. As he handed the glass of claret to Wakeham, the ladies returned, and Hart busied himself pouring glasses of ratafia.

The footman brought in plates of appetizers for their guests and set them on the table.

When Hart sat, the conversation began with the usual topic: the weather, blustery for this time of year but not much rain.

"Did you ride today, Lady Madeline?" Hart asked her when the discussion petered out. She sat primly, a slight distance from her uncle, on the opposite sofa to him and Diane. He had not seen her during his brief ride before luncheon, and later was shut up in his study, achieving little, while his indomitable sister turned the house upside-down.

"I rode quite early," Madeline said. "Your sheep are safely on the Montford side of the fence. It has been repaired."

"Good thing," Wakeham commented. The man was exceedingly dour. Hart could see he didn't want to be here. "What about the rest of the fences? One of these days, your bull will get in with my cows."

Hart smiled. "Rest assured, sir, I shall not charge you for any births that might arise."

Wakeham nodded, his mouth a thin disapproving line.

Diane coughed and held a gloved hand to her mouth.

He looked at his sister warily, but biting her lip, she contained herself. Madeline's large brown eyes were alight with laughter. Surprised, he smiled at her, as if they were coconspirators. He saw no fondness in his uncle toward her, and none for Wakeham from Madeline. Did she dislike her uncle as much as he did? If that was so, he hoped she would go soon to London to enjoy the Season and find a husband. Although the thought of her marrying didn't appeal to him as much as he expected it to.

"Would you care for an hors d'oeuvre, sir?" The footman held the plate before Wakeham. Diane leaned forward. "The biscuits are cucumber and cream cheese, but I prefer the toast triangles with smoked salmon and egg. Delicious with the dill."

Wakeham eyed them as if they might poison him. He gestured to the footman to move away. "I don't eat after dinner. Disturbs a man's digestion."

Madeline took one topped with smoked salmon and bit into it with even white teeth. "What a shame, Uncle," she said when she'd eaten a piece. "These are delicious. I agree the dill is a perfect addition."

"Cook is quite capable. Although his menu is rather uninspiring," Diane said. "I imagine that was the way it had to be. Papa insisted on simple dishes. He suffered dreadful indigestion."

Hart addressed Wakeham as he nursed his half glass of wine. "Perhaps we should address those problems before we begin our card game?"

"Indeed, there are several areas along the boundary your father left neglected," Wakeham said ungraciously.

"Shall we seat ourselves at the other end of the room? Will you forgive us for a few minutes, ladies?"

"Of course," Diane said. "What shall we do, my dear? Do you play the pianoforte and sing?"

"I do," Madeline said. "But I confess to being a trifle rusty. My uncle does not have a pianoforte."

"Shall I play then while you sing?"

"That would be preferable," Madeline said with obvious relief.

They rose together and went to the pianoforte while Hart led her uncle to the group of chairs nearer the long windows overlooking the terrace. He would have much preferred to remain to appreciate the music, but could not suggest it now. He seated himself where he had a clear view of them. Madeline and his sister agreed on a piece and Madeline stood, slim and elegant, her hand resting on the piano. Soon her soprano voice rose sweetly in the room in a country song.

"Your niece sings well with delightful expression," Hart said.

"Years of practice. She was much indulged by the earl and countess."

Hart had been right. Wakeham's voice lacked any fondness for his niece.

"Surely being gifted with loving parents hurts no one." Hart struggled not to protest at the man's unfair condemnation. Hart barely knew Madeline, but found nothing spoiled about her. It became increasingly apparent her life had taken a starkly tragic turn since becoming an orphan and the ward of this man. "Hasn't Lady Madeline yet made her debut?" he asked, aware he was rudely inquisitive but now quite happy to forget his manners.

As expected, Wakeham looked affronted. "Madeline is barely out of mourning and still very distressed. Her come-out must wait until the following year."

Hart could say nothing to this, although he disagreed. He suspected it suited Wakeham to keep her here. But why? It wasn't because he was fond of her. It pointed to a certain disregard for Maddie's wishes, which made Hart see red.

They agreed on the necessary repairs, while Hart worried about where he would find the money to satisfy Wakeham's demands. Then they joined the ladies at the green baize-topped gaming table. Hart, as banker, removed the cards from the pack. "You sing beautifully, Lady Madeline," he said as he shuffled them.

Her cheeks flushed. "You are kind. I'm afraid I am not in good voice. Lack of practice, I suspect."

"It was a pleasure to listen to you." He turned to Diane. "Plus my sister's skill at the pianoforte, of course."

"My, Hart, what have I done to deserve such praise?" Diane asked, obviously amused. "I remember when we lived under the same roof, my playing came in for some criticism. Which I thought most unjust."

"You have improved immensely," Hart said, dealing the cards.

Madeline giggled.

Her uncle glanced sharply at her.

They settled down to play.

As he studied his cards, Hart said in a casual tone, "It was most fortunate that Lady Madeline did not hurt herself when she fell from her horse, was it not?"

Madeline met his gaze and gave a small shake of her head. Why? What was she afraid of?

"An unfortunate accident." Wakeham stiffened in his seat.

"The strap appeared to have been cut." Hart watched his reaction. "Odd that, don't you think, Mr. Wakeham?"

"Careless," Wakeham said. "I'd fire the fellow, except he'd be difficult to replace, and is usually reliable."

Hart nodded and desisted, as Madeline obviously didn't want him to pursue it further.

The subdued game followed with light, trivial conversation, mostly led by Diane. Hart could sense Wakeham's eagerness to depart. He took his niece home early after their game of whist, which displayed Madeline's proficiency. When Hart complimented her, she admitted she often played with her parents after dinner. "I worked very hard at it, I confess. Determined to beat my father." She smiled wistfully. "But I never did." It offered a sad view into the life she had left behind and increased Hart's sympathy for her.

After the door shut, Diane joined him in the salon for coffee. It was still too early to retire, in Hart's opinion. He refused to adjust to country hours. "What do you think of Lady Madeline?" she asked.

Aware his observant sister might have picked up some signal from him as he played with Madeline as his partner, he chose his words carefully. "I find her a remarkably strong-minded young woman, considering all that she has had to endure."

Diane smiled. "Is that the best you can do? She is lovely and has a very pleasing manner. I liked her immensely."

"She can be very firm in her opinions," he said to throw her off. He sensed she was matchmaking again and, much as it amused him, he would not allow it. He would choose his bride, not his older sister. Her days of directing him by the leading strings ended many years ago.

"And you find that unacceptable?"

"No. Not at all. I'm glad of it for her sake," he admitted. "I think she will need it."

She nodded. "I did not take to Wakeham. He seems a charmless and unpleasant man."

"Neither did I."

Diane looked uncomfortable. "When we were upstairs, Madeline told me how much she wanted to go to London for the Season. And hoped that her aunt might be her chaperone. But her uncle refused even to consider it. She pines for some gaiety. I feel so very sorry for her. I suppose there is nothing to be done?"

"We cannot interfere. It is none of our concern. In any event, I must leave for London tomorrow to consult the bank manager. I'll remain for their answer to my request for a mortgage. The quicker I show some improvements here, the faster I will receive my inheritance." He eyed her. "Father was a darn skinflint where I was concerned."

"Apparently, his finances have been sadly depleted for some time."

"Father could have put the colliery in Newcastle-on-Tyne up for sale, although the Heaton Colliery disaster in '15 might have made it hard to find a buyer a year ago. I will advise my solicitor to sell Grandmama's Devon estate." He frowned. "Why the devil didn't he tell me he was in such bad straits? The last time I saw him, he said nothing about it. Just the usual carping, which only served to get my back up."

"I suppose he thought you needed to…to find your way."

He returned his cup to the saucer and sat back, observing her, aggrieved. Then he shrugged, abashed. "I wish my relatives didn't feel I need improving. I am not a wastrel."

"You are not," she said soothingly. "But you've been enjoying your time in London, have you not? I've heard the gossip. It's been on everyone's lips since you became marquess. How you are one of the most desired bachelors in London. That is true, although much of your inheritance is at present tied up. You are not judicious, Hart, you must admit. I was also told you gave money to one of your previous lovers when she fell into debt."

"How do you come to hear such things?" He shook his head, disconcerted. "Is it time for me to pay the fiddler?"

"You could solve your immediate problems by marrying a wealthy woman."

He scowled. "Marry an heiress for her money? That's not for me."

"Then don't consider Madeline."

"I wasn't…" he blustered.

"No? I saw how you looked at her. She is very attractive. I'm not sure how she is placed financially, but I am sure her father would have left her a generous dowry. It's doubtful her ghastly uncle would agree to a proposal before she's out, though. And she has told me there are no immediate plans for her debut."

Hart rubbed his hand along his jaw, feeling the prickle of stubble. "She should make her curtsey to the queen this year."

"Does that mean you might consider her when she's made her come-out?"

"No. I must marry soon. And I shall choose a bride who fits into my life and causes little change."

"A lady who never crosses you?"

Hart laughed. "Precisely."

"Even when you are wrong?"

He raised an eyebrow. "I am rarely wrong."

"How mind-numbingly dull." Diane yawned. "I'm sure you'll write and tell me when you become engaged to some milk-and-water miss. Forgive me. I simply must retire. I leave first thing tomorrow. My dear ones will be missing me. And I've promised to take them to the local fair on Saturday."

"Thank you for coming and for your invaluable help, Di. I appreciate it very much."

"No need. It was a pleasant change from my domestic life."

She should remarry, he thought, but didn't express it. Diane was too young at twenty-nine to spend the rest of her life alone. But she had dearly loved Edgar. For some people, there was only one true love. With a brief smile, he rose from his chair. His thoughts took a remarkably romantic turn tonight. "Give my love to Tom and Charlotte. I hope to see them soon."

She rose with him, and they walked to the stairs. "Make sure you do."

"Are all older sisters nags?" he asked conversationally as she climbed the stairs.

"I daresay we are. After all, it is necessary."

He rested a hand on the newel post and grinned at her parting thrust. Then he went to the library and poured himself a balloon of brandy. He wanted to go over this evening with a fine-toothed comb before he slept on it, although he was dashed if he knew why. He supposed he needed to understand what was occurring on that property a few miles down the road. Perhaps when he returned from London, he might persuade Madeline into telling him more.

⁂

IN HER BEDCHAMBER, Maddie rose from removing her stockings. She took off the pendant at her throat and her earrings, placing them in the jewel box on the dresser.

Jane helped remove her gown.

"Did you have a pleasant evening, milady?" she asked as she carefully arranged the fragile material over a chair and returned to untie Maddie's stays.

"I did. It was good to be amongst bright company again."

She hadn't expected to enjoy it so much. An evening with her uncle portended a solemn affair. But she had sung for the first time in ages. How good it felt to laugh. She feared she'd forgotten how. Lord Montford made her laugh. Just his presence lightened the air around her. She stepped out of her petticoat. When their hands touched briefly during the card game, a spike of electricity lifted her gaze to his. His eyes searched hers for a moment before he continued the game. She liked him too much. How foolish. She must not make him the subject of her dreams. Nor should her morning rides take her closer to his estate with the hope of a glimpse of him. She had seen him earlier today, riding with a dog at his heels. How at ease he was in the saddle. She kept well behind a screen of bushes, afraid he might think she lurked for a sight of him. Which, of course, was true.

"My lady?" Jane had removed her shift while she was barely aware of it and now held up the nightgown.

"Thank you, Jane," she said, smoothing it down. "You may go to bed. I will brush my hair myself."

The door closed. Maddie went to the window and looked out at the dark night. The wind had washed the sky clean. The moon shone down and alighted on three figures slipping through the grounds. She shivered in her nightgown and, rubbing her arms, stepped back behind the curtain. Her uncle's strange visitors were back again. They'd been gone for over a week, making her believe they would never return. And here they were.

She washed her face in the washbasin and cleaned her teeth, then sat before the mirror to brush her long locks. One night, she would creep to the top of the stairs and try to hear what was said. Tonight, she only wanted to think about the evening. And how wonderful it had been to be in society again, and have Lord Montford's blue eyes smile into hers from across the table.

Chapter Four

B EFORE HE LEFT for London, Hart took his gelding, Blaze, for some much needed exercise, Rasputin running behind, tongue lolling. He spied Madeline riding up a hill about half a mile away. Thinking it was very early for her to be out, Hart urged Blaze into a canter, jumped the small stream which divided their properties, and rode after her.

Reaching the top of the hill, he again caught sight of her, galloping over a long, straight stretch of ground. He had the impression she wanted to keep going, riding away into the early morning light. She rode skillfully, unconstrained by both her cumbersome dark gray riding habit and the sidesaddle. Impressed, he spurred Blaze into a gallop to catch up with her. His more powerful horse quickly reached her mare. She looked elegant in the riding habit, but he couldn't help wishing she wore the breeches. Would he see her in them again? An erotic image flashed into his mind, which made him laugh and shake his head.

She saw him, her surprise turning to pleasure. Reining Pearl in, they slowed their horses to a walk. "Good morning, Lord Montford. Weren't you traveling to London today?"

"Shortly. After I've given Blaze some exercise." He gestured to the lush green landscape, breathing in the smell of pine and oak and damp earth, which evoked childhood memories. "I will miss this while in the city."

She raised her slender, dark eyebrows. "You enjoy the country?"

"I grew up in the country." He wondered if that was censure he detected in her voice.

"There's always Rotten Row."

"Doesn't really compare, does it?"

Her lips lifted in a smile. "I imagine not. I've never been there."

"Then you must visit it when in London."

She ducked her head. "I will, one day."

"Do you often gallop that mare of yours?" He admired how at ease she seemed on the gray.

"Pearl enjoys a gallop." She frowned. "You're not about to tell me I should be accompanied by a groom, are you?"

He faked alarm with a rise of his eyebrows. "I wouldn't dare."

A hint of a smile lifted her lips. "I suspect you were about to do precisely that."

"I knew you would take me to task, and it's too delightful a morning to argue, is it not?"

"Then I am glad you saw the sense of it," she said.

He grinned. Having made her point, she looked far too satisfied. "Sense is not jumping your horse over high hedges."

She sighed. "Oh, must we go over that again?"

He sighed heavily, but a grin hovered on his lips. "No. I can see it's quite useless."

"Quite tiresome, in fact."

"You will be careful, though, won't you, Lady Madeline?" he said suddenly, disconcerting her.

She frowned. "Of course. Why the concern?"

He wasn't entirely sure why he'd said it. The sense of unease persisted. "No particular reason."

"Because you think me reckless?"

"I suspect you have an adventurous nature," he said, attempting to be tactful but apparently failing woefully, as she frowned at him.

"And what is wrong with that?" she asked indignantly. "Is it only men who can enjoy an adventure, Lord Montford?"

"The world is safer for men. Regrettable, but true, unfortunately."

She nodded her head, acknowledging the fact.

"As we are neighbors, will you call me Hart?" It surprised him he'd asked it and wondered if he'd be rebuffed.

She tilted her head and observed him. "Hart? A nice name, although I cannot call you that in company, you understand." She hesitated, adjusting the reins in her hands. "My parents and friends called me Maddie."

Was he now a good friend? Pleased at the prospect, he smiled. "Maddie," he echoed, glancing at her curls escaping her black riding hat, more red than chestnut, with paler streaks, making it a color all of its own. "It suits you." *An unusual name for an unusual lady. And a very pretty one.*

Blaze pawed the ground. "Alas, I must take leave of you," Hart said, conscious of the hour as he steadied his mount.

"Enjoy your time in London."

She sounded wistful.

"It's business mostly," he said, which was not quite true.

"The metropolis offers many wonderful entertainments during the Season," she said longingly. "I trust you will make the most of it."

"I shall endeavor to. Goodbye…Maddie."

"Goodbye, Hart."

Black braid and toggles decorated her military-style gray gown. Still in half-mourning, and even when she smiled, there was a hint of sadness in her brown eyes. She should be among friends and bright company to lighten her grief. It wasn't his business, but he had a powerful urge to make it so, if in some way he could help her. Wakeham wasn't her father's heir. What sort of control did he have over Maddie? Surely she would cease to be his ward once she came of age? Hart heartily disliked what he suspected was going on here. It was obvious Maddie was not reclusive by nature. She was filled with fire. No girl who rode with such passion wished to let life slip by. She would not have been left without money of her own. He didn't know the circumstances, but her father, the earl, had been a wealthy man and would have ensured she was well placed should he die. Perhaps it was just as well Hart was leaving, or his temper could get the better of him. He might stir up more trouble for Maddie with that difficult uncle of hers. She was such an independent young woman, he doubted she would turn to him for help in any event. And he could just be jumping at shadows. But while in London, he'd make it his business to find out more about Wakeham.

It was full dark by the time he reached Mayfair and left his curricle in the mews stables, his grays in the care of a groom. Mixed feelings assailed him as he approached the double front doors of the family's London mansion. When he was alive, his father had not felt obliged to keep the house open for Hart, renting out the furnished property for two years, with most of their servants.

Even after his death, his father's disfavor remained a sore point with Hart. The animosity began between them when Hart, a young lad, had stood up for his mother, resenting his father's harsh treatment of her. But long after she was gone, he still visited Pembury without complaint whenever his father requested it, even though those visits were inexorably painful. What hurt him deeply was why, despite a litany of complaints about his aches and pains, his father had never asked for Hart's advice or confessed to being incapable of running his estate. Their relationship remained stiff and formal, and he kept Hart at arm's length. When his mother was alive, she moderated his father's difficult moods, but after she was gone, his tempers worsened, and he seemed to plunge into misery. Hart wondered now if his father felt some guilt and anguish over his behavior in the past. But it was impossible to say. His grandfather had been the same: an abrupt, cold man. Such things were often perpetuated each generation. But such behavior would end with Hart. He was his mother's son, not his father's. She had guided him through his childhood. It was her wise words that stayed with him. He tightened his jaw. Would she have approved of his London lifestyle? Perhaps not. Well, that was about to end, although he still worried about the new role he was about to adopt. Marriage.

With the lease at an end, Montford Court was Hart's to rattle around in. It seemed a cold place after his mother died and didn't fill him with joy.

A footman opened the door.

"Welcome home, milord." The butler, Crispin's, voice echoed in the lofty hall as he hurried with a slight limp to welcome him. He had served the family for thirty years and looked older and balder than Hart remembered.

"It is good to see you again, Crispin." He shook the man's hand, feeling a tremble in his fingers. Perhaps he would welcome retirement and a pension, but Hart wasn't about to suggest it until he was sure.

"Your suite has been made ready, milord." Crispin snapped his fingers, his authority apparently undimmed. Two footmen scurried to take Hart's luggage. Hart piled his hat, gloves, and greatcoat into one footman's arms. "Your valet awaits you in your chambers. Should you require anything, the housekeeper, Mrs. Hatton, will deal with it."

A sense of lightness surprised Hart. He was home. But with no family, was it really a home?

"Will you be in for dinner, milord? Shall I alert Cook?"

"I'll take a tray in my room. A cold collage will do, Crispin. Leonard will bring me coffee in the morning, and I'll be down to breakfast at eight."

With a pang, Hart noted the blank places on the walls where paintings once hung. But the stately marble statue of Aphrodite and a lecherous Pan still took pride of place at the foot of the stairs. The sculpture held a great deal of fascination for Hart when he was young.

The stone mansion would fetch a good price should he choose to sell it. But it seemed wrong to sell what had been home to Montfords for over two hundred years. And his mother's touches remained in every room. He could imagine her here, quietly going about her day.

As he climbed the curved marble staircase, he faced the fact that he must begin his search for his future bride. It must be someone who understood his way of life and fit smoothly into it. Someone he liked and liked him. A woman he found both attractive and interesting. It was a tall ask in such a short space of time.

In the marquess's hereditary apartments, Leonard sorted through Hart's luggage. After the valet's effusive welcome, Hart requested a bath, which sent Leonard swiftly off to arrange.

Hart read long into the night by candlelight, finding it difficult to sleep. So much importance rested on his shoulders. He had treated life lightly, but could do so no longer. Finally, he snuffed out the candles and sleep claimed him.

After breakfast the next morning, Hart, dressed for the city due to the ministrations of his meticulous valet, squared his shoulders and stepped out onto the street to hire a hackney to go to his bank.

A crowd had gathered, and a constable stood in the street outside, the doors still closed. Inside was in an uproar, the staff in a huddle, talking in hushed voices.

Hart turned to the constable. "What has happened here?"

"The bank was robbed, sir," the constable said.

"Robbed? When was this?"

"This morning. As soon as the bank opened. In broad daylight, sir," the constable said, outraged. "A gang of robbers muscled their way in armed with pistols. Demanded all the money and shot the man who'd just arrived. Got the lot, apparently, and they were clean away before the alarm went up."

"Brazen of them," Hart said. "The man they shot. How is his condition?"

"Deader than last week's mutton, sir. The bank manager, it was."

Hart swore under his breath. Graves was a decent fellow, always with an earnest expression behind the glasses perched on his nose. "Why the devil did they shoot him? Unnecessary, surely."

The constable shrugged. "As a warning, I suppose. Such devils have no conscience."

It would be days, if not weeks, before they would find a replacement for Graves. Hart could do nothing other than return to Montford Court. He hoped for some good company tonight.

At home, he sent a footman around to the Broadstairs residence, belatedly accepting their invitation to their spring ball.

At eight that evening, Hart's closest friend, Tarleton Fanshawe, Duke of Lindsey, strode into The Running Horse inn in Mayfair where they had arranged to dine.

The inn was busy, the air filled with tasty aromas, causing Hart's empty stomach to protest. Tate shook Hart's hand. "Good to see you."

"And I you. Marriage agrees with you." Hart had been Tate's best man at he and Ianthe's wedding. "Is Ianthe with you in London?"

"No. She's at home in Cloudhill. Spends most of her days working with the horses, setting up a breeding program. I am here on business for a few days, but eager to return home. We're in the process of building a glasshouse."

Their life sounded idyllic. Hart suffered a twinge of envy. "You intend to grow exotic plants?"

Tate nodded. "Fruits and vegetables from different climes. We'll have cucumbers all year round." He laughed. "I'll send you some pineapple when we have a crop." His expression changed to one of concern, and he leaned closer. "But what of you? Have matters improved since your father died?"

"Father let Pembury run down, and his finances are in a muddle." Hart shrugged. "Nothing that can't be resolved, but here's the rub..."

He explained about his Uncle William's will.

Tate looked concerned. Then a wry smile lifted his lips. "So, you are to join Ianthe and me in wedded bliss?"

Hart rubbed his chin. "I hope for wedded bliss. It will have to be a rushed affair."

"You have a lady in mind?"

"Not yet. I am due to attend the Broadstairs ball tonight. You never know, I might find her there." Inexplicably, an image of Maddie encroached on his thoughts.

"Take care. Choose the right woman and marriage really is bliss. The wrong one and it's hell on earth."

Hart grimaced. "I shall be very circumspect in my choice of bride."

Tate raised a dark eyebrow, his green eyes serious. "Might be wiser to choose with your heart."

"As you did." Hart knew what a difficult road Tate had traveled to marry his childhood sweetheart.

"I wish you the same good fortune, Hart," Tate said.

"Thank you, my friend."

Love was all very well and good, but Hart didn't have the luxury of time and must choose with his head and hope his heart got involved. As he'd never fallen in love, he wasn't confident.

A few hours later, in a Mayfield mansion a few streets from his own, Her Grace, Georgina, Duchess of Broadstairs, greeted Hart at the door of the festooned ballroom. Statuary, columns, urns of flowers, and orange trees decorated every available spot. Well-dressed guests filled the long, elegant room, moving about the fringes or forming a square for the cotillion. Candle smoke drifted in the overly perfumed air.

"You have been a stranger in London as of late, Montford," the dark-haired duchess, dressed in gold satin, said teasingly. "Broadstairs and I thought perhaps a lady had taken you away from us."

"Unfortunately, no, Your Grace. Matters pertaining to my country estate," Hart said. "And as I must soon return there, I welcome such delightful company."

"You shall find it here tonight." She pointed her fan at no one in particular. The gesture was enough to draw Hart's eye to an attractive brown-haired lady. Aware of his gaze, she slowly raised her fan to her face with her left hand. Over the top of the painted sticks, her smiling eyes met his. If Hart read her message correctly, she desired his acquaintance. He nodded and smiled.

"Now who has caught your attention?" With an innocent expression, Georgina followed his gaze. "Mrs. Vivian Spencer is delightful company. Lost her husband to the sea two years ago. Spencer was Vice Admiral. No children from the marriage," she said, giving him a potted history of the lady. "Come, I shall introduce you."

After she presented him, Georgina excused herself and slipped away.

Mrs. Spencer's vivid blue eyes surveyed him as if she approved of what she saw, and he certainly approved of her. Diminutive and stylish, she seemed much at ease within society.

The waltz was announced, and Hart promptly invited her to dance before another gentleman with the same aim claimed her.

In his arms, she smiled up at him as he swept her around the floor.

"I have not seen you about in London this Season, Lord Montford."

"I've been away. Matters with my estate."

"How distressing for you to be trapped in the country. It's bad enough that we must stay among the rustics during the hot months. I hope you are done with it."

"Not quite, I'm afraid."

"You are not about to vanish for the rest of the Season, are you?" she asked, tilting her head.

He smiled, finding her charming. "I shall hurry back."

They spoke of mutual acquaintances, and when the dance ended, he escorted her to her friends. Hart stayed in her company for another half hour, and after securing a promise from her for the supper dance, excused himself to speak to the earl, Dominic Thorne, and his wife, Olivia, who seldom came to town. It was good to see them here tonight.

Another example of a successful marriage, Hart thought. It had been just as difficult for Dom to marry the girl he loved as it was for Tate. Perhaps the true test of a man's love was the struggle he faced before he could call his beloved his own. He wished the path he took could lead to love, but he had to be brutally honest. Unless the love of his life appeared under his very nose, it seemed unlikely.

At the announcement of the supper dance, Hart made his way to Mrs. Spencer. A witty woman with an attractive laugh, she proved good company. While they ate supper, she inquired if he planned to attend the Browns' card party on Friday. He hadn't intended to go, but he agreed to see her there. When he headed home in the early hours, he considered the evening a success, which had, temporarily at least, pushed the worry about the bank from his mind.

HART HAD PERSISTENTLY lingered in Maddie's mind all day. She spent her time indoors avoiding her uncle, pretending to be the woman he wished, reading, although the words seemed difficult to absorb; embroidering, which she disliked; and sketching, which she did. None of it was enough to make her sleepy when she retired, her mind still busy. In her nightgown, she stood at the window, gazing out at the sky. It had rained earlier, but had cleared away, and a slice of moon threw light and shadow over the garden. Movement on the path through the gardens alerted her. Her uncle's three guests were back.

Curious, she slipped into her dressing gown. She had to know if her uncle told the truth about their card games. She quietly opened her door and crept along the corridor to the top of the stairs.

The front door opened, and the men's excited voices rose, subdued at once by a curt response from her uncle but still loud enough for her to pick up a word or two. Something about a successful venture. What would that be? She stepped down another tread to hear more as they filed into the drawing room. The boards creaked. Maddie jumped back. How foolish, she knew every loose board on the stairs. She'd been too eager to listen to remember it.

Two men came back into the hall. "Someone's up there," one said gruffly. They stared up at the landing, but couldn't see where she crouched in the shadows behind a wooden pillar.

"It's an old house. It creaks. I'll check on my niece." Her uncle went to fetch a lantern, which gave Maddie time to run back to her bedchamber and slip into bed. She blew out the candle and pulled the covers up to her chin to hide her dressing gown.

Moments later, the door opened, and light flooded into the room. "Are you awake, my dear?"

She raised her head. "Is there something wrong, uncle?" She yawned. "Did I fall asleep with the candle still lit?"

"No. Go back to sleep."

The door closed.

Was he suspicious? Her body stiff as a poker, Maddie steadied her breath as she listened to his noisy descent down the stairs. She must learn more about these men, but the sound of that rough, menacing voice that first spoke left her with no illusions about the danger she would be in should they discover her spying on them.

Chapter Five

URING THE WEEK, Hart escorted Vivian Spencer to a dinner
party held by Baron and Baroness Fortescue. A charming couple
whom he had never met, but were good friends of Vivian's. He
enjoyed Vivian's company. She was engaging and undeniably lovely,
mature, and experienced at twenty-six, with no qualms about inviting
him into her bed. He was tempted. What man wouldn't be? But he felt
the timing was wrong when he must return so soon to the country, so
he made his excuses.

The bank had reopened. Assured of a modest loan to tide him over
until they could sell the property in the north, he promised Vivian to
return to London by Saturday and escort her to Ascot. Instantly, she
forgave him for declining her invitation to her bed. They would mix
with royalty and imbibe champagne as the thoroughbreds raced over
the flat. Hart left the lady, expressing her earnest desire for him to
return quickly. The next day he was on the road at dawn.

As soon as he arrived at Pembury, Hart rode out with his steward
to inspect the land. He ordered the work agreed upon with Wakeham
to begin.

The following morning, Hart followed the boundary between his
and Wakeham's properties on Blaze, searching for Maddie along the
path he'd spotted her on earlier. He found no sign of her. In case she
rode later, he went out again in the afternoon, the air crisp and dry

with no sign of rain, which spelled problems with the newly planted crops. He wasn't sure why Maddie's absence concerned him, but as the freedom riding afforded her was important to her, he doubted much would keep her from it. Might she be ill, or could it be something even more worrying? The cut strap loomed again in his mind. While he couldn't demand to see her, he could call in and give Wakeham a report on the work set to begin tomorrow.

That evening, he retired early, but ended up reading until late. He hadn't given a thought to Vivian since he left London, he realized with a grimace. She would expect him back in London to escort her to Ascot. His young neighbor occupied his mind. Had he just missed her out riding? He couldn't dismiss the possibility she might be in trouble.

With no sign of Maddie in the morning, Hart went to Wakeham's house. When no servant came to take his horse, he continued around to the stables. The groom worked in the stable yard. He put the broom down, and recognizing Hart, hurried over. "Can I help you, Lord Montford?"

Hart dismounted. "What is your name?"

"Henry, milord."

"I'm here to see Mr. Wakeham, Henry. Take care of my horse."

"Yes, milord." Henry took the reins from him. "He's a fine animal."

As Hart pulled off his riding gloves, he glanced over at a horse who'd thrust its head over the stall gate. Maddie's Pearl. "I didn't see Lady Madeline out riding this morning. Might I have missed her?"

Henry turned from admiring Blaze. "Lady Madeline has gone away, milord. Left the day before yesterday."

"To visit a relative?"

"Milady didn't say. She…went without a word to me."

"I see the coach is in the coach house. By what means of travel?"

"I can't say, milord."

His neck prickled. "I see her horse Pearl is here."

"Yes. She didn't ride. She must have walked to the village."

Hart rubbed his nape. "Why would she go on foot? Do you know if something occurred to upset her?"

Henry frowned and shrugged. "I don't know, milord. I wasn't told. But she didn't go alone. Her lady's maid, Jane, went with her."

"Have you seen Wakeham since she left?"

Henry nodded. "He came and questioned the staff. Wanted to know if any of us knew where she'd gone."

So Maddie had run away. Hart thanked Henry and strode around to the front door. He rapped smartly on the knocker. After several minutes, a maid answered.

Hart offered his card. "I wish to see Mr. Wakeham."

She bobbed and hurried away.

A moment later, she returned to admit him into the parlor. Wakeham rose from his chair.

"Good day, Mr. Wakeham. I bring you news about the repairs," Hart said, crossing the carpet to shake the man's hand.

Wakeham's handshake was limp, his appearance disorderly. His neckcloth appeared to have been tied hastily. The lines around his mouth seemed deeper. He looked unhappy to see Hart, but that wasn't surprising. He didn't like Hart any more than Hart liked him. "Good of you to keep me informed. May I offer you a drink?"

"No, thank you. You'll be pleased to hear our lands have been banked up in that section of the river, which floods. It was not in our agreement, but as I had to do it, I made sure the change was beneficial to you as well."

"Thank you," Wakeham said in his cool voice. He nodded toward a chair.

Hart sat and studied the man. "All the broken-down fences are up. I have turnips and wheat sown in the south fields and I hope for rain."

Wakeham grunted. He appeared to want nothing more than to be left alone.

Hart refused to oblige him without learning more, whether the man welcomed him there or not. "The groom tells me Lady Madeline left without leaving word of her direction. Surely that cannot be true?"

Wakeham paled. He straightened in his chair, holding the arms as if for support. "The wretched girl ran away."

"Do you know why?"

"No. She didn't bother to leave a note of explanation." Wakeham shrugged. "Madeline has never been happy here, always wanting something else. Something better." He glowered. "Her mourning period is barely over, although to her, society's rules don't seem to count for much. She'll be back soon enough when she discovers how hard it is out there without my largess. I took her in out of the goodness of my heart. And this is the thanks I get."

"Do you have any idea where she might have gone?"

"Her aunt in Bath, I imagine. I have written to her and await her reply."

Hart fought to keep his temper at the man's lack of affection and concern for his niece's safety. "You did not think it prudent to look for her?"

"I saw no sense in careering around the countryside when she could be anywhere. It is best to wait." Wakeham stood, his pretense as a polite host at an end. "If that is all, Lord Montford?"

Hart could do nothing other than put on his hat and leave. Outside, he turned and stared up at the second-story windows. They looked blankly back down at him. It looked like Maddie had left with little thought to her safety. What made her take such a step? Wakeham must have something to do with it. His lack of concern for his niece bothered Hart as he walked back to the stables to retrieve Blaze.

"Henry," he called as he approached the groom oiling saddles. "That strap on Lady Madeline's saddle. How do you think it came to be cut?"

Henry's blue eyes flared angrily. He checked to make sure they were alone before answering. "Someone sliced a knife through the leather, leaving just enough to hold it together until put under strain," he said, lowering his voice.

Hart rubbed his neck. "It was deliberate?"

"I'd stake my life on it, milord."

"Did you mention this to Mr. Wakeham?"

He shook his head. "Lady Madeline told me not to."

"Do you know who Lady Madeline's relatives are?"

"Yes, milord. I worked for the family before her parents died."

"It was a coach accident, was it not?"

Henry nodded. "The drag-shaft broke, and the horses bolted."

"A tragic business. Where might I find her?"

"Lady Madeline visited her old nanny in Malmesbury occasionally. And more often, her aunt, Lady Dalby. She and her daughter, Catherine, live in Bath. Never known milady to visit anyone else."

"Did you accompany her on these visits?"

"Yes. Always."

"Can you give me their directions?"

"Certainly, milord." Henry went into the stable and returned with the addresses written on a scrap of paper. "If you find her ladyship, will you bring her back?" he asked, his eyes shadowed.

Hart pulled on his gloves. "I must find her first."

"Lady Madeline won't appreciate being returned here, if you'll forgive me for saying so. And should she return, milord? With that cut strap and all? She doesn't trust her uncle. Told me some ruffians come at night to play cards after she is abed. Said she wanted to find out more about them, but I warned her not to."

"Strange. Have you seen them?"

"Once when I was up late at night with a horse in foal. Not that well, though. They hugged the shadows, like they were up to no good, and had a carriage waiting for them farther down the road."

Disturbed, Hart swung his leg over the saddle and took up the reins. "Thank you, Henry. You've been very helpful."

"I'm glad of it, milord. I pray you find her before something bad befalls her."

Hart nodded. "That is my aim."

Hart rode out the gate. After walking the five miles to the nearest village, Maddie and her maid must have traveled to Tunbridge Wells where she could purchase tickets on the stage. He looked down at the paper where Henry had written down the addresses. The nanny lived in Malmesbury, which was closer than Bath. Maddie might choose to go there. He tossed up in his mind where to go first and decided on Malmesbury and rode home to pack a portmanteau.

Hart ordered the curricle to be brought around and glanced at the sky as he walked to the house. He had about five hours of daylight left.

⇶⇷

IN THE LATE afternoon, the coach reached Bath and pulled up beside the Crown Inn. Maddie and Jane climbed gratefully down. As they gathered up their bags tossed down onto the pavement, Maddie took a deep breath of fresh air. The coach stank of sweat and meaty odors after the man opposite brought out a sausage and took a painstakingly long time to eat it. A young child sniveled on her mother's lap. The woman looked exhausted, but she shook her head when Jane offered to hold her child so she could rest.

Maddie stretched and gazed around to get her bearings. They must find a hackney in Milsom Street to take them to her Aunt Libby's townhouse. It would be a long walk uphill, and she and Jane drooped with fatigue.

"Aunt Libby will be pleased to see me," she said, attempting to sound cheerful, although she longed for a cup of tea and a sandwich, followed by a good long rest. They barely had time to eat when the stage stopped at the last inn, and the rocking of the coach took away her appetite.

On reaching Milsom Street, Maddie saw a hackney coming along the road. She ran out to hail it down.

The jarvie put them down outside her aunt's terraced house on Bathwick Hill. Maddie paid him, and they carried their luggage to the door.

With the lure of comfort and friendly faces, Maddie grasped the knocker and rapped smartly.

A moment later, a maid in a mobcap opened it. The girl's mouth formed an 'o.' "Lady Madeline?"

"Yes, Mary." Maddie walked past the astonished girl and removed her soiled gloves. "Is my aunt in?"

"No, milady. Your aunt is in London."

Maddie's heart sank. "London?"

"Yes. I'll fetch Mrs. Wilmot. The housekeeper will explain."

Maddie and Jane sank down on the sofa in the parlor. Mrs. Wilmot bustled in a few minutes later. "Lady Madeline! Lady Elizabeth and Catherine left yesterday for London. They'll be gone for two months."

"I wasn't aware they were to leave so soon," Maddie said, her hopes dashed.

"I believe your aunt wrote to advise you of their plans and invite you to make your come- out with Catherine. Did you not receive her letter?"

Maddie stared at her. "No, I didn't."

"Your aunt told me your uncle wrote back. He said you were unwell and would not go to London this Season."

Furious at her uncle's cruel lie, heat surged up Maddie's neck. She put her hands to her hot cheeks. "I wasn't aware he'd written."

"Are you better now?" Mrs. Wilmot asked carefully, observing her. "Would you care for some tea?"

"I am well, thank you. As we traveled by stage, my maid and I sorely need a wash and some food, if you would be so good, Mrs.

Wilmot."

The housekeeper rose and went immediately to the door. "Of course. I'll see to it." She turned her hand on the latch. "I'll have chambers prepared for you, and one for your maid. Do you plan to stay long?"

"Only a few days." Maddie's mind worked furiously. Her aunt would be gone for two months! Where could she go now?

After a thorough wash, a change of clothes, and a satisfying meal, Maddie felt more positive as she and Jane retired for the evening. Dismissing her tired maid, Maddie slipped off her shoes and lay down on the pretty embroidered coverlet. Her widowed aunt was a keen embroiderer, something she'd never mastered. Bitter tears blinded her at the missed opportunity to go to London. Her father thought it best to make her uncle her guardian because after her uncle died, her aunt became very unwell. How wrong he was. Maddie's father would turn in his grave to see how her uncle controlled her with lies. At least he couldn't touch her dowry, which would be held in trust. It made her so angry she was glad to run away and never wished to return. Uncle Arthur would be determined to find her, so she and Jane couldn't stay here long. This would be the first place he would look for her, and without her aunt here to assist her, he would surely take her back.

Hart's absence had made her feel oddly cut adrift. Foolish to think of him as a friend when she hardly knew him. It didn't matter now. She would most likely never see him again.

Maddie wiped her eyes with her handkerchief as she remembered what had occurred beneath her uncle's roof three nights ago, which gave her no choice other than to flee.

From the safety and comfort of her aunt's bedchamber, their mad dash flooded back. Determined to discover what her uncle was up to, she'd crept to the top of the stairs again. The men had been closeted in the drawing room with her uncle. Maddie descended the stairs, studiously avoiding any of the creaking treads. She darted across the hall and listened at the drawing room door. "It takes brains to plan these operations," her uncle snarled in a tone that brooked no dissent. "And if you want to be paid rather than land in jail, don't you numb-skulls forget it." His growling voice sounded so menacing, a gasp forced its way through her lips.

Inside, the room grew quiet. Had they heard her? Maddie turned, and moving swiftly and as light-footed as she could, flew up the stairs, sick with fright. In her bedchamber, she quietly shut the door.

In bed, heart pounding, she lay still and listened. The staircase creaked with a heavy tread. Was her uncle coming to check on her again? She screwed her eyes shut and tried to regulate her breathing.

The door opened and someone crossed the floor to peer down at her. It wasn't her uncle. The unwashed smell and the heavy breathing made her sure of it. A scream rose in her throat, and she clamped her lips shut. *Go away,* she silently cried. *Go away!*

Finally, the rogue moved so close that his stinking breath touched her face. Panic made it difficult to stay still. She wanted to leave the bed and escape, but when she almost couldn't bear it another minute, he moved away and left the room. Once the door shut behind him, she released the breath she'd been holding. Throwing off the covers, she left the bed, running to listen at the door. She was certain she'd come close to being ravished. Would her uncle care? Had he sent the man up to her room?

The next day, Maddie wandered around in a daze, trying to decide what was best to do. At dinner, when Uncle Arthur commented on her quiet demeanor, she said she was tired and tried not to wriggle as he studied her.

But that night, when she heard heavy footsteps in the corridor, she muffled a scream with her hands over her mouth. Her door opened. Lying curled up on her side, her eyes tightly closed, she heard the ruffian's raspy breathing above her and smelled his sour body odor again as he moved closer. It was all she could do not to cry out and order him from her bedchamber, but she firmed her lips and resisted. She wasn't sure why, but instinct told her it wouldn't be wise to let her uncle know she'd seen these men. After a few terrifying minutes, which seemed an eternity, the man left the room. At the sound of his footsteps stamping down the stairs, she left the bed. Quickly dressing, she crammed a portmanteau with a few articles of clothing, donned her warmest cape, took the lighted candle, and left the room.

Maddie climbed the stairs to the servants' wing where Jane's bed-chamber was located. Jane had the room to herself after one of the maids had been put off.

She opened the door. The bedchamber was in darkness. Her candle lit her way to the bed, and she shook Jane's shoulder. "Jane," she murmured. "Wake up."

"Milady...?" Jane sat up and stared at her, sleepily rubbing her eyes.

"We have to leave, Jane. Pack your bag with enough clothes for a few days. I'll explain as we walk to the village. We can get a ride there to Tunbridge Wells and join the stagecoach."

Jane scrambled out of bed and dressed while Maddie worried if she was doing the right thing. Should she take Jane away? What if she couldn't keep the girl safe? But she didn't trust her uncle not to dismiss Jane. Maddie couldn't return there. The man would come to her bedchamber again. He might become emboldened and touch her, and it would be useless to appeal to her uncle.

Even here at her aunt's, the horror of it still made her tremble. Maddie moaned. *Where now?* Impossible to go to London without decent clothes. She would have to seek her aunt's help, which meant asking her to go against the wishes of Maddie's guardian. Even if Aunt Libby would agree, Maddie could not ask it of her. But where could they go that was safe from him? When Uncle Arthur found her again, he only had to appeal to the local magistrate, and she would have no power against him. It was more than a month before she could claim her independence. Until then, she must find somewhere she and Jane could stay in safety. But with very little money, there was only Nanny. Although she hated to alarm her when she was getting on in years, Maddie had no choice.

Chapter Six

MISS GREYSON, MADDIE'S nanny, lived in a tiny cottage in the old town of Malmesbury. Although she was far from young, the lady had a brisk manner. Hart saw wisdom in her eyes as she invited him inside for a cup of tea.

Hart stood, feeling overlarge in the neat parlor, which smelled of beeswax and lavender. Embroidered chair covers and tapestries decorated every available surface.

"You were about to leave?" He had noted the small piece of luggage at the door. "I shouldn't wish to delay you."

"My brother has fallen ill and requires my nursing. But there is time for a nice chat and a cup of tea."

In the adjacent room, Miss Greyson lifted the kettle off the stove. She stared anxiously at him. "Has something occurred? Lady Madeline isn't unwell?"

"No. The last time I saw her, she was in excellent health. But I understood she was to visit you."

"She didn't mention a visit in her last letter." She fussed over the tea cannister. "Did Maddie tell you she was coming here?"

"Not exactly, but as I was in the vicinity, I thought to call on her. I'm a neighbor of Mr. Wakeham's."

She frowned. "Maddie is impulsive, but she's a sensible girl. I cannot imagine her going away without saying where. Please do sit, milord."

He eased aside a ball of wool and knitting needles and sat. "I was told she planned to visit someone, but must have mistaken her direction," he said, not wishing to worry her. "It's of no consequence; it was merely a courtesy call."

She poured the tea into flowery cups, then brought the milk jug and sugar bowl to the table. He thanked her as she placed a plate of buttered scones down within his reach. He saw she would have been an excellent nanny. Small and efficient, but with a softness in her features which told him she would be kind to the children in her care.

It was some hours since he'd eaten. He ate one of the delicious scones appreciatively and reached for another while Miss Greyson expressed the view that Maddie would have gone to her aunt in Bath.

"Ah, I see, my mistake."

She scrutinized him. "What is your interest in Maddie, sir?"

"Only as her friend and neighbor."

"I see." Miss Greyson looked doubtful, but said no more.

Hart spent an hour with her, talking, or rather listening. He came away knowing more about Maddie than he suspected she might like, her nanny painting a picture of a determined girl, sometimes difficult to constrain, but good-hearted and excited for the future when she left the schoolroom and could put up her hair and go to London.

Maddie was not that girl now, he thought, as he set the horses on the road to Bath. But, given the chance, she would be again. If she arrived safely in Bath. Hart didn't doubt her courage, but the thought of her, alone and at the mercy of unscrupulous men, pickpockets and the like, drew a curse from his lips. He would ride through the night if he could, but instead must put up at a coaching inn to rest his horses. If he left at first light, he'd reach Bath around midday.

The following day, the sun was high in the sky when he reached Lady Elizabeth's townhouse. It was one of a long row that swept down the hill. A small, drooping figure hovered uncertainly on the steps. Hart had seen the girl before. As he approached, he recognized the freckle-faced maid who had peered at him over the top of the boundary wall between his and Wakeham's properties. "You are Lady Madeline's maid. What is your name?"

"Jane Frost, Lord Montford." She sniffed and wiped away tears with a finger.

"I wish to see your mistress. Shall we go inside?"

Her eyes widened. "But Lady Madeline is not here, milord. Her aunt is in London."

He raised his eyebrows. "Where is Lady Madeline?"

"I don't know." She shivered, alarm in her eyes. "Milady and I were on our way to buy tickets for the stagecoach when it happened."

"What happened, Jane?" Alarmed, he curbed his impatience for the girl was on the verge of hysteria.

"A carriage pulled up beside us in the street. The door opened, and a rough-looking man jumped down. He grabbed Lady Madeline and pushed her into the carriage." She paused to take a breath. "Then the coachman whipped up the horses and they went away at a cracking pace with her inside."

Fear rocketed through him. "How long ago was this?"

"I waited for ages, hoping they'd bring her back. When they didn't, I walked up the hill. Her aunt is not here, and I wasn't sure who to turn to."

"An hour ago, do you think?"

She hesitated and then nodded.

It could have been longer, the girl wasn't sure. Hart tightened his jaw. Could he catch up with them when they'd been gone so long? "Did you see which way they went?"

"I don't know... I was that shocked." She rubbed her arms. "I almost lost my wits."

"Try to think."

She nodded. "The carriage turned off at the bottom of the street.

That way." She turned and pointed.

"Are you sure?"

"Yes…yes. I remember now."

On their way back to Tunbridge Wells? Where else could they take her? "Come inside, Jane." He climbed the steps and knocked. When a maid answered, he handed her his card and requested to see the housekeeper.

While they waited in the hall, the lady hurried in.

When he explained about Maddie's abduction, the housekeeper, Mrs. Wilmot, put her hand to her chest, alarmed. "Dear heaven. I hope she is all right."

"I don't know. But I intend to go after them. Would you take in Lady Madeline's maid until she returns?"

"Certainly, my lord. I hope nothing bad has befallen Lady Madeline. I wondered why she had arrived here unaccompanied and without notice. Most odd, I thought. And she did not know her aunt had gone to London, despite Lady Dalby writing to tell her of their changed plans." She sighed. "These family affairs are never easy. Especially with young ladies. So unpredictable. Would her uncle have come to take her home? If not he, perhaps I should advise him?"

"There's no need. I'm sure it was Mr. Wakeham," Hart said shortly.

Before he left, he asked to see Jane again. "You mustn't worry, Jane. I'll find your mistress. Why did she leave home? Did she tell you?"

There was not much Jane could tell him. Struggling to understand her, Hart calmly questioned her. Some men who visited her uncle had frightened Maddie. In what manner, Jane wasn't sure, but it became clear they came after her on Wakeham's orders and grabbed her off the street. Hart's anger and disgust toward Wakeham grew.

"Describe the carriage to me."

"It was old, gray…or a light green."

"Anything else?"

She shook her head.

Untying the reins, he climbed into his curricle. Hart ordered his thoughts. Was it even possible to follow them? Jane had failed to offer a helpful description of the vehicle. Might it be better to return home and force Wakeham to tell him what this was about? He was obviously in deep with some rough types. Did they take their orders from him? He dismissed any notion of approaching Wakeham. He didn't trust the man. It would waste precious time, and every minute Maddie spent in their company was dangerous. His heart turned over at the disturbing possibilities which came unwelcome into his mind. What might she be going through? What would they do to her? Surely Wakeham would have instructed them not to hurt her. Or would he? There was no understanding the man's motives. And no time to call in the Bow Street Runners who must come from London, although Hart wouldn't hesitate if he failed to find her.

Hart turned his curricle into the road at the bottom of the hill. Anger caused him to urge his horses into a fast trot. Passing a slow carriage, there was only light traffic ahead. The few carriages were neither gray nor green. Disheartened, he passed them, and getting a clear run, urged his horses on. He would not turn back. He had to find her.

The road ahead was now clear, and the horses settled at a steady pace, enabling Hart to consider those things he'd left undone during this mad dash. He groaned aloud. Oh lord, and he must send a message to Vivian Spencer to say he would not be in London by Saturday. Would it reach her in time? A shocking lapse in manners. She would never forgive him. What troubled him more, he realized, was that he'd hurt her and behaved in an ungentlemanly fashion, not that he might lose her favor. But then there'd been no time to get to know her, and for a relationship to develop into something deeper would take time. Time he didn't have with his uncle's trustees on his back. His own predicament rose to worry him, and while he wrestled with it, he almost failed to notice the muddy old carriage up ahead. It was cream, not gray, or green, but so dirty the color was almost indecipherable. It lurched at an angle in a deep ditch. Hart reached down and drew out the pistol he kept in a box under the seat. He cocked it and tucked it into the back of his breeches beneath his coat.

THE CARRIAGE WAS grimy, the seats smelling of ale and smoke, and something undefinable but nasty, which she didn't try to put a name to. Maddie tried to breathe slowly, but her heart galloped, and her knee ached, so badly bruised she wasn't sure she could run if she tried to escape. One scoundrel went away with the wheel to find a wheel-wright. A dark-haired man sat opposite her in the carriage, leering at her as she crammed herself into a corner. The third stood at the horses' heads.

"You'll be in trouble when the authorities get hold of you," she said to him. "They'll toss you in jail for life, or hang you."

He rubbed a scar on his pale cheek. His eyes looked jaundiced.

"If you live that long," she added.

His thick red lips parted to show stained teeth. "Why wouldn't I?"

"You look liverish."

"None of your lip," he growled. "Or I'll teach you a lesson. Arrogant bunch, you nobles, think you own the world." He laughed. A raw, grating sound. "There are ways of bringing you down."

"What nonsense." These were her uncle's men. She recognized his voice. She wanted to keep him talking, afraid he might think of something else to fill the time.

"We can take whatever we want and live as high and mighty as you."

She tapped her cheek with a finger. "Let me see. Who was the last highwayman to be hanged? James Snooks, wasn't it? The streets are safer now. Bow Street will catch up with you. Few robbers get to grow old."

"I said none of your lip!" He bent forward and leveled a stinging backhand across her cheek.

Tears flooded her eyes, but she refused to rub it. "You'll be in trouble when my uncle learns how you've treated me."

He shrugged his thin shoulders and grinned, showing off his yellow, broken teeth. "Your uncle? Who might he be?"

Maddie shivered and her blood ran cold. Her uncle never cared for her. His behavior toward her was cruel. She couldn't make sense of it.

Turning away from the man's ugly face, she gazed out of the window, not allowing him to see her distress. Craning her neck, she saw a curricle draw into the side of the road a few yards behind them. A tall figure jumped down and tied off the reins. He strode toward them. Hart! Her heart pumped hard as excitement and fear for him made her tremble. She sat back against the squab and clasped her gloved hands together.

"You've decided to behave," the man said. "Pity. I would enjoy teaching you a few tricks about how to treat a fellow."

She wanted to jump up and bang on the window to alert Hart, but she couldn't see where he was. Suddenly, a thud and an *oomph* came from the front of the carriage. The horses lurched and whinnied.

"Eh, what was that?" The rogue opened the door and leaned out.

Thrilled, her stomach fluttering with nerves, Maddie watched Hart drag her jailer out of the carriage. A fist to the man's jaw sent him reeling back, but the rogue merely staggered and came at Hart with a knife in his hand. Sneering, he waved the blade about. As he lunged, Hart stepped aside and chopped the back of the man's neck with the side of his hand. He went down like a stone and lay still.

Her rescuer looked remarkably unruffled as he turned to her and held out his hand. "Maddie. Are you all right?"

"I am now," Maddie said with a faint smile. She put her foot on the step and fell into his arms. "I've hurt my knee." She leaned into him, enjoying his clean, masculine smell and his reassuring strength. So welcome after those who held her captive. Her bonnet hanging by its strings, she gazed up at him dizzily with the urge to laugh.

"We'll have your knee attended to." He scooped her up in his arms and carried her toward his curricle just as a smart landau swept by. Three ladies in flowery hats stared back at them. They turned and watched until the vehicle disappeared around the corner.

"The doyens of Bath." Maddie still trembled as she held onto a solid, muscled shoulder. "Gossip will be everywhere before nightfall."

Hart settled her in the curricle. "They don't know who you are."

She sank back against the seat with a relieved sigh. "They would. I visited my aunt frequently with my mother. We took the waters and went to the theater...and attended..."

"Let them." Hart untied the reins and leaped aboard the curricle. "Did these men cause you to run away?"

"Yes, they came up to my bedchamber in the night. I was frightened."

Hart scowled. "I wish I'd known that. They wouldn't have gotten off so lightly."

She very much doubted they had. The crumpled, dark-haired man lay like a bundle of dirty washing when they passed him.

He set the curricle in motion. "Shall I take you back to your aunt's home?" he asked, pulling her back to reality. Her newfound energy at just being with him drained away. What could she do now?

"Yes please, I must get my maid, Jane, who waits for me there. I'm sorry to be such a nuisance." She glanced at him. "Why are you here? This cannot be a coincidence."

"When I heard you'd run off with your maid, I came after you."

"I didn't just run off, I began to doubt my safety from my uncle's men. Why did you come after me?"

"Why?" He hesitated. "Because I thought you'd need help. It's what any decent man would do. And I'm dashed glad I did."

He made her sound like a flibbertigibbet, an expression Jane used. A helpless woman and a dreadful burden. Despite the thrill at seeing her handsome rescuer make short work of disabling her uncle's men when she had little chance of escaping, she wished to reassure him she was ordinarily quite capable. "You doubted I could get myself to Bath? I am in Bath, am I not?"

He turned to her, one eyebrow raised. "Maddie. You need my help, don't you?"

She sighed and rubbed her sore knee through her skirt, a little ashamed at how ungrateful she sounded. "I do. I am indebted to you, Hart." She sighed again. "If you'll return me to Jane, we will leave Bath on the next stage. My nanny will take me in."

"She won't. When I saw her, she was about to leave to visit her brother."

"You went to see Nanny?"

"I did. Gracious lady."

She stared at him. "How did you know about her?"

"The groom, Henry, told me."

"Oh, yes, of course." She frowned. "I hope Henry can look after Pearl."

"He will. He seems a decent enough fellow."

"Henry is. But I would prefer neither he nor my horse were there."

"We'll discuss that later. The most important thing is to find you somewhere safe to stay. Where these cutthroats can't find you."

The name cutthroats made her gasp. That's exactly what they were. How wise Hart was. He surely must want to be somewhere else than dealing with her problems. Perhaps some lady expected him to call. She hated to be his problem. Maddie suppressed a moan as her hope to find refuge with Nanny evaporated. Her last haven had disappeared. "Just put me down at my aunt's house, if you will be so good. Jane will be anxious about me. I cannot stay there overlong, however. Those biddies who saw you carrying me will have created a fine scandal for my aunt's ears when she returns from London." She put her hands to her face. "My uncle wants me home. I can't bear to return there," she said, her voice muffled. "But I worry about Pearl."

"Go home? The devil you will. What is that man up to?"

"I don't know, but it has nothing to do with me."

"Those men are criminals."

"Yes, I'm sure of it. But what would my uncle want with them?"

"I don't yet know."

"If I had the right clothes, I could go to London. Perhaps I should anyway. I shall have to bear the scandal, which is sure to follow." She hesitated. "But I hate to embarrass and upset my aunt." She sighed. "Aunt Libby hasn't been well."

"Do you know what your uncle plans for you?"

She shook her head. "I wish I did. He refused to allow me to make my debut. He wants to keep me close, but he doesn't like me. I didn't want to think him capable of evil, but now..." She shook her head. "I had intended to stay with him until my birthday, but those men made it impossible. When I turn twenty-one in six weeks, I will receive a little money from the trustees, and there's my dowry, should I wish to marry. After that, Uncle Arthur will have no hold on me."

"What is in your father's will?"

"I don't know precisely."

"Why not?"

"I wasn't present when the will was read. Uncle Arthur handled everything. Because I was under age, the whole business was taken out of my hands. But it is within my uncle's rights to force me to return."

"And after your birthday? What will you do then?"

"I don't know. I haven't thought that far ahead. My birthday seems a long way away at this moment." Maddie watched him. His hands lightly clasping the reins, he passed a slow cart at a good pace, his polished boot resting on the footboard. He seemed so calm it was difficult to feel the weight of her predicament. But putting her experience into words had brought it all rushing back and made her stomach clench. Hart was right. She couldn't go back there. But what about Pearl? She rubbed goosebumps on her arms. And where could she go? She supposed she could remain at her aunt's, but she doubted it was right when Aunt Libby would be away in London until summer.

Hart pulled the curricle up outside her aunt's townhouse, then sat back and looked at her. "There has to be something more behind your uncle's behavior."

"But what could it be?"

"I don't know, but I don't intend to let him get his hands on you again. If he does, I fear he might kill you."

She frowned at him. "I don't understand why he would. He can't get hold of my dowry." She shivered. "You don't have to be so blunt about it."

"Maddie, right now, he owns all the cards." He took her hands and gave them a gentle shake. "I don't know what he's up to, but by God, you are not going back there."

Chapter Seven

MADDIE WAVED TO Jane, where she waited at the door. Then she turned back to Hart. "I appreciate how you've helped me, Hart, but now I must deal with this myself." Her voice was tight as she fought for control. She didn't fool him. She was reaching the end of her tether.

He had given some thought to Maddie's plight as he drove here. "I own a small rural cottage near Box Hill on the North Downs, left to me a few years ago by a relative. It will need some attention to make it comfortable, as it's been empty for close to a year. But you will be safe. I doubt they'll find you there."

"How kind you are," she murmured. She tied the ribbons on her bonnet more firmly with quick fingers. "I hate to trouble you further."

"It's no trouble." He pushed aside the thought of Vivian's outrage and his uncle's trustees. "I can take you and Jane there now. You can remain at the cottage for the following month, or longer if you wish." He frowned. "But even after you turn twenty-one, you could still be vulnerable to whatever your uncle has in mind for you."

She frowned. "Father never intended it to be this way."

"Nevertheless, it is. You have to face the situation you are currently in. I will help you all I can."

He assisted her down, breathing in her fresh lily of the valley scent, her hand resting lightly on his shoulder.

Her gaze met his and the reluctance in her expression told him how difficult this was for her. He remembered her nanny's words, how independent she'd always been. "Thank you, but if you will take me back to my uncle's house, I shall be grateful."

"But why, Maddie? That is madness."

"He might hurt Pearl if I don't go back. And I can't draw you into this. Those men won't hurt me once my uncle gets his wish."

"Won't they?" Hart swallowed his anger at her uncle and modulated his voice. "What if I fetch Pearl and bring her to the cottage?"

She stared at him, obviously tempted. "No. I can't let you. It would be stealing."

"Isn't Pearl your horse?"

"Yes...but..."

"I'll get the mare. Henry will assist me."

Relief fought with apprehension on her face. "Oh, Hart, you make it so hard for me to say no."

"Then say yes."

"What if those men see you? They will try to hurt you." She put a hand to her mouth. "They would kill you given the chance."

"You saw how I dealt with them."

A half smile lifted her lips, reminding him of how pretty she was. "Yes, but still..."

"Ye of little faith," he said bracingly. "Fetch Jane. We are wasting daylight. As it is, we will have to put up for the night at an inn somewhere along the road."

After she thought for a moment, the struggle evident on her face, she nodded. "I shan't tell the housekeeper about the cottage. Only that you are assisting me. I'll write to my aunt as soon as I can to explain."

When Maddie and Jane appeared on the steps with their luggage, he stowed it in the curricle and ushered them onto the seat.

Before he left Bath, Hart stopped in the town to send a letter to Vivian with his apologies. With the women crammed snugly beside him, the curricle bowled along the road toward Guilford. While greatly relieved at having Maddie safe, he was uneasy about the state of the cottage. It might have fallen down for all he knew. He'd been a neglectful landlord. Was this the best answer? He should consult his solicitor, but feared the law would be on Wakeham's side, and he'd be forced to hand Maddie over to him. As things stood, Wakeham's men didn't know him. He'd acted swiftly to deal with them, catching them unawares, so their description of him would be unreliable. He doubted Wakeham would suspect him, and when he fetched Pearl, he trusted Henry to remain silent.

They spent a night at an inn. After dinner, Maddie and Jane left Hart alone and retired to their room, as their start tomorrow would be early. When a fellow guest invited him to play a game of cards, he accepted, glad of the distraction.

Night was drawing in when they reached the village high street where there was a bakery, a food store, and a haberdashery. Hart stopped and left the curricle to purchase a few necessities, and they drove down the lane, stopping before a sign for Lilybrook Cottage. Hart drove along a pot-holed driveway through crowded, neglected gardens, a riot of spring color, and waist-high grass, and pulled up before the dwelling. In the gloom, it looked abandoned, with weeds growing in the thatched roof, shutters closed over the windows, the walls in need of paint. It was very much run down externally, at least. He hoped the interior would be in better condition.

They left the curricle, and as if to emphasize Hart's growing concern, a cool breeze sprung up. An enormous chestnut tree overshadowed the roof. Hart put the box of food, candles, and cleaning supplies down at the door and tried the handle, wondering if the last tenant had locked it. The door creaked open.

"That's in need of some oil," he said unnecessarily. "We can keep these candles spare if we find some." The tiny hall led into a snug parlor. "Ahh, yes." Hart went to the fireplace. He lit the candle in the candelabra on the mantel and added two more from the box. The room, now bathed in a soft candlelight, exposed cobwebs in the corners of the low-beamed ceiling, and dust thick on the sofa and tables.

Jane sneezed.

"It is charming," Maddie said, rather hastily, he thought. She came over to the inglenook fireplace. "We can light a fire in the hearth."

"A lick of elbow grease will put it to rights." While he wished to reassure them, his voice lacked enthusiasm. What was he thinking of bringing them here?

But apparently, the women were undaunted.

Jane explored the other rooms. "There's wood stacked outside the back door," she called. "I can light the kitchen stove."

Hart went outside and carried in the logs. When he tried the pump near the backdoor, the rusty water soon cleared. Ridiculous that the sight of it heartened him.

Maddie busily removed items from the box. "Good, you bought tea." She checked the pantry and found a teapot. "Once we have the stove lit, we can make some tea and heat water for washing."

Jane began to fill the stove with wood while Maddie took out plates and cups. "There's bread and cheese, potted beef and lamb's lettuce, gooseberry tart and strawberry jam. That will do us for several days."

Hart could do with a decent meal, and he imagined they could too. "Shall we dine at the village inn?" he asked. "I'll stay the night there and rest the horses." He waved his hand to encompass the dusty room. "Leave this for now."

With the smell of burning wood, the stove lit, and welcome heat radiated into the parlor. Maddie, on her knees, encouraged the flames in the inglenook to blaze into life.

"No, Hart." She smiled up at him. "I'd rather stay here. But you must dine at the inn. You need a proper meal and a good night's sleep."

He'd never really considered women in this light. The ladies of his acquaintance seldom lifted a finger, some not even to open a door. He watched, impressed, as they rolled up their sleeves and dealt with the mess. Maddie and Jane were much stronger than they appeared and went about things in a far more practical manner than most men might.

"Jane, come upstairs. Let's see what bedding there is." Maddie turned to Hart from the small landing. "Go, Hart," she urged him, relief brightening her brown eyes. "Enjoy an excellent dinner. We shall see you in the morning."

Hart realized he'd become irrelevant. He mounted the narrow staircase he'd never climbed before. Both of them worked in one of the two bedchambers, Maddie dusting, Jane shaking bedding out of the window. "I'll bring something for your sore knee."

Maddie turned and wiped her forehead with the back of her arm. "Oh, that. No need. It feels better now. But thank you, Hart."

"So there's nothing I can do? Move furniture around?"

She shook her head, smiled, and walked over to him. "It's fortunate there is no sign of the roof leaking. We will manage nicely." She put a hand on his arm. "Don't worry about us."

"You seem to be managing, but no amount of scrubbing will turn this cottage into decent accommodation," Hart said.

"Oh, but it will. You'll see."

He gazed at her doubtfully while inordinately pleased to find her less troubled. This was only a reprieve. Her problems were far from solved. "I'll bring food in the morning for breakfast."

Hart left the cottage, unsure whether he felt relieved or sorry to be of no further use. But as busy as Maddie now was, as soon as she sat down to think, her plight would loom large again. He would wrestle with the problem over a glass of wine at the inn, after he'd bedded down his tired and hungry horses for the night.

⤜⤜⤜⤛⤛⤛

MADDIE HAD PUT on a good act, but now, with Hart gone, her shoulders slumped, and annoying tears filled her eyes. The horror she'd faced would haunt her forever if she let it. She blinked them away, sniffed, and wiped her face with a handkerchief. Turning to Jane, she said brightly, "Let's go down. I'll slice the bread while you make the tea. We'll eat by the parlor fire."

"I could do with a bite, milady." Jane, at least, appeared to enjoy the adventure.

Later, when Maddie climbed into her bed, and pulled up the cover, which needed a good wash, her only hope was for it not to rain tomorrow. She'd spied an overgrown vegetable garden, a few turnips and carrots pushing up through the weeds.

The fine weather held the following morning. They drank horrid black tea sweetened with the jar of honey Hart had bought. More of the bedding hung out the upstairs windows. With the shutters and windows thrown open, fresh air and sunshine flooded into the rooms, highlighting the neglect while they cleaned. Fortunately, the last tenant had left a broom, mop, and dusters in a cupboard.

When Maddie heard Hart's curricle come down the drive, she rushed to the murky mirror in the hall to straighten her hair. Good grief, she looked like a waif! She scrubbed at a smudge of dirt on her chin and hurried out to greet him.

Hart jumped down, took a basket from the seat, and turned to greet her carefully, carrying a pail in his other hand. "You didn't run away in the night then."

She grinned. "We are made of sterner stuff."

He smiled. "I believe you are."

She rushed over and peeked into the basket like a child at Christmas, breathing in the delicious aromas.

He laughed. "Some goods from the bakery. I'll leave money for you to buy more necessities in the village. It's only about a three-mile walk. A pleasant stroll on a fine spring day."

"Come inside. Jane will make some tea." She sighed. "Is that milk?" She eyed the pail he carried.

"Yes, I was able to buy a quart from the innkeeper's wife. She said the farmer down the road might sell you some." He smiled. "Until you get a cow."

He stood in the parlor and gestured to the jug of yellow daisies on the table. "Well, this is an improvement. You've done a fine job of removing the dust. It smells a good deal better. But it's small, isn't it?" With a worried frown, he glanced around.

"Quite big enough for the two of us." Maddie took the pail and basket from him. "Jane has found a hidden door behind the parlor paneling. We were quite excited, but it only leads to a space beneath the roof." Her smile faded. "It might be useful if we should ever have to hide."

"I hope you never have to use it." Hart took a chair in the kitchen as Jane placed the delicious fare onto plates.

"So do I," Maddie said, joining him at the table.

"Spiders." Jane gave a shudder as she carried over the teapot.

While they ate the freshly baked warm muffins, his blue eyes grew serious. "As you can't stay here long, I've given some thought as to what you might do."

"Oh?" Maddie had not. Every time she tried, the painful thoughts skidded away. It made her realize how tired and fraught she'd become. And she'd been that way since…she feared remembering her parents' deaths could bring those pesky tears again. How sad they would be for her.

Hart gazed at her so carefully that Maddie feared he'd guessed, and she curled her fingers, resisting an impulse to rub her eyes.

"I'd like to get your thoughts on something," Hart said when Jane left the room.

She nodded, wondering what it was.

"I am in need of a wife, Maddie."

At first, she thought she must have misheard him. Her hand shook, and she almost spilled her tea when she saw he was serious. She put the cup down carefully. "I believed…" She could hardly reveal what her cousin said about his rakish lifestyle in her letter.

"You believed…?" he said, coaxing her.

She could hardly tell him her cousin had heard he didn't wish to marry.

"You seemed happy to be a bachelor," she said lamely.

He didn't dispute it. "I'll explain in more detail later, but briefly, in order to inherit from my uncle, I require a wife. He left some unusual conditions attached to his will." He leaned toward her, searching her eyes. "And you need a husband. It is the only way to safeguard your inheritance, not to mention your life."

Maddie traced the edge of the table with a trembling finger, wondering where this was leading. "Hart, is this a proposal of marriage?"

"You might call it that."

Her chest was tight, and she could hardly breathe. "I've always considered my marriage would be one of romance, even love."

"Love? That cannot be a concern when your life is at stake. This could be a mere formality. You cannot leave things as they are for long. Eventually, Wakeham will find you. If you must marry, why not me?"

She looked at him, askance. "You can't just thrust this on me… I need to think…"

"It makes perfect sense," he said warmly. "You will rescue me from a difficult situation. If I marry and restore my estate in the manner my uncle stipulated in his will, I will gain my inheritance, and all will be well."

"All will be well," Maddie echoed, staring at him. Hart made it sound so reasonable. Not a declaration of love. A mere formality to safeguard her life and his inheritance. It seemed so cold-blooded. Although he'd proved to be a stalwart friend, he didn't love her. Not once had he even flirted with her. When they first met, she doubted he'd even liked her. And there was the undeniable fact of his rakish reputation. Her cousin had said as much. Although he'd never shown that side of himself to her. Apparently, she didn't appeal to him in that way.

"I have heard of such arranged marriages." She fought to keep the disappointment from her voice. She supposed she should be grateful. After all, Hart offered safety. A way out of her predicament. But gratitude was not an ideal way to begin a marriage.

He lifted his dark eyebrows. "Yes. Arranged marriages are popular because they often make perfect sense. They can be quite successful."

Was she mad enough to condemn herself to such a life? When she wanted love and tenderness from a husband. And fidelity. If Hart was unfaithful, she doubted she'd be a wife who pretended not to know, or took a lover herself. He wouldn't know that about her, or he might not ask her. "But you don't know me. Or I you."

His blue eyes sought hers, questioning. "We have a lifetime to discover each other, do we not?"

Although casually said, a frisson of sensation settled low in her stomach, and she almost gasped at the force of it. Would lovemaking be part of this arrangement? She wanted to ask, but didn't dare. Hart was handsome and would be a fine lover, of that she was sure. She frowned. But that would not be enough for her. She wanted far more from a husband. And she feared she would be badly hurt.

"Why the frown? I know I've rushed this. But we have little time. Can you see the sense of it? Unless you find me a bad bargain?" His uncertainty only made him more attractive to her. No sign of the accomplished rake she had expected after reading her cousin's letters.

"I... I..." She struggled for words, wanting to reassure him. He was anything but a bad bargain. Any woman in her right mind would want to marry him. "I really must have time to think," she said at last.

"Of course. But remember, such a marriage can be whatever you choose it to be."

"Oh?" Maddie was stunned at the deep regret his words caused. Would he wish to continue his bachelor lifestyle after they married? Or was he suggesting it would be all right for them both to stray? She wanted to ask him that too, but it might sound insensitive and insulting if she was wrong. This would be a marriage of convenience, she firmly told herself. Hart was not looking for a love match.

"But I will need an heir sometime in the future," he said after a pause. He ran his hand through his dark, wavy hair. "I'm making a terrible hash of this, Maddie. But I think we will deal well together. Friendship is an excellent basis for a marriage."

Heat flooded her neck, and she put her hand to her throat. Of course, an heir. She hadn't thought of that. How intriguing he made it sound. She stared at his mouth and envisioned him making love to her. Her knees weakened as such thoughts threatened to sweep away her good sense.

He stood. "I'll say goodbye. I must return home." He smiled as he put on his hat. "Think about it, Maddie. The next time you see me, I will have Pearl with me."

Maddie followed him outside. He was a good man and a wonderful friend. She watched him jump athletically into his curricle. He seemed to do everything with ease. Her cheeks burning, she went inside, where Jane stared at her. "Is everything all right, milady?"

"Yes, Jane." She put a cool hand against her cheek. "Lord Montford is to bring Pearl here." How calm she sounded while still stunned by what had just occurred.

"Oh, that is good news." Jane began mopping the floor.

Left alone, Maddie's fears crowded in. If they married, the trustees and Hart's solicitors would reach some sort of agreement as to her dowry. Her uncle had explained about her father's will. Papa left her a dowry of twenty-thousand pounds. The bulk of the estate went to her aunt, whose husband left her in difficult circumstances after he passed away. But she trusted Hart instinctively in this. She knew when someone lied to her as her uncle did. And she would know if Hart lied about a mistress. He was dreadfully appealing, as all rakes were, she imagined. But she didn't have to marry him. She would be free of her uncle's control within a month and have no need to sacrifice her hopes of making a love match. And Hart would have little trouble finding a suitable lady to wed.

Would he safely rescue Pearl? What if her uncle's men attacked him? He'd handle two, but three against one? They might be ready for him, armed with knives and pistols. She shivered, suddenly cold, and went out to fetch more wood.

Chapter Eight

HART FELT A little bemused as he slowed his horses to negotiate a tricky corner. He had just asked Maddie to marry him. Normally, he'd give a considerable amount of thought to a weighty decision before he acted. And this was the biggest and most important decision he would make in his life. But his uncle's will had put a time limit on his bachelorhood. To ask Maddie seemed a perfectly reasonable arrangement when he'd broached it. But had he badly erred? Without a declaration of love, what woman would welcome such a proposal?

Nor had he considered the social consequences when surely Vivian, a delightful companion who would move seamlessly into his life in London because she understood society's expectations, might have been a better choice. He had only ever known such women. There was a clear understanding between them they might take a lover, and many of the *ton* behaved in that way, albeit discreetly.

Maddie was young and had seen so little of the world. Would she expect her husband to be faithful? She had not experienced London society, and the *ton* could be heartless if they took against someone. She would be a big cat's prey to be devoured if she put a foot wrong. However, she was intelligent and strong-willed, and when it came down to it, quite brave. He admired those qualities in her, which he supposed was why he'd rushed to help her. And why he felt no regret at having asked her to marry him. Well, he'd proposed, and had only to wait for her decision. Surprising how the anticipation of Maddie's answer caused a nervous tightening of his stomach. Had he acted subconsciously, without understanding the strength of his feelings for her? Surely not. He was a rational being. Might London life have left him so jaded he didn't know the real thing when he stumbled upon it? He didn't yet know the answer. But he suffered an uneasy feeling he'd handled this badly.

He arrived home, sorely tempted to visit Wakeham and find out just what he was up to. But because his men could be there and one of them might recognize him, it wasn't worth the risk. He'd wait until the evening, then alert Henry to his plan.

The improvements to the estate continued steadily, eating up the money from the bank. Some of the more important modifications, especially the marchioness' suite, might not be finished in time to satisfy his uncle's trustees, which added to Hart's worries. He could sense his relative, Willard Frompton, eagerly waiting for a windfall he had no right to, counting on Hart's failure.

Later that evening, the moon high in the sky, Hart crossed the acres between his property and Wakeham's on foot. Hugging the shadows, he approached the stables, above which the coachman and grooms slept. He'd have to think of a way to rouse Henry without waking everyone.

The cool breeze carried the smells of manure, hay, and horses as he crossed the cobbles to the stables. He was in luck. A lighted lantern hung from a beam, illuminating the interior. He crept to the door. Inside, two men attended a sick horse. "Colic," the veterinarian said, removing a bottle from his bag. "This will help. But I'll call back tomorrow."

"I guessed as much," Henry said.

When Henry left the stall and went to the tack room, Hart stepped out of the dark, a finger to his lips. He beckoned Henry outside.

"Have you come to tell me where Lady Madeline is, milord?" Henry asked, out of the veterinarian's earshot.

"She is somewhere safe. I've come for Pearl."

Henry stared. "You wish to take her horse?"

"Don't tell me the mare isn't here?" Hart asked with a sense of foreboding.

"Mr. Wakeham came this morning. Said he planned to sell her. The horse will be gone tomorrow."

"He's in for a surprise in the morning then."

Henry's eyes shone in the lantern light. "I am mighty relieved, milord. If you can wait until I finish up with the vet, I'll saddle her."

Hart shook his head. "No, I don't want you implicated. Go to bed. I'll saddle her."

"It's no trouble, milord," Henry said. "I'll saddle Pearl and meet you in the stable yard."

Hart returned to the shadowy wood and waited. Twenty minutes passed. Wakeham was still awake. Loud voices drifted through a window downstairs. While Hart hoped to get away before the men left, right now he wanted to know what they were up to.

He sprinted over the drive to the wall of the house.

Cautiously raising his head, he peered inside the brightly lit room. Four men sat around a table. One was Wakeham. Two others he recognized as those who he'd dealt with earlier, looking a little bruised but no worse for their experience. At first, he thought they played a game of cards, but when a man shifted on his chair, Hart had a clear view and saw how they divvied up money from a stack of notes and gold coins piled in the center of the table.

Voices came from the stables. The veterinarian emerged. Hart slipped back into the trees and watched him climb into his trap. After it disappeared down the drive, Hart ran into the stable courtyard, where Henry led Pearl out by the reins.

"Here is milady's horse."

"I fear this will get you into trouble, Henry." Hart mounted the gray. Unused to a heavy male rider, she danced about until he settled her. "There's some bad business going on in there." He nodded to the house. "Should you decide to leave Wakeham's employ, come and work for me. I'll leave word with my steward."

"I planned to seek new employment," Henry said with a pleased grin. "Wakeham's a penny-pinching miser with never a good word for anyone. I'll be there first thing tomorrow."

"A sound decision. You'll be welcome." He frowned. "Make yourself scarce if Wakeham comes looking for Pearl. I'll instruct my staff."

Hart rode Pearl along the bridle path in the woods toward Pembury. Not a bad night's work. A horse for Maddie and an excellent groom for his stables.

The next morning, painters were still at work in the house. Glad to leave the unpleasant smell of paint, he rode over the estate to see how matters stood. After which, he'd be off. He would have Maddie's answer. Last night, he spent some hours dwelling on the idea before he fell asleep. Today, the more he thought about it, the more he liked it. He hoped she would see the sense. Now that he had committed himself to wedlock, he would be deeply sorry should she refuse him. For both their sakes. He feared what might happen to her should she fall into Wakeham's clutches again. The heartless man appeared to be a crook. Although Hart thought it unlikely Wakeham would wish to draw attention to himself by notifying the constable about a stolen horse, he might come to inquire after it at Pembury. Hart would leave instructions to admit them. They would find no sign of Pearl at Pembury, because Hart planned to depart with the horse at first light.

"It's a fine day again, my lady." Jane put a cup of unappealing black tea sweetened with honey on the table, then went to draw back the curtains.

"So it is." Maddie threw off the covers, noting the sunny day beyond the window. She'd finally fallen asleep at a late hour and woke to the sound of a cockerel somewhere nearby announcing dawn. Hart stayed in her thoughts, his blue eyes dark and intense as he asked her to marry him. She tried and failed to find anything behind his words to reassure her he wanted her for more than a sensible arrangement to suit them both. Marriage! It was such a big step to take. And this was not the way she envisaged being proposed to. It would have been somewhere romantic. Her suitor down on one knee… She shook her head. Well, maybe not that precisely, but certainly with a heartfelt declaration of love.

What should her answer be when he came today? If she refused him, what could she do when she left here? Hart had invited her to remain until her birthday. Then she supposed she could join her aunt in London, although she must first claim her inheritance, visit the bank, find accommodation, and have an appropriate wardrobe made. And that meant going to London in these clothes, which by then would be little more than rags. She might buy a readymade gown in one of the bigger towns. But then, how would she get there? She would not be able to rely on Hart. Then, after she contacted the trustees, she would have to inform them she had left her uncle's house. And the trustees would, in turn, write to him. Even though he would no longer be her guardian in the eyes of the law, he still might be a danger to her. She found it overwhelming.

If she refused Hart, she supposed he would rarely come here to see her, if at all, for he would seek another bride. She disliked thinking of him with another woman. She didn't want to face a future without him in it. During her restless night, she'd realized that. But it made it harder rather than easier to make a decision, for she must guard her heart.

She grimaced and put the cup down. "After breakfast, we'll walk up to the farm and ask if they will sell us milk and eggs."

"I've boiled a large pot of water," Jane said. "I found an old tin hip-bath if you wish to bathe first."

Gritty and still tired, Maddie would love to soak in a hot tub. After all that had occurred, she did not look her best when she very much wanted to. Her appearance had mattered little to her while with her uncle, but now... "That sounds heavenly, Jane. You can wash my hair."

Maddie's thick locks were still damp, and it was past midday when they set out on the road.

The farm looked prosperous, the farmhouse recently whitewashed with green shutters on the windows. The farmer's wife, Mrs. Lester, a slender woman with gray-streaked dark hair, enthusiastically showed them into the parlor. Whipping a dust sheet off the sofa, she invited them to sit. "How nice to have company. Lester is out in the fields or with the pigs most of the day. Will you have coffee, Miss Burrell, Miss Frost?"

"We would welcome a cup, thank you," Maddie said, a little guilty at deceiving her about her title. But she feared any word of her staying in the area might reach her uncle.

Mrs. Lester chatted about the history of the old cottage while they ate an excellent pound cake with their coffee. "The cottage belongs to a handsome young lord, but you would know him, for didn't I see him drive past yesterday? There were tenants, but it has been empty since before Christmas. I hoped somebody would come to live there. It has a certain charm." She glanced at Maddie curiously, but was too polite to ask about her circumstances.

"We think so, don't we, Jane?"

Jane put a hand to her mouth full of cake and nodded.

After they drank the coffee and consumed the last crumb, Mrs. Lester stood, all business. "Now, is there anything else you might need? Cups, plates, blankets?"

"How kind of you, Mrs. Lester. We are well catered to."

As they prepared to leave, the farmer's wife insisted they take some of the cake wrapped in brown paper, along with the china jug of milk and the eggs. She refused any payment. "The hens are laying, and we have more than we can use. Come again when you need more. It would please my husband to meet our new neighbors." She saw them to the door. "Lester will come and scythe the long grass. You have only to ask."

"What good people they are," Maddie said as she and Jane walked back down the road. "They have little compared to those far wealthier, yet they are happy to share it. And often the wealthy are not."

It was late in the afternoon when they arrived back at the cottage, Jane walking slowly, careful not to spill the milk. As they turned down the cottage driveway, Hart appeared with Pearl's lead tied to the curricle.

Maddie handed the package she carried to Jane and ran to greet him. "You brought her! Thank you!"

He scrutinized her face. "How are you coping with all this, Maddie?"

She laughed. "I'm in much better spirits, thanks to you," she said in a rush. "We have visited the farmer's wife. Such a generous woman," she added over her shoulder as she ran to her horse.

Pearl whinnied and Maddie threw her arms around her neck.

Hart chuckled as he stood and watched. "Your mare would have liked to throw me off last night."

"Pearl would do nothing so unladylike."

"The horse only wants you, and I can see you return her affection."

Maddie rested her head against the horse's glossy neck, familiar with her sweet, warm, and musty smell. "Pearl is all I have from my old life."

"Then I am glad to have brought her," he said soberly.

"Did you have any trouble?" she asked, coming back to him. "What about Henry?"

"No difficulties. He works for me now."

"I am so pleased for him. Shall we put Pearl in the stables? I can offer you tea and cake." She grinned. "A decent cup this time. We have milk!"

Hart laughed. "Allow me." He untied Pearl and led her across the drive. At the stable door, he turned to look back at Maddie. "Afterward, we can have that talk."

Maddie nodded, her pulse racing. What could she say to him? She would follow her instincts and see where it led her. Without giving away too much of her feelings, which she feared he might not wish to hear.

Chapter Nine

A COOL BREEZE rose in the late afternoon. At the look of the heavy dark clouds gathered on the horizon, it might be best for Hart to stay at the inn tonight. Maddie went with him to the dilapidated stables to settle the horses. Pearl neighed a welcome as he gave them feed bags, hung up the traces, and filled the water troughs from the pump. When everything was done to his satisfaction, he approached Maddie. "Shall we go for a walk? I've yet to see the garden."

Her eyebrows rose. "You've never seen the garden?"

He eyed her with amusement. "I was a young lad when I inherited this cottage. I guess I didn't appreciate my good fortune."

"And do you now?"

He laughed and held her arm to guide her over the pebbled ground. "I am warming to it," he said, appreciative of their closeness and her familiar sweet scent.

She drew away to look at him. "I believe you turned up your nose at it earlier."

The teasing smile in her brown eyes was altogether too attractive. Tempted to kiss her, he wondered what she would do. He didn't expect this fiercely independent woman to fall into his arms. She might think he was trying to coerce her, to urge her to accept his proposal. And perhaps he was. He had chosen this path to matrimony with little thought and was now committed to it.

"You like to argue, Miss Burrell." He used the name she'd given herself, her mother's family surname. The desire to draw closer lingered. He turned to view the rundown state of the cottage with a critical eye. "I admit its sorry state is entirely because of my neglect, which I intend to rectify." As soon as he had the money to do it, he'd engage carpenters, painters, and plasterers to bring the cottage up to standard. But he wouldn't go into that now. He still hoped she'd take the second option and come to Scotland with him to marry. Get everything tidied away, and have her safe, he told himself, watching as she stooped to pick a flower.

They strolled through the overgrown gardens, a riot of spring color with floral smells sweetening the air, both avoiding what they said the last time they met.

"I'll arrange for a gardener to tidy the garden beds." Hart moved aside the branch of an azalea for Maddie to pass. A brief vision came to him; removing the pins and allowing her burnished gold locks to fall over her shoulders. Naked shoulders. With a quick indrawn breath, he took himself to task. To crowd his mind with thoughts of making love to Maddie affected his reasoning, and did not help his intention to convince her to marry him. It was merely because they were often alone, and she was undoubtedly alluring, and now that he'd decided they should marry, she became more so each time he saw her.

But now on this course and committed to it, he brought up the subject of his proposal. "Have you given any thought to what we discussed?" *Damn. It sounded like he was referring to an invitation to ride in the park. He was seldom clumsy with women, and yet Maddie set him back on his heels, unsure how to proceed, like an inexperienced youth rather than the man he now was.*

Maddie turned to face him. She twirled the stem of a daisy she'd plucked in her fingers. "Of course. I've thought of little else."

His pulse quickened. "And...?"

"It seems too rushed..." she began.

"As English law prevents you from marrying until you're twenty-one, you have a month to consider the merits," he said hastily before she put an end to the scheme. "Unless we travel to the Scottish border to marry."

Her tense shoulders relaxed. Obviously, a flight to Scotland was not something they would agree upon. "I'd like to stay here with Jane if I may. So much has happened recently that I need to catch my breath."

"I understand." He nodded, shelving his disappointment. "This is what we first decided. There's no reason for haste unless something forces us to act." *His impatience, his uncle's trustees, and Maddie's criminal uncle, for instance.* He had debated whether to tell her what he witnessed through her uncle's window, but decided against it. Maddie had enough to worry her. He would deal with Wakeham later. When he'd first considered informing the local magistrate about his suspicions, he'd decided against it, because with no guarantee of success, it could draw everything into the open, including the question of where Maddie and her horse were. These things had a way of being reported in newspapers, and would end up involving Henry. In the meantime, Wakeham, whatever he was up to, might become careless and bring the law down on himself.

"You'll come to see us now and then?" As if afraid she asked for too much, or gave something away, she rushed to add, "But I understand if you'll be too busy."

Would she miss him? "I'll come whenever I can. I must go to London tomorrow." To beg for more money from the bank, although he kept that to himself.

"Oh. I didn't know." Was she disappointed? "Will you be away long?"

"I'll return in about a sennight. I have to go on to Pembury after I've completed my business in London." Although he thought them safe here, he disliked leaving the two of them alone, and wished he could stay for a few days. He was even prepared to sleep on that sofa in the parlor. "You'll be all right? Is there anything you need? I'll give you some money before I go."

"No, nothing, thank you. Jane and I will be snug here."

He failed to see the cottage in that light. It would be drafty in windy weather. Fortunately, summer approached. "I'll return as soon as I can," he promised. "Would you both dine with me at the inn tonight?"

Maddie looked torn. "Do you think that's wise? People might wonder about us."

She was right. It was unwise. But he didn't like to think of them scraping together a meal while he dined on oysters and a plump bird with all the trimmings. "Shall we chance it? I'll be gone tomorrow. You're the new tenants of Lilybrook Cottage. They'll soon have little to gossip about."

She grinned. "I am weak. I cannot resist your invitation." She put a hand on her stomach, drawing his eyes to the swell of her breasts. "And longing for a decent meal."

As if she sensed his thoughts, with an indrawn breath, she ducked her head over the daisy she'd picked.

"Have you ever tested a theory with a daisy?" He nodded toward the flower she held. "My sister used to when she imaged herself in love with someone."

Maddie laughed and turned the stem in her fingers. "I remember my friends doing it."

"Will you put it to the test?"

"I don't believe in such things." She threw the daisy away.

"Coward," he murmured. But that only drew another laugh. Was he a crass fool to want to draw her down on the grass and enfold her in his arms? He took himself to task as he strolled beside her along the path. Minutes passed. The drawn-out silences between them seemed to speak louder than their words. Her cheeks had become flushed. Did she feel a burgeoning passion, as he did?

The path led them back to the cottage, and whatever magic the garden held for him dissipated as reality rushed in. She was attracted to him. A man recognized the sensual language between a man and a woman. Those small, subtle movements when he touched her. The way her gaze roamed his face. How she tilted her head when she laughed. The softening of her expression when she teased him. But none of that meant anything if she was loath to marry him. It spoke more to what she thought of him as a prospective husband. And her lackluster response to his proposal did little to make him sure of her answer.

They entered the parlor, where Jane, on her knees before the fireplace, encouraged the kindling to burst into life. The nights were cool here and next winter would be bitter. "I must hire a cook," Hart said to push away the nagging worry that he might be left to seek a bride among the debutantes in London when he had made up his mind to marry Maddie.

"No, please don't. I plan to try my hand at preparing the meals." Maddie nodded toward her maid. "Jane can be my guinea pig. You don't mind, do you, Jane?"

Jane smiled over her shoulder. "I cooked for my mum when she was under the weather."

"Well, there you are," Maddie said with a satisfied glance at him. "We have two cooks."

Amused, he raised an eyebrow. "What do they say about too many cooks?"

She narrowed her eyes at him and then laughed. "Be warned. I might cook dinner for you when you return."

And he would eat every bite even if it was burned to a crisp, he thought, admiring how game she was.

WHEN HART LEFT Maddie to check on the horses, she turned her attention to what to wear tonight. The gown she wore had dusty skirts and a little dirt on the hem. She had only brought two gowns suitable for daytime and travel, plus her spring green with the satin sash and the lace, which would have to do. It was far from her best. She sighed, wishing she'd thought to pack her lavender gown, but as it was, she'd crammed in too much. It would have been wiser to refuse the dinner invitation, but Hart's decisiveness made it impossible. Although he never tried to coerce her, he often got his way. While it annoyed her, she came to agree with him. If she was honest, she wanted to dine with him, and not just because she was hungry. She enjoyed his company. He made her laugh, which was something she had not done for a very long time. Something passed between them while they walked in the garden. Something unspoken, a feeling, which grew stronger every time she saw him. Did he become too important to her? She feared her ability to know what was right for her would be lost in the intensity of his blue eyes.

Maddie went back inside to Jane, who, having successfully got the fire going, was now sweeping the upper landing. "We are to dine at the inn tonight." Maddie took down the green dress hanging on a hook. It had suffered being crammed into her bag. "Is it possible to steam the creases out of this dress?"

Jane took it from her and shook it out. "I think so. I'll put the kettle on. What a pity I didn't bring the hot iron."

Maddie laughed. "And haul it all the way on the stage?"

As they climbed the steps of the old stone inn, delicious aromas wafted out, promising a good meal. Inside was warm and inviting, the tables arranged around a crackling fire. This was the first time Maddie had dined with Hart. He had changed into a dark blue coat, his cravat crisply tied, and looked very handsome, his dark hair burnished by candlelight. When he raised his glass of wine to her in a silent toast, she responded with a smile. As if they'd shared a secret. His gaze took in her simple gown, cut low over her bosom where the trim of lace failed to conceal her decolletage. Then he raised his eyes to hers, and her heart skipped a beat. He had never looked at her quite that way before. It made her toes curl. Did he judge her as a prospective bride? Was that approval? She was hardly at her best, although Jane had performed miracles with the gown and arranged her hair nicely and Maddie had tucked a yellow primrose into the curls.

This was hardly an intimate dinner for two with Jane seated at the table. Did she want to be alone with him? Really alone? Maddie wondered what it would be like for him to take her in his arms and kiss her, to make love to her. She rubbed her arms in response to the frisson of sensation rushing through her body.

"You're warm enough?" Hart asked.

She nodded, wanting to touch her hot cheeks. Why must a flush always give her away? She was probably the same color as the coals burning brightly in the fireplace.

The proprietor brought their meals to the table, placing the plates before them with a flourish. He hovered, eager to please, until Hart sent him away for a bottle of wine.

Suddenly very hungry, Maddie gave herself up to enjoying the roasted meat and vegetables. Every bite, heaven. She couldn't rely on poor Jane to cook for them, as well as the rest of the tasks she performed so cheerfully. But to employ a cook and have them bustling about in the tiny kitchen and sleeping in the narrow servant's room at the back of the house would intrude on their peace. And right now, Maddie valued peace, but knew she would soon yearn for excitement, to see more of the world, and she hoped Hart would be there. But in what capacity, lover, or friend? She had never been so indecisive, so unsure. She'd always known her own mind. But her criterion for marriage was love and being able to trust one's partner, as it always had been, and remembering her cousin's letters, she was grateful for the month he had given her to decide.

After a delicious almond cream pudding, Hart drove them back to the cottage and Jane went inside, leaving them alone on the drive.

"Thank you for dinner." Dismayed, Maddie put her fingers to her lips. "I am always thanking you, Hart. You've done so much for me. One day, I hope to repay you in some fashion for your kindness." She realized the connotations of her remark and groaned inwardly.

Amusement brightened his eyes as if he'd guessed her inner turmoil. He took her hand, raising it to his lips. "You are under no obligation to me, Maddie." He paused, and his mouth curved in a smile. "I wish for nothing unless it's freely given."

Freely given? Did he mean what she thought he meant? Her pulse quickened. Was he flirting? She was so new to this. Having always been strictly supervised by her mother, she couldn't be sure. Before, in the garden, she'd resisted a powerful urge to throw her arms around his neck and draw him down to her. To kiss him. That would have served as her agreement for their marriage. Foolish, when she was still so unsure. She drew her bottom lip through her teeth, hoping he hadn't read her thoughts. It was becoming so hard to resist him, and yet she must rely on her common sense, and not allow herself to be swayed by emotion.

He put a hand to his hat. "I shall see you in a few weeks."

She watched him climb into the curricle, realizing she didn't want him to go.

"I'll have a hot meal ready for you next time," she called as the horses started forward.

He grinned and waved as the horses gained speed. Then he was gone.

He didn't believe her, and rightly so. At her childhood home, she'd only ever ventured into the kitchens to sneak some of Cook's freshly baked biscuits. How they were prepared before they appeared on the plate failed to interest her, but the warm room smelled delicious, and she'd stayed to chat to the kitchen staff and stroke Sooty, the black mouser.

Maddie paused on the path to pick another daisy. She pulled off the petals. "He loves me, he loves me not..." Fearing the answer, she threw it away, and shook her head that she could give relevance to something so ridiculous.

By the time she reached the front door, she had turned her mind to more practical matters. Would the farmer's wife have a cookery book she could borrow? The need to prove her worth to Hart and have him admire her seemed suddenly important.

"His lordship has left?" Jane asked.

"Yes."

"He is awfully nice for a lord, if I might say so, milady."

"He is. Awfully," Maddie agreed. There was nothing toplofty about Hart, despite his title. "Jane, there's a brook at the bottom of the garden. We can wash the spare bed linens and our clothes when it's sunny." She laughed to herself, visualizing the two of them pounding the sheets with a rock and hanging them out to dry over the bushes. What would her mother say if she could see her now? Mama had much loftier hopes for her. But Maddie believed she would approve of her fortitude. And one day she might be married to a handsome marquess! She put a hand to her chest and dragged in a shaky breath. A marquess with a history of rakish behavior, she sternly reminded herself, which he was unlikely to give up for a woman he was obliged to marry.

Chapter Ten

HART DROVE THROUGH green fields and meadows on the outskirts of London. He pictured Maddie at the stove wearing an apron. Something stirring about a woman cooking him a meal, one who was nothing like the succession of solid, middle-aged cooks his mother had employed over the years. If only Maddie had given him her answer. The longer they delayed, the more dangerous it became for her. He recalled her response to his proposal; marriage for her meant romance, even love, and sharing her life with her husband. When he'd proposed, he viewed their marriage as a mere formality, a strategy to solve both their problems. It was hardly romantic, but he was all for romance, although love meant little more than a word to him, something bandied about by poets. He imagined it took courage to love someone with your whole heart. To give yourself up to them and risk heartbreak.

He hadn't missed the way Maddie looked at him while they dined, her softer, more intimate smile. She was considering him as a husband. She must have been aware of the powerful attraction between them, but wanted more from him, which he wasn't sure he could give her. Commit himself to one woman for the rest of his life? He supposed he had never loved a woman enough to promise undying love and fidelity. Even though he could take on the fiercest adversary without a second thought, he had to admit it scared him. The sadness of his childhood, and his unhappy mother a constant reminder.

An hour later, after threading his way through the traffic to the calmer streets of Mayfair, he drove the curricle into the stable mews and handed the reins to his Irish groom. "Rub them down well, Will. They're tired."

Will untethered the horses from the curricle. "I'll treat 'em like me own, milord."

Hart laughed and crossed the mews to enter Montford Court. After a bath and a change of clothes, he sat in a comfortable wing chair in the library, sipping a cognac while sorting through his post. Among them was an invitation to a card party. Vivian might be there, and he could offer his apology.

He sipped the excellent cognac and rolled it on his tongue. The tulip glass warmed over the candle-flame; the flavor was dry with a hint of oakwood and orange zest. Leaning back in the chair, he watched a painted lady butterfly fluttering around a flowering bush outside the window.

Hart missed Maddie. He was already very fond of her. So, maybe he was looking at this the wrong way. If he allowed himself to risk his heart, he could fall in love with her, which would be far better than this cold arrangement he pursued. If she agreed to his proposal, he would try to be the loving husband she wished for. Maddie at least deserved that.

During the evening at the Robinsons' card party, two of Vivian's friends cut him. It was no mystery why they did. They considered his treatment of Vivian as bad *ton,* and he admitted it was.

When he entered the gaming chamber, the volume of noise in the room lowered. Some watched him with speculative glances. Must society always involve themselves in his affairs? Hart strolled around greeting those he knew who would still speak to him, then decided not to play and left the room. He was certain gossip only lasted until the next juicy scandal. He found Vivian in the drawing room, lovely in a violet gown embroidered with silver moons. The friend at her side murmured to her and moved away. Burying a sigh, Hart crossed the carpet to her.

"Mrs. Spencer, how charming you look tonight."

"My lord." She curtsied, her eyes frosty.

From a distance, her friend gazed at him critically. Damn, anyone would think he had left Vivian standing at the altar. Wondering how he might justify his behavior, or whether he'd remain forever in her bad books whatever he said, he spoke softly, foiling the lady to her right who leaned closer to catch his words. "May we talk privately?"

She inclined her head regally, the soft feathers in her hair fluttering as if in protest. "I believe the small parlor is not in use tonight." The parlor was blessedly empty. She turned to him with an ironic smile. "I imagine it's your intention to apologize, Montford. But there really is no need."

"There's every need. Did you get my letter?" Hart was determined to smooth over the matter. "I let you down badly, and I am profound-ly sorry for it. It was unavoidable."

She put up a gloved hand to stop him. "I received it just before we left for Ascot. A little late, don't you think? Fortunately, Lord Bolton kindly took me up in his carriage as one of his party. We drank champagne and watched his horse win. It was a lovely day."

"I'm pleased, but it was never my intention…"

"Where were you? Not in London," she asked, her voice mild, deceptively so, he suspected.

He cleared his throat. "No. My neighbor had a problem and re-quired my help."

"Oh?" Her eyes searched his, doubting him. "What sort of prob-lem?"

"His niece was missing. I went to find her."

"And did you?"

"Yes. Happily, I was successful." Hart's fingers itched to loosen his cravat, but he resisted.

"So, a happy ending. How wonderful! I trust the little girl was unharmed?"

"Yes, but er, she's not so little." He found himself led helplessly down a dangerous path.

"How big is she?" she asked, frowning.

"Lady Madeline is twenty."

"Twenty?"

"I believe so."

"It is unusual to get lost at twenty. Is she pretty?"

"One might say so, yes. Vivian, I wish I could tell the whole, but I'm afraid I've promised discretion in the matter."

Vivian stepped closer. Her expensive perfume scented the air as she placed a gloved hand on his chest and gazed up at him. "I might forgive you if you'll escort me at the Forsters' dinner party on Saturday."

"My deepest regrets. I am in London only to visit my solicitor and the bank, and then I'm away to the country. Matters at Pembury need my urgent attention."

Vivian nodded as she smoothed her gloves. "How disappointing."

"Indeed, it is. I am deeply sorry," he said, feeling like the worst scoundrel. "I shall return to London as soon as I am able."

"Yes. We might dance, perhaps." She walked to the door. "When you are sure that miss whoever she is hasn't wandered off again."

She went out the door and closed it with a sharp click.

It left Hart with the uneasy feeling Vivian had not finished with him. He spied a flash of emotion, like revenge, in her beautiful eyes. He disliked leading her on, and had been clumsy. And to think he'd once considered joining the diplomatic service.

In the morning, he visited his solicitor who acted on Hart's behalf to sell the colliery in Newcastle-on-Tyne. "Matters move slowly, milord," Upton said. "There are still quibbles over the contract." He drew the papers out and placed them before Hart. Leaning across the desk, he pointed to items on a page. "I've marked them here."

Hart read it through, then pushed the pages back to him. "That seems reasonable. I would like the matter concluded as soon as possible."

Upton removed his glasses and gave them a quick polish, then replaced them on his nose to stare at him myopically. "One cannot hurry the law, milord."

"So I see." Frustrated, Hart rose and offered his hand. "Keep me informed, Mr. Upton."

Forgoing the rest of the invitations which had landed on his desk, Hart dined with friends that evening and played cards at his club until late. Two friends who suspected he had a new lady in his life teased him unmercifully. But how could explain his relationship with Maddie when, should she decide against the marriage, it might disappear like a wisp of smoke? And Hart refused to mention her in the same breath as his previous brief affairs. All he would say was 'in the fullness of time, gentlemen,' which only made them more curious. Tate threatened to tie him to a lamppost until he gave the lady's name up. Fighting them off good-naturedly, Hart went home to grab a few hours of sleep. He left the city for Tunbridge Wells right after breakfast.

Arriving back at the Pembury stables, Henry came to greet him. "Any interest in Pearl?" Hart asked him as he dismounted.

"Not a murmur from that quarter, milord," Henry said.

"Good. Be sure to make yourself scarce if Wakeham should decide to visit. It's best to admit him and let him have a good look around if he wishes."

"I'll keep an eye out, milord."

The work done to the house, now finally close to completion, pleased him until he read the stern letter from his uncle's trustees, which mentioned a visit at the end of the month, three weeks away.

Hart rubbed at the creases forming on his forehead. Unless he and

Maddie married, he had no time to satisfy their demands. There was still work to be done on the estate. The tenant farmers Hart visited barely managed, and their crops suffered. What if he failed to meet the solicitor's conditions? Would they be harsh enough to turn him down flat? It seemed unbelievable, and yet he could not afford to take it lightly.

The clatter of horse hooves sounded on the driveway. Through the library window, Hart saw a cream-colored carriage pull up outside the house. One he recognized. "Speak of the devil," he murmured.

Wakeham alighted and strode up the steps to ring the bell.

Moments later, a footman appeared in the library.

"Will you see Mr. Wakeham, milord?"

Hart rose from the desk. "Show him in."

"Mr. Wakeham." Hart waved him to a chair. "Do you still have concerns about the fences? I assume that's why you're here?"

"No. The repairs are acceptable." Wakeham took a chair and sat upright as if a poker had been stuck down his back. "I wondered if you might have seen my niece's gray mare while riding over your acres, my lord."

"I cannot say I have." Hart forced a smile as he sat on the wing chair opposite him. "But then I've only just arrived from London."

"The mare did not wander into your stables?"

"No. My groom would have informed me of it. I trust Lady Madeline has returned safely?"

"Not as of yet. But I know where she is." Wakeham's small gray eyes hardened. "As she is safe, I shan't insist on her return."

"She stays with a relative?" Hart was immediately on the alert, but the man must surely lie.

"My niece is like a wild filly. I am giving her a little rein. She'll return when she tires," Wakeham said with a mendacious smile.

Had his ruffians traced Maddie to the cottage? It was possible. "I am sure you are most concerned about her," Hart countered. "She must be unhappy here."

Wakeham's mouth formed a sour expression. "Young women are hard to please."

"They yearn for the bright lights of London. Understandable, when they look forward to attending the Season after they emerge from the schoolroom."

"Yes...I daresay." Wakeham stood abruptly. "Funnily enough, I have also lost a groom."

"You suffer extraordinary bad luck," Hart said as he led him to the door. "I hope Lady Madeline is found and your groom returns."

"He won't come back if he values his life. He most likely absconded with the horse, in which case I'll have him tracked down and dealt with." A vicious expression changed Wakeham's face. Hart inhaled a breath. Wakeham showed his true colors at last. It worried Hart a good deal. He hoped Henry would take his advice and hide himself away.

❯❯❯❯❮❮❮❮

TWO DAYS AFTER Hart left them, Maddie, unsettled but refusing to admit she missed his company, rode Pearl to the farm. She hoped Mrs. Lester could spare a recipe book. There was a limit to what culinary delights she could create with the old cottage oven, but she was keen to try her hand.

Mr. Lester answered the door. "That is a fine animal you are riding, Miss Burrell," he said, studying Pearl where the horse stood tethered to the fence.

"I am fortunate to have her. The mare was a gift. I am very fond of Pearl."

"Then you wouldn't consider selling her."

"Never." Maddie smiled. "I come hoping Mrs. Lester will share some of her recipes."

100

Mrs. Lester appeared. "Leave us women to discuss domestic matters," she said, shooing him out of the parlor. "Lester loves his horses." She shook her head. "As if we could afford to buy such an animal. Please sit down, Miss Burrell, while I fetch coffee, then we can have a pleasant chat."

A short time later, a maid entered with a tray. Mrs. Fletcher placed a cup of coffee and cake before Maddie on the occasional table. "You wish to borrow one of my recipe books?" She went to a bookshelf and chose a volume.

"I confess to being a novice," Maddie said. "We always had a cook at home."

Mrs. Lester sat and flicked through the book. "Where was that, dear?"

Maddie realized she'd given too much away. She was terrible at building a web of untruths to hide behind. "A small village in the north. I'm an orphan. Both my parents passed away two years ago."

"I am sorry. But why come here?"

Maddie sighed. "My aunt lived in this district, and I loved it when I came to stay. I suppose I wanted to get away and begin a new life."

Mrs. Lester lifted her gaze from the book. "Oh, that is sad. I am sorry. You are young to be on your own in this world." She turned to another page. "Now these are quite easy recipes to follow. You can purchase the ingredients at the village shop. These meals are for you and Jane?"

"Mostly, yes. And the occasional visitor."

Mrs. Lester glanced at her thoughtfully. "Well, you'll have to adjust the recipe accordingly."

Maddie quickly finished her coffee and put down the cup. "I intend to bake biscuits and a cake, although I fear they will suffer compared to yours."

Mrs. Lester grew pink. "How nice of you to say so. I shall wrap some biscuits for you to take home. To tide you over until you make your own."

Maddie tried to dissuade her, but soon saw it was hopeless. She would insult Mrs. Lester should she refuse.

Handing her the package, Mrs. Lester accompanied Maddie to the door. "Might we see you both in church on Sunday?"

Maddie had initially thought it better not to make herself known to the community. But if she remained a recluse, might that spark more interest in her than her appearance at church?

She made a vague reply and before Mrs. Lester probed deeper into her past, as Maddie was sure she'd like to do, mounted Pearl. She rode home. For now, until her birthday at least, home was the cottage. As the horse slowly walked down the hill beneath the oak tree bows, Maddie gazed over at the fields, the boxwood, the flowering hedgerows, the sheep, startling white against the greenery. The lane was beautiful, with clusters of white snowdrops in the grass. If here was home for a while, it wouldn't be so hard to bear.

At the beginning of the second week, Hart returned when Maddie was on her knees in the vegetable garden, weeding her turnip, carrots, and lettuce seedlings.

He strode down the path to meet her, hat in hand, dressed in snug-fitting riding breeches and boots, his greatcoat swirling around his long legs.

At the sight of him, Maddie's heart beat faster. She took a quick breath and stood, brushing her knees, and walked over to greet him.

"You look in excellent health, Maddie. I believe the air here agrees with you."

She smiled. "You rode, Hart?"

"The carriage horses need rest, and Blaze needs exercise. I'll put up at the inn tonight. Would you care to ride? We can see something of the countryside, known for its beauty."

"I would like to. It is glorious here."

"You don't find it too quiet?"

She pushed her hair off her face with her arm, conscious of her dirty hands. "Not at all. I am always busy."

"You enjoy gardening?"

"I do, although it's not something I've tackled before, as well as other household things. Come inside. It's long past midday. Have you eaten?"

He shook his head. "No. And I missed breakfast. I came to invite you and Jane to—"

"Nonsense. I shall feed you." She thought of the meat pie she made this morning, hoping he'd come. The pastry was a little crumbly around the edges, but the beef and onions were tasty.

"Who scythed the grass?" Hart asked, gazing around before stepping into the narrow hallway.

"Our neighbor. Mr. Lester, a farmer. He and his wife have been very good to us." She feared she looked dreadfully untidy. "Excuse me while I wash off the dirt." Upstairs, she washed her hands and face, rubbing roses into her cheeks before the mirror, tidied her hair, then hurried down.

Hart turned as she came in, concern in his eyes. "I hope no one has recognized you."

"Why would they? I've been careful. I am the orphan, Miss Burrell, the new tenant of Lilybrook Cottage," she said. "And Jane Frost is my maid. We hail from the north."

"No one has called or inquired after you?"

"After we attended church, two ladies came to welcome us to the village. Flibbertigibbets, Jane calls them. I served them tea and cake, but told them very little about myself, although their curiosity was palpable."

"Church? Was that wise?"

"It would have seemed odd if we hadn't attended, and drawn more attention to us."

He sat down on the sofa. "I suppose so. But you must remain

vigilant, Maddie. Your uncle visited me. He is furious with you, and Henry. I don't like to guess what he is capable of should he get his hands on either of you."

"Is Henry safe?" Maddie asked, alarmed.

"He is while he remains in my employment."

"My uncle won't find me here."

"I'm sure he has his men scouring the countryside for you." His blue eyes searched hers. "Have you given any thought to my proposal?"

Because she wanted him, it only made things worse. She would be open to hurt, which would be constant throughout her life. If she could remain indifferent to Hart, she might manage an arranged marriage. But becoming the wife of a rake would not suit her. She sighed and shook her head. "I see no need to rush." She must keep a cool head and take all the time allotted to her, to be sure it was wise. "There remains a few weeks until my birthday." Was that disappointment she saw in his eyes, or something else? Affection? She dared not hope for love. She wished he would do or say something to show her he wanted her. As badly as she wanted him? Dreams of them together filled every night and embarrassed her. Where such passion came from, she did not know. When he wasn't here, she could imagine herself living here, with the cottage at its best, pottering about the gardens, and reading by candlelight, becoming a spinster. But when he was here before her, so big and manly that his very presence pulled her toward him, she knew herself to be in love with him. It was useless to fool herself. She pressed her lips lest she be tempted to ignore the warning voice in her head and accept him.

Apart from a sigh, which might be impatience, he did not reveal his feelings, leaving her wishing for something more. "Of course, you must be sure. It's a big step to take."

"It is, Hart," Maddie said, hoping the disappointment in her voice didn't give her away. About to say more, edging closer to a statement of her true feelings, she was glad when Jane entered the room and dropped into her usual curtsey, which Hart hadn't been able to cure her of. "Milord."

"Do you enjoy your stay here, Jane? You are more accustomed to working in big houses with many staff."

"That is true, milord. But this is closer to the way I lived as a child. I am quite content here." She turned to address Maddie. "I've set the table in the kitchen, milady, and the pie is hot."

"Please, share a meal with us, Hart." Maddie tried to keep the proud note from her voice. How silly to give a pie so much importance. Her father would scold her. He would not have wished what he considered dreary domesticity upon her. Poor Papa, he had promised her the world.

After Hart took a chair at the small table, Maddie placed the pie in the center.

"That smells delicious," he said. "Mrs. Fletcher's?"

"No. I made it." Maddie fought the silly grin on her face.

"You are a lady with many gifts." Hart served himself some of the salad from a bowl. "And celery from your garden?"

"You are teasing." She laughed. "It is shop bought. We have not been here long enough to grow celery."

"But this pie," he said, watching as she cut him a hearty slice and ladled it onto his plate. "Looks delicious."

"You'd best reserve your praise until you taste it."

Once Hart and Jane were served, Maddie sat down. Her stomach churned too much to enjoy it herself. She hoped the golden pastry would be as crisp and tasty as it looked. Her first mouthful reassured her.

"This is the finest beef and onion pie I've eaten." Hart sounded sincere, but it didn't fool her. The pie was acceptable as plain fare, but hardly the sort of meal usually served to him. She smiled. "That is generous of you, Hart."

"I mean it," he said. "May I have another piece?"

"Certainly. Jane? Do you care for more?"

"No, thank you, milady."

As Maddie served him, she felt more pleasure than she'd experienced in the year since her parents' accident changed her life. She marveled it took something so simple to make it so. But would she feel the same if Hart wasn't here?

Chapter Eleven

AFTER LUNCHEON, HART suggested he and Maddie go for a ride over the fields, which flowed away in an endless green swathe from the bottom of the garden.

On horseback, Hart opened the bottom gate, and they set out in the early afternoon on a fine day when the sun cast sharp shadows beneath the trees, the air fresh and scented with the wildflowers which grew over the hills. Hart jumped Blaze over a low fence. He glanced back as Maddie's horse sailed over it behind him. Hart smiled, admiring her gumption. His smile faded when he considered her reluctance to respond to his proposal, which he had to admit, spoke of a reluctance to marry him. Or to place her trust in him. Hart couldn't deny it was a blow to his male pride, but more than that, he found it profoundly disappointing.

They reined the horses in at the top of a hill to survey the beautiful downs; the ribbon of the River Mole threaded its way through the green, and the small village nestled in the shallow valley below. They could see villagers going about their day, and the small piece of land on which Lilybrook Cottage sat looked like part of the garden with its thatched roof and leafy bower.

Hart tensed and leaned forward in the saddle, watching a man ride down the lane. Outside the cottage, he dismounted to open the gate and led his horse inside.

"We have a visitor," Hart said.

Maddie held a hand up to shade her eyes. "I can't see anyone."

"He's walked beneath the chestnut tree. You wait here. I'll go back."

"You're not leaving me here, Hart. I'll come with you."

He turned to her, exasperated. "It's best they don't see you, Maddie."

When Hart turned to look again, the man had mounted his horse. He rode away up the lane.

"It's all right. He's gone. Could be anyone, but let's ride down and see what Jane says."

When they reached the cottage, Jane rushed over, high color in her cheeks. "Milord, milady," she cried as Hart dismounted.

"What is it, Jane? Who was that man?" Maddie asked as Hart assisted her down.

"He came while I swept the porch, milady." Distressed, Jane put a hand to her chest. "He asked to see the lady of the house. I told him you weren't in. Then he asked if Miss Burrell lived here. I didn't know what I should say, but I thought it best to admit it, because you're known by that name in these parts." Her voice fell away. "Did I do right, milady?"

"You did, Jane," Maddie said admiringly. "It was well done."

"Take a breath, Jane," Hart urged. "Tell us slowly. What did he look like?"

"He was thin and had dark hair." She thought for a moment. "There was a scar on his cheek."

Maddie stared at her. "It sounds very much like the man who held me captive in the coach. Did he say anything else?"

Jane took a large breath, the red fading from her cheeks. "He asked when you would be back, and I said you'd gone away on a journey. He said his master knew of a lady who he thought might be her. That a relative of his in the village sent him word of her. Then I said I didn't think so because your people came from Scotland." She looked panicked. "Should I have said Scotland? I couldn't think of anywhere else."

"What quick thinking, Jane," Maddie said.

"A horrid-looking man, with sunken cheeks. I was so relieved when he left."

"How distressing for you. I am sorry." Maddie cast a worried glance at Hart.

"This is a blow," Hart said. "He will most likely come back. We have to move quickly."

Maddie looked distressed. "I should not have gone to church."

"You don't know that. They might have seen you at the store, or the inn, or even walking in the street."

"Must we leave here?" She cast a longing glance at the cottage.

"Wakeham will have his spies about." He took her by the shoulders and searched her troubled eyes. "Do you wish to find another hiding place?"

She shook her head.

"Then it has to be Scotland. I know a ceremony over a black-smith's anvil is not what any woman wishes for, but will you come, Maddie? Are you willing to marry me?"

"Yes." Her lips trembled.

"I won't be able to hire a carriage in this small town. I'll go back for the coach." Hart pulled his pistol from his saddle. "Have you had any experience with firearms, Maddie?"

She gazed at the gun in his hands. "Only a hunting rifle."

"It is quite simple. Let me show you." He explained about the workings. "Remove the safety catch. Then aim it." He pointed the pistol at a fence. "And squeeze the trigger." An explosion followed by wood chips raining down. He handed it to her. "I'll reload it. It will fire two shots."

She turned the small deadly gun in her hand. "I hope I won't have to use it."

He prayed she wouldn't. Could Maddie shoot when faced with the scoundrel? Even if she managed it, nerves played a big part in accuracy. "Did you have some success with the rifle?"

"I only shot at targets. But I managed well."

"Good. I'll ride home for the coach. Remember the ladder to the roof space Jane found? Hide up there if anyone comes. I know it will be uncomfortable, but it would be wise to spend the night there."

Jane gave a shudder. "There will be mice and spiders."

"Better that than Wakeham's men. I'll leave now, Maddie, and be back by dawn."

She put a hand on his arm. "You'll ride through the night? Surely that's not wise?"

"It won't be the first time." He gazed up at the sky. "The clouds appear to have blown away. There will be a moon." He took Pearl by the rein and mounted Blaze.

Maddie clutched her hands, alarm in her eyes. "Can you manage both horses for such a long distance?"

"It's less than thirty miles to Pembury. Pearl will be safe in my stables. If the men were to find her stabled here, it would confirm they'd come to the right place." He gathered up the reins. "You wouldn't want them to get hold of Pearl?"

"No...of course I wouldn't, but..."

"I'll return in the early morn with the coach. Pack and be ready to leave." Hart rode out into the lane. He gazed over his shoulder to where Maddie stood with her hand raised. God keep them from harm until he could return. At Pembury, he'd grab a bite to eat and set out immediately. There was no time for rest. He was happy to forgo sleep to see them safe.

As he rode up the high street, Hart kept a sharp eye out for any of Wakeham's men. They would stand out here lurking about. If they were here, he would go back to the cottage. But he saw no sign of the rogues and urged the horses on. Pearl soon gave up pulling at the rein and kept pace with Blaze.

While he hated to leave Maddie, he had no choice. He hoped the women would take his advice and hide in the attic. Once night fell, they were vulnerable, and now Wakeham knew where she was. He would waste little time sending his men to capture her, or worse.

When Hart arrived home, he dismounted at the stables, weary, his thigh muscles sore. He left the horses with a groom and gave the order to his coachman for the coach to be brought around. Then he went into the stables in search of Henry. He found him in a stall with his sleeves rolled up, raking straw. "Toss your clothes into a bag and join the coachman," Hart said. "You are to accompany us to Scotland."

Henry threw down the fork, his eyes shining with the sense of adventure. "I've few clothes to bother about. I'll be but a minute, milord."

"Good man."

While the kitchen staff prepared him a hamper, Hart ordered his valet to pack a portmanteau while he quickly washed and shaved. Leonard remarkably kept his tongue as Hart dressed. Downing a cup of coffee, Hart took a piece of toast from a kitchen maid. A short time later, he climbed into the coach, sat back, crossing his arms, and wearily closed his eyes.

As the sun cast a warm glow over the fields, the coach reached the toll road on its way to Box Hill and Lilybrook Cottage. Hart raised the hamper and took out a chicken leg. He chewed without tasting it, tossed down the bone, and wiped his mouth and hands with a napkin. Then he turned to watch the countryside pass by while anxiety for the women's safety filled his thoughts. Should he have dealt first with Wakeham? He had no proof. Probing his reasoning, he realized his aim had always been to take Maddie far away from all this and marry her.

An hour later, he awakened, surprised that he'd fallen asleep. Hart felt a good deal better as he planned their long journey to the Scottish borders in his mind: the best inns where he could exchange the horses and dine along the Great North Road and the women could spend a comfortable night. He would not waste a day once they arrived in Scotland. He and Maddie must marry immediately. Hart waited for the expected alarm at saying goodbye to his bachelorhood. When it failed to come, he allowed himself a small smile before apprehension about what he would find at Lilybrook cottage consumed him again.

⁂

THROUGHOUT THE REST of the day, Maddie and Jane took turns to watch out for any sign of her, uncle and his men. Their spirits rose when neither he nor his cohorts appeared. But they dared not light the stove, and dined on cheese and biscuits left in the pantry.

Once the light ebbed, Jane opened the panel she'd found in the parlor, exposing the tall ladder leading up to the windowless space beneath the roof.

"I'll pass up a blanket and pillows to you," Maddie said. "We might as well make ourselves as comfortable as possible."

Before it grew too dark, they chose a spot and settled down.

"I shan't sleep a wink," Jane said, moving about and prodding her pillow.

"Nor I." Maddie had brought up a candle and the tinderbox for emergencies, but wouldn't light it unless absolutely necessary. She lay crammed into a space between wooden struts and prepared for a long, uncomfortable night. "Talk to me, Jane. Tell me about your childhood."

Jane spoke about her life growing up on the farm. "My brothers and I had to do our share. It was my job to feed the pigs, collect the eggs, and help Mama in the house. The boys worked outside on the farm. After Papa died, everything changed. Mama remarried, but her new husband didn't take kindly to us. As soon as my brothers were old enough, one joined the army and the other the navy, and I went into service at fourteen."

Maddie felt a rush of sympathy. "How did your father die?"

"Spreading fodder. The wheel of the cart he stood on hit a rock. A fork tine stabbed into his leg. It wasn't a big wound, but deep. We expected him to get better. He'd had plenty of accidents before working around the farm, but he got worse. The doctor came and bled him, but..." Her voice trailed off.

"I'm so sorry, Jane." Maddie was a little ashamed at not having asked Jane before this. There would be many servants with sad stories to tell about how they came to work in service.

Upset, the maid turned her head away.

Maddie didn't disturb her while she dealt with her own distress as she revisited those halcyon days when her parents lived. But tomorrow, they would go to Scotland! The thought buoyed her until the fear that Hart would come to grief on the dark road upset her.

A little while later, soft snores told Maddie Jane slept. She was glad of it. She closed her eyes, but they popped open again, staring sightlessly into the dark.

A scuffling sound came from below them, outside the building. She stiffened. Moving carefully across to Jane, she gently shook her and whispered in her ear.

Jane sat up.

A loud banging was followed by the shatter of breaking glass. A window was thrown up. Then the heavy tread as footsteps crossed the floor. Someone searched for them.

As his foul threat rose, Maddie took the gun out from under her pillow and carefully removed the safety catch. With a deep breath, she used her other hand to keep the gun from wavering about and aimed at the ladder.

They silently waited.

More furious mutterings below. Then a loud exclamation. The

panel slid back, and the ladder slammed against the beam.

"He's found it. He's coming up," Maddie whispered. She wished her hand didn't shake.

The man appeared at the top, holding a lantern high. Stepping off the ladder, he stood before them. His face a rictus of evil, he stared at them both. Saw her gun and sneered at it. "You won't shoot me." He pulled a knife from his belt. "I'll please the boss with this night's work," he said. "Pity I can't take me time wit' yea. Who wants to die first?"

Maddie steadied the gun, aimed it at him. "Go back or I'll shoot you."

He stared at her for a minute and then laughed. "You couldn't hit the back end of a barn."

"Don't be so sure."

Holding the knife by the blade, he raised his hand to throw it, forcing Maddie to squeeze the trigger. The sound almost deafened them in the small space.

The knife clattered away as he crumpled to the floor and lay still. Blood seeped from the wound on his head.

Maddie reached down and grabbed the blade. She held it out to Jane. "Keep hold of this!" Jane took it from her gingerly, as if it was boiling hot.

Jane gasped. "Is he dead?"

Maddie moved closer to check on him. Her bullet had grazed his forehead. He hadn't moved, but his chest rose and fell. "No. He's not dead." That she thought she had killed him sent a shudder rocketing through her. She held the gun aimed at him and nudged him with her foot. Then hurried back. He groaned, but didn't open his eyes. "We shall have to tie him up."

Jane shuddered, holding the knife away from herself. "We have to touch him?"

"Yes, we must. Quickly, before he wakes."

"What with?"

"Cut the bedsheet and tear it into strips, Jane. Use the knife."

Jane hurried over to her bed, and while Maddie watched the man, sounds of ripping came from behind her.

"Will these do?" Jane handed her two long strips.

"Good. Help me tie his hands. Quick, before he comes to."

They tied his hands and feet and fashioned a bandage for his head while he thankfully remained senseless. "I know him. He's one of those who kidnapped me in Bath," Maddie said. The horrid man who threatened her in the carriage. She trembled and sank down on the makeshift bed, fearing her legs wouldn't hold her up. "I've never shot anything that actually lived and breathed. Papa wouldn't allow me to go out with him on shoots." Her father would never have imagined she'd be in a situation such as this.

"You did well, milady," Jane said.

"More luck than skill, Jane. We'll watch him until Hart arrives. I don't trust those bindings to hold him long if he gets into a rage."

"He'll certainly be annoyed," Jane said, "but I learned my knots from my brother in the navy. They'll hold tight."

Maddie rested the pistol on her knee. She swallowed. "My throat is terribly dry."

"I'll go down and get you some water," Jane said.

"No. Never mind, Jane. Another of my uncle's men might come looking for him."

"Then I'd best just go down and close the panel."

"Good idea."

Jane climbed nimbly down beside the ladder. A bang as the panel closed, then her head appeared at the top.

Maddie was profoundly glad to see her. She hated to be alone with this man for even a moment. He planned to kill them, to slit their throats. She recoiled in horror and thought she might be sick. "Now we must wait until morning," she said, aware Jane would wish her to remain calm. "We'll take turns to watch him. You rest first, Jane, and then I'll wake you."

"All right." Jane lay down on her makeshift bed. After a moment, she said, "I can't sleep, milady. I'm not sure I'll ever feel safe enough to sleep again."

"Let's talk to keep ourselves awake," Maddie said.

"We might sing," Jane suggested.

"Yes, sing, Jane, but softly." If Maddie tried, she would sound strangled.

Jane sung in a sweet, shaky voice. Some country song Maddie had never heard. It made her feel better somehow. Jane's voice drifted away. "I'm sorry, milady. I've forgotten the words. It must be the shock."

They fell silent and were drooping with fatigue when the man's voice suddenly cut across the room. "Ow, me head. What have yea done? When I get free I'm going to…"

Jane put her hands over her ears.

Maddie picked up the pistol and pointed it at him. "You'd best be quiet. I shot you once. I can do it again. And if I must, be sure I will."

He took her at her word, his cruel mouth forming a thin, hard line.

In the gloom with the candles fluttering, his yellowed eyes glared at her, reminding her of some dangerous jungle beast she'd seen in a picture book. But at least he'd fallen silent, and his head lolled.

A ribbon of blood ran down his cheek. She checked to make sure he was still breathing. She leaned back, satisfied. "I'm sorry to have dragged you into this, Jane."

"Dragged me in?" Jane sounded shocked. "I've never had so much fun in all m' life!"

Maddie disbelieved her, but was grateful, and even managed a breathy giggle. "I can't imagine coping with him on my own. I would certainly have panicked."

"We must look like a couple of ghosts covered in all this dust!"

Jane shook out her skirts and sneezed.

"We shall both need a bath." Maddie sighed, thinking of the state Hart would find them in. "Although I don't know when we can manage it."

"A bath?" Jane asked, as if the idea of immersing herself completely in water had never occurred to her. "A good wash will do me."

Outside, an owl hooted in the chestnut tree and somewhere, a fox barked. "We'd best be quiet," Maddie said. "We don't know who else might be out there."

Rain pattered on the roof. It forced Maddie to move to avoid a steady flow of drips from a hole in the thatch. She chose a dry spot and settled down again, her gaze remaining on the slumped figure. It was important to show Jane she was in charge of the situation, but so difficult with her nerves strung tight. Horribly stiff, she sat as still as a statue with her eyes wide open, her stiff fingers cramping around the gun.

They spent the rest of the night in tense silence. Finally, the dark, windowless space grew lighter with the warm glow of dawn. They heard the rattle of carriage wheels in the lane. For one fearful moment, Maddie feared it would be her uncle.

"Shall I go down?" Jane whispered.

"No. Wait," she whispered back.

The front door opened with a creak. Footsteps crossed the floor. A rasp as the panel opened. Then the ladder shook as someone climbed it. Maddie stopped breathing, her heart banging against her ribs. She aimed the pistol at the top of the ladder, steadying the firearm with both hands.

Hart called, and then his head appeared at the top. "Don't shoot me. Good God." He stared at the man who had roused himself and was spitting curses with fury. He turned to Maddie, surprise in his eyes. "You shot him?"

"I had to. He won't die, will he?"

Hart crouched down and looked at the fellow, who spat at him. "Unfortunately, no. Excellent work, ladies."

Maddie couldn't decide whether to burst into tears or fall into his arms. She did neither. Setting an example for Jane and for Hart, if she was honest, she calmly allowed him to assist her down the ladder.

"It must have been a long, terrifying night." His hands released her waist, leaving some of his reassuring warmth. He turned to help Jane, who scurried down after them.

"Fire up the stove and have a hot drink while I take this fellow to the constable. We shall have to appear before the judge at the Assizes when they next sit. It will be after we return from Scotland, but we won't worry about that now." He scaled the ladder again and came down with the runt of a fellow over his shoulder.

Maddie watched the coach pull away up the lane while Jane stoked the fire. They sat with their second cup of tea when Hart returned.

"The fellow refuses to talk. Perhaps a stint in jail will refresh his memory." He rubbed Maddie's arm, concern in his eyes. "I'm sorry you had that terrifying experience. I wish we could go somewhere safe and let you rest awhile. But we must leave for Scotland straight away." Hart smiled. "There's a hamper of food in the coach, and warm rugs. You can sleep until we stop at an inn for the night. Take the ladies' baggage," Hart said to Henry, who stood waiting.

Maddie smiled. "It's good to see you, Henry. You and Jane must have met when you worked for my father."

"We did, milady." Henry nodded to Jane.

Jane's cheeks turned rosy as Henry gathered up the bags.

Well, what have we here? Maddie thought, then forgot about it, her eyes raking the gardens for a sign of the rest of her uncle's men. Reassured, she settled into the luxurious equipage as the coach trundled away on their long journey north.

They soon left the village behind, and as Hart had promised, the food in the hamper was delicious. Maddie ate bread and cheese, and

Jane had a scone. After some lemonade, they lay tucked up beneath fur rugs while the coach carried them smoothly along the road on its superior springs. The tension which held her in its grip since the man appeared in the loft slowly ebbed away. Maddie leaned against the soft, padded squab, smiling at Hart opposite her, seated with his back to the horses. He reminded her of a brave and handsome knight of old. What would she have done if he hadn't come to her aid in Bath? She still wasn't sure why he did. Or why he wanted this marriage. But she was very glad he did.

Beside her, Jane slept. Maddie's eyelids grew heavy. She pulled the rug up around her shoulders and closed her eyes.

Chapter Twelve

AN HOUR HAD passed and, exhausted, Maddie was still sleeping. Her slender fingers curled beneath her chin, long dark eyelashes feathering her cheek. Incredibly brave, she had been through so much. Relieved to have her safe from her uncle at last, Hart didn't forget that much lay ahead of them. Wakeham could remain a danger. Hart didn't know enough about him to understand his motives. It had become clear he wanted his niece dead. But why? Thinking about how much Maddie had suffered at her uncle's hands, anger twisted his stomach. As soon as they returned to London, he and Maddie would visit her solicitor. She told him Wakeham explained her father's will, and she'd seen no reason to suspect him of lying. But now she doubted everything he'd said to her. Hart remained convinced the will would give a clue to Wakeham's behavior. Although it left the mystery of the man's involvement with scoundrels unsolved.

When dusk fell, they stopped for the night, dining at a well-appointed inn. Afterward, they played whist with two of the guests, a married couple, Mr. Brocklehurst, and his wife. Brocklehurst kept a full glass of brandy at his elbow and played badly. His wife's attempt to flirt with Hart became blatant and embarrassing. Hart could sense Maddie growing restive after she and Brocklehurst lost the first game. He struggled not to chuckle when Maddie asked Mrs. Brocklehurst if she was feeling all right. "You are fidgeting so," she said with concern.

"Perhaps your laces are too tight?"

The lady glared at her and did not deign to reply.

Not something a lady should say in male company, but Hart approved. While he silently applauded Maddie, he wished she was enjoying the evening. After a game in which he and Mrs. Brocklehurst won, Hart stood and put an end to the evening.

He bowed. "Forgive us. We have an early start and a long day ahead."

As he settled Maddie's shawl around her tense shoulders, he expected her to speak of it, but made light of it, considering it best not to allow Mrs. Brocklehurst's behavior to come between them before they'd even tied the knot.

⇒⟫⟪⇐

MADDIE WAS RELIEVED when Hart cut the evening short. Mrs. Brocklehurst failed to say goodnight to her, while her husband clumsily climbed to his feet and swayed over Maddie, smiled sadly, and kissed her hand.

She might have enjoyed the game if his wife behaved. The well-dressed, attractive woman of some thirty years, on learning that Maddie was not yet Hart's wife, flirted outrageously with him all evening. She eyed Maddie's green gown with obvious disdain, and smiling at Hart, leaned forward over the table in her low-cut dress. Maddie saw her fingers touch Hart's with a light stroke when he handed her the cards. Hart failed to respond, giving his attention to arranging his cards. Mr. Brocklehurst drank steadily through each play. He was too far in his cups or too used to his wife's behavior, for he ignored it. While Hart did nothing to encourage the woman, neither did he stop her; Maddie had itched to slap her face.

When the clock struck eleven, Hart escorted her to the chamber she shared with Jane.

"Mrs. Brocklehurst's behavior was outrageous," she said on the stairs, unable to hold her tongue a moment longer.

Hart raised his eyebrows, the picture of innocence. "Mm? She played well. The last was an excellent winning hand."

Maddie narrowed her eyes. "You must have noticed she simpered at you all evening."

"If she did, I missed it. I was more interested in the game."

Maddie frowned at him while he infuriatingly continued to deny all knowledge of the woman's behavior. "At one stage, she almost climbed into your lap."

The uncomfortable thought struck her that society expected wives to be blind to such things. Well, she would not be.

Hart shrugged. "We won because Mr. Brocklehurst was drunk, and you, by the sound of it, became distracted."

Maddie fell silent. Was Hart so used to the way women behaved around him that he barely noticed? She doubted any man would ignore such a flagrant play for his attention. Didn't such a disgraceful absence of good manners also bother him?

Did men care that much about manners?

When they reached her chamber door, her annoyance faded when she considered his side of the situation. It wasn't fair to accuse him when he'd done nothing to encourage the woman. If the woman had wished to pass Hart a note, she'd had no opportunity with Maddie watching like a hawk. But what would stop Hart from returning downstairs if he wished to spend time with the lady? Maddie couldn't bring herself to believe it, but this was exactly what she feared. Because there was no love between them, she could never be sure of his fidelity. And she hated how Mrs. Brocklehurst had turned her into something resembling a jealous, possessive woman. Was this the way their marriage would be? In which case, hell awaited them both. She knew herself to be passionate, and didn't deny she had a temper, although it usually took a great deal more than this to provoke it.

What was wrong with her? Was it only because she felt so insecure? Should she have agreed to marry him?

"Sleep well," Hart said amiably, their disagreement forgotten.

"I shall." She smiled at him regretfully. "Thank you for a lovely dinner."

He caught her hand and pressed a kiss to her palm. The touch of his lips caused an unfamiliar yearning low in her stomach. When he spoke, his words were like a dash of cold water. "We both benefit from this marriage, Maddie. When we return to Pembury, you will be free of your uncle's tyranny, and I will go to the trustees as a settled, married man."

She withdrew her hand. "Yes, it works well for both of us," she said dryly, and moved toward the door, then turned back. "Shall we go straight to Pembury from Scotland?"

"Would you like to spend some time in London?"

"I would love to."

"Then we shall. I'll send word for Montford Court to be made ready for us. I am eager to show off my lovely bride to society."

The idea of facing the *ton* also unnerved her. She felt as unprepared for that as she did for this marriage. There was sure to be talk. And if her cousin was to be believed, Hart was one of the most sought-after bachelors in London, apparently with a well-earned reputation as a rake. The women Hart would associate with would dress elegantly and be at ease with society's customs, while Maddie knew only what she'd experienced at assemblies, and her mother's tutoring. Right now, in her crumpled gown, she felt like a country bumpkin. An unattractive, bad-tempered bumpkin.

Hart could have his pick of brides. He might marry an heiress keen to find a titled husband, no matter how he behaved. If he married Maddie just to save her, she would be forever in his debt. That troubled her. It was hardly a good way to begin a marriage. Could she dismiss all that bothered her? Would being well-dressed give her confidence? She must find a dressmaker as soon as she arrived in the city, although she didn't know quite how to go about it with no one to advise her. "I shall need to dress well in London," she said, hoping he'd understand. She could feel the women's eyes on her already, taking in every detail and talking behind their fans.

"I'll send a footman to fetch your possessions from Wakeham," Hart said. "You can have everything else you need made in London."

His words drew her reluctantly back to the danger her uncle represented, although she'd tried to put him and that dreadful night out of her mind. It terrified her to think anyone would hate her so much they wanted her dead. "Should we alert him to our marriage so soon?"

Hart looked surprised. "We wish him to learn of it, do we not?"

"Yes, of course, eventually..." She rubbed goosebumps on her arms.

Hart stepped close to her. Close enough for her to study the thick dark lashes rimming his blue eyes, and a small scar at the corner of his lip. She wanted to touch it and ask him how he came by it.

His hands on her shoulders, he searched her eyes. "He won't get close enough to hurt you again, Maddie." His soft voice carried a warning that her uncle, should he hear it, would be wise to heed it. "He will have other things to worry him soon enough."

Maddie wanted to lean against him, fearful for him at this moment rather than herself. "I don't trust him. When he learns what we have done, he'll act."

"What could he do?"

She considered her uncle a danger to them both. "He'll find a way."

"He'll be busy with his own affairs." Hart told her what he had seen through her uncle's window.

She hugged her arms. The memory of that man raising his knife to throw at her, intent on killing her, made her tremble.

Hart sighed. He drew her into his arms. "You've had to endure so much, Maddie."

She rested her head against his chest. His strength and masculine scent made her feel better somehow. "What bad business is my uncle involved in? Do you have any idea?"

"Not yet, but I intend to find out. And when I do, you'll have no more trouble from him."

That sounded like a dangerous venture. She didn't want Hart involving himself in her uncle's affairs. What if those men hurt him, or worse? Losing him would be as bad as losing her parents. The possibility made her stomach clench. She was well acquainted with the pain of losing those she cared about. She drew back to look up at him. "Surely it would be best to let the law deal with him?"

"With no proof, the magistrate won't act. And in the country, a Bow Street Runner will stand out like a scarecrow in a plowed field. He can't do much except lurk around Wakeham's estate, trying to discover what goes on there. I doubt your uncle acts alone. There will be someone higher in charge. Wakeham must grow nervous and fear discovery, and that will make him vigilant. But I'll engage a runner, although right now I have little to tell him. I'll return to Pembury after we reach London. See if I can discover more.."

Hart planned to leave her alone in London? "Can't I go with you to Pembury?"

"I don't think it's wise with your uncle so close. You would have to be guarded and remain in the house, which you would hate. In London, you can stroll in the park with my sister. I intend to invite her to join you. You'll enjoy Diane's company. She will advise you about dressmakers and where the best shops are to be found."

Relieved, Maddie smiled. "An excellent idea, Hart." She had taken to Diane immediately. A warm-hearted, sensible woman.

He dropped a kiss on her cheek. "Good night then, my sweet."

"Goodnight, Hart."

Resigned now she'd committed herself to this loveless marriage,

Maddie slipped through the door, wishing he'd kissed her on the mouth. He had been kind and caring. She supposed that should satisfy her.

In the truckle bed, Jane raised herself up on her elbows. "Did you have a good evening, milady?"

"It was pleasant." At least the last bit.

Jane threw back the covers to help her undress.

Maddie put a hand on her maid's shoulder. "Go back to sleep. I've become quite adept at changing my clothes."

"You won't need me at all soon." Jane settled down again, her voice drowsy.

"Of course I will." But Jane had fallen asleep. Maddie undressed. She witnessed the exchange between Jane and Henry when the coach stopped at the last inn. Their fondness for each other was solace to Maddie's troubled heart. Why could life not be simpler and more straightforward for her? She doubted it would ever be. Hart was kind and would be an affectionate husband. But she, unreasonably, wanted passion. Her outrageous Aunt Gabby, referring to her own experiences, had told Maddie something that stayed with her: *Once a rake, always a rake. A married woman might briefly enjoy their attention, something to fill their dreams, perhaps. But rakes cannot be cured of their love of women, Maddie,* she had warned. *So never fall into that trap. Unless you can accept their philandering, a miserable life awaits you.*

After breakfast, pulling on her gloves, Maddie walked with Jane to the coach. Jane's gaze immediately sought Henry's, where he stood at the horses' heads. The groom's eyes were warm, filled with a yearning that made Maddie catch her breath. She wanted that kind of love. Would she ever have it?

Seated in the coach, they waited for Hart to settle the bill. Maddie glanced at her maid, whose flushed face told her all. "Did you speak often to Henry when he worked for my father?"

Jane ducked her head and smoothed her skirts. "Yes, milady."

"You seem on good terms."

Jane blushed furiously. "We are, milady."

Maddie smiled. "He is a fine fellow."

Hart climbed into the coach. "Who is a fine fellow?"

"Henry!" Both Maddie and Jane said as one.

"My goodness." A corner of Hart's lip quirked up. "And I thought you were speaking about me."

Maddie laughed and shook her head.

Hart took out *The Times* newspaper and folded it in two. He leaned back, crossed his legs, and perused it.

"Any news from London?" Maddie asked after a while.

"Yes. Another bank robbery. A man killed."

"Dear heaven. In the city!"

"Yes."

"How blatant."

He gazed at her thoughtfully over the top of the newspaper. "The robbers are." He rattled the paper and disappeared behind it.

Left to her thoughts, Maddie studied him from his glossy black top boots to his snug-fitting cream pantaloons. The cream-and-tan striped waistcoat stretched over his chest, his carmelite brown coat unbuttoned. His tall beaver hat was on the seat beside him. Her gaze rested on his elegant hands and long fingers holding the newspaper when he suddenly lowered it, and his blue eyes met hers with a question.

Had she just sighed? "I was thinking about that bank robbery."

"Yes?"

"The money you saw on my uncle's table. Could he be behind these robberies?"

"I can call several criminal activities to mind." Hart put down the newspaper and uncrossed his legs, drawing her eyes to another part of his anatomy. She hastily looked up at him. "My initial thought was Wakeham ran a smuggling gang," he said. "They land smuggled goods on the Kentish coast from where they're whisked inland." He stroked his chin. "But I suppose these audacious bank robberies are a possibility. I need to find out more about them."

"How might we do that?"

"We?" Hart sat forward to place a hand on her knee. "Not you, Maddie, never you. That's impossible, surely you know that."

"How will you find out?" she amended with a frown. "Rather than leaving for Tunbridge Wells as soon as we arrive in London, why not consult Bow Street?"

"Yes. I intend to have a word with the Bow Street Magistrate before I leave for the country."

Hart picked up the newspaper again.

Subject closed, she thought. That her uncle might be behind the robberies had occurred to him, although he'd generously allowed her to first suggest it. That was thoughtful, but it was all he would allow, and being wrapped in cotton wool and tucked away somewhere safe never appealed to her. If she thought he needed her help, she would act on her own initiative. It made her smile.

Hart raised his eyebrows and looked at her. "Why the smile?" He folded the newspaper and held it in his lap.

Didn't he trust her? "Nothing worth mentioning," Maddie said airily.

Chapter Thirteen

A FTER FIVE DAYS of travel, Hart's coach reached their destination, Coldstream Bridge. Surrounded by lush countryside, the fine stone bridge spanned the River Tweed, and beyond it was the large village and parish church with a square clock tower. The Marriage House, which was also the toll house, sat snug against the approach to the bridge on the Scottish side of the border. The unassuming, single-story sandstone dwelling with a small garden walled off from the road shocked him. He wasn't sure what Maddie made of it. But, believing they should not delay, left the coach, and went inside to make the arrangements.

He booked them into an inn on the High Street where they would spend the night, and he and Maddie, with Henry and Jane as witnesses, returned to the Marriage House an hour later. They met another young couple emerging from inside, who looked curiously back at them. Hart and Maddie entered a small parlor, where the celebrant awaited them. The small room smelled of the river. He warmly greeted them and invited them to sit at a long table. What followed was shockingly brief. Hart insisted on a document he supplied to be signed, although the celebrant assured him no certificate was required. Hart removed the signet ring he wore on his little finger and slipped it onto Maddie's wedding finger. It would do until he retrieved the family rings from the bank.

Less than half an hour later, Hart paid the man and escorted Maddie back to the coach.

"Is that it? We are married?" she asked as he helped her inside.

Hart tucked the document into his pocket. "Yes, our marriage is legal." He smiled at her. "Although we must be seen to have spent the night together."

She flushed. "Oh, of course,"

His gaze lingered on her face. They had avoided this aspect of their agreement, and he remained unsure of her feelings.

"I wish it could have been a lavish wedding with all the trimmings," he said.

"Did you want that, Hart?"

"No." He grinned. "Men seldom do."

She smiled. "A simple church ceremony would have been nice. But I'm relieved to be finally free from my uncle."

It wasn't exactly what he wanted to hear. But they were man and wife. "We'll dine at the inn. Celebrate with champagne."

It was colder here with a brisk wind, the skies a flat, dull gray. He would have liked Maddie to remember her wedding as something special, but it was hardly an auspicious start. She had been quiet during most of the last few days' travel. If he had a daughter, he would want something far better for her than this hurried affair in that humble little Marriage House. But in the future, there was nothing to prevent them from having a church wedding if Maddie wanted it.

Hart regretted the necessity to return immediately to London. He would prefer to honeymoon in Scotland, just him and Maddie, staying at quaint inns and enjoying the beauty of the countryside, but the closing date set by his uncle's trustees drew near. He would send a letter in the post tomorrow to advise them of his marriage, although it would do little to delay matters. The wording of his uncle's will still bothered him. When he'd spoken of it to Tate, the duke was incredulous. "It's a ruse," he said after some thought. "Designed to make you pull up your bootstraps. What sort of fellow was your uncle?"

"Eccentric, I have to say. But a nice fellow, and decent. I was fonder of him than of my father. But whether or not it was a ruse, the fact remains, unless I comply with the terms of his will, I won't inherit." Remembering their conversation, Hart smiled. It was only a few months since Tate married the girl of his dreams, and he still believed in fairytales. Hart hadn't believed in such things, but hoped his life would take a decided turn for the better. He clasped Maddie's hand in his and, feeling relieved, and a little triumphant, smiled at her.

She smiled back as the coach took them back to the inn.

Once they arrived in London, all the pressures would return. Maddie's father's will, dealing with her uncle, not to mention her introduction to society—a lot for her to face while they learned more about each other in their rushed marriage. Hart was determined to be as considerate a husband as he could, but knew he'd have to change. He was used to being alone. Making his own decisions. Not having to consider another's feelings. And he'd had no example to follow. Certainly not his father, who was neither a good parent nor a decent husband. Hart considered himself not cut out for the role. He liked his freedom too much. If not for Uncle William, he would have remained a bachelor until the need for an heir forced him to consider marriage. And then it would have been on his own terms. So it came as a surprise when he faced the parson's mousetrap without alarm. And that was because of Maddie. He smiled at her again and squeezed her hand.

His sister, Diane, could be a great help to them with her knowledge of London society. He would write and invite her to spend time with them at Montford Court. Diane's children often stayed with their grandparents, so she might be free to accept. He was sure Maddie would appreciate Diane's guidance as she settled into her new role.

Arriving at the inn, Maddie and Jane left him to do some shopping. Hart bathed and dressed and took a short walk before returning to the foyer to wait for his bride. He turned and saw her coming down the stairs in a lemon-colored muslin gown he hadn't seen her wear. She had washed her hair, and damp curls the color of autumn leaves clustered charmingly around her face.

His gaze roamed over her, and he smiled. "A new gown? You are the veritable picture of a spring bride."

"I think the shops here must cater to elopements."

Hart ordered champagne. They entered the inn's parlor and sat on the sofa by the fire. The innkeeper bustled in a few minutes later, holding a bottle Hart hoped would contain some resemblance to champagne. He raised his glass in a toast. "To us, Maddie. A joyful life. I'm sorry it was such a humble ceremony."

Maddie put her small, slim hand over his. "I have no complaints. I am free of my uncle's control at last. It's a heady feeling. And married to the nicest man in the world. My parents would be happy for me."

Hart would make her happy. He had wanted to kiss her in that plain little room where their marriage took place without a shred of pomp and ceremony. But it seemed inappropriate. And he wasn't sure of Maddie's reaction. She looked a bit stunned by the simplicity of the service.

He had made a mistake couching his proposal in those terms. While he no longer thought that way, perhaps Maddie still did. The problem was that he found it difficult to make things right other than demonstrating how much he cared for her. They had become friends, but he hoped for more, or their life together would be a dismal failure. Impatient to take her upstairs and make her his, he looked for a sign she would welcome it. But she seemed to hold herself at a distance, due, he supposed, to his clumsiness. He hoped for a wedding night to bring them closer.

After dinner, they returned to the parlor for coffee. "It's a shame we must return to London so soon," Hart said. "My trustees will await me at Pembury. I wish I did not have to leave you so soon."

Hart saw the uncertainty in her eyes. "I should prefer to go with you to Pembury." She drew in a breath. "But if Diane comes to stay, I shall cope nicely."

He wasn't sure how well he'd manage without her. He appreciatively watched his bride select a chocolate, her sweetly curved lips pursed in concentration, lips he was impatient to kiss. "My sister will come if she can. Diane loves London and misses the life there since her husband passed away."

"What happened to him?"

"Heart trouble when he was only forty-one. His death left her with two children to raise."

"Poor Diane. That is sad."

"I would like to see her marry again, but I doubt she will. She loved Edgar and remains committed to his memory."

"Perhaps time will soften her pain. It lessens grief a little."

She was speaking of her own tragic experience. "We might spend a month on the Continent later in the year," Hart said. "When all of this is behind us?"

"How thrilling," she said. "I've always wanted to visit Rome and Paris." Her coffee sat untouched, turning cold. "It's hard to imagine this will be over. My uncle finally beaten."

She seemed to doubt their marriage would put an end to her uncle's villainy—didn't trust him to get the better of Wakeham. As a boy, he hadn't been able to help his mother when she suffered because of his father's anger. But now, he would save Maddie from that brute, whatever it took. "As soon as we reach the city, we'll meet with your solicitor and learn what was in your father's will. Then we will make an informed decision about Wakeham."

She pushed her half full coffee cup away. "I hope it gives some clue to my uncle's behavior."

Hart didn't want to talk anymore about Wakeham tonight. He wanted this to be a happy time for them. But the man's hold on

Maddie was insidious. While his rational mind told him Wakeham could do nothing more, he struggled to believe it would be resolved with their marriage. "It should make his motives clear. I'm surprised the solicitors didn't ensure the will was explained to you."

She scoffed. "To an underage female? They wouldn't consider it necessary."

"You have a right to know." He held her hand, threading his fingers through hers, impatient to put an end to this unhappy conversation. "Where is Jane?"

"She and Henry are dining alone. Do you mind?"

He raised his eyebrows, then shrugged. "Love must be in the air here."

Her eyes rested on him for a moment.

Why had he mentioned love? He was not yet ready to confess he loved her, and he thought Maddie was not ready to hear it. He'd never said those words to any woman. Such a declaration must come from the heart. "Care for a walk by the river? Or would you rather go up to our chamber?" He knew which he preferred. His body grew warm, and he could think of little else.

"I'D ENJOY A walk." Maddie was nervous about their first night together. Was it disappointment she saw in Hart's blue eyes? Did he desire her? She wanted them to make love so badly it made her tremble. But it was not yet dark, and she was suddenly afraid she might disappoint him. His well-known reputation seemed to stand between them.

Hand in hand, they strolled along the river bank breathing in the fishy smell of the water, mud, and reeds. Across the river, a man reeled in a salmon with a cry of triumph. Maddie enjoyed Hart's strong hand clasping hers. Experience had taught her life seldom turned out as one expected. But this was her wedding day. And a nervous yearning for him to make love to her blotted all other thoughts from her mind.

As if he sensed it, he bent his head and kissed her. Their first kiss. His lips were warm and soft against hers, and held an intriguing promise of what was to follow. She trembled against him as his hands, firm on her back, pulled her closer, deepening the kiss. She had dreamed of this. The musky smell of his soap tantalized her. The kiss was brief, but made her heart thud and her stomach tighten.

With his arm around her waist, they walked on, watching the sun setting over the river turn the water to liquid fire as he talked about their future. Hart described the changes made to Pembury.

"Are you anxious about meeting people in London?" he asked suddenly.

That he understood surprised and pleased her. "A little," she confessed. "I know no one in London except my Aunt Libby and cousin Cathy. My cousin is pretty and very likeable. She must have suitors, and her days and nights will be busy."

"Everyone will like you. How could they not?" He hugged her against him. "You will become a trendsetter. All the young women will look to you as an example."

She laughed. "Is that supposed to make me feel better?" She smoothed her skirt. "I am certainly not that at the moment."

"Ah, but you will be."

His faith in her touched her deeply. She wished she could be as confident. But as the daughter of an earl, she was meant to one day become the wife of a distinguished, titled gentleman. Had her parents lived, she would have embraced such a marriage without a doubt in the world. Taught since childhood to be well versed in English, poetry, botany, and mathematics. She had dance instructors, French and Italian tutors, and spent endless hours at the piano, and singing with a music master. Maddie had learned how to conduct herself on all social occasions. She'd been told the pinnacle of a lady's achievement was to be seen as an elegant wife, engaging and graceful among her peers. While she considered she had more to give than that, she wanted to be that for herself and have Hart proud of her.

But she could not forget how difficult it would be after their scandalous elopement became known in society.

She glanced at Hart, glad of his support and hoping she would always have it. If it was within her power, this marriage would be as loving and happy as her parents' had been. But it wasn't all within her power, was it?

In the fading light, Hart turned to her. "Shall we walk back to the inn?"

She nodded and took his arm, calmer now because she'd discovered something more about him she approved of. They strolled toward their first night together.

Chapter Fourteen

MADDIE TURNED TO Hart as they approached the inn. "Jane will be upstairs, waiting to assist me." She glanced away as a flush warmed her cheeks.

Hart smiled, understanding her hesitancy. "I'll have a brandy in the parlor and read the newspaper." He grimaced. "Scottish news. It won't make good reading."

She smiled at that and left him to climb the stairs.

In the parlor beside the crackling fire, Hart sipped his brandy and attempted to read the day-old newspaper while a man in the chair opposite, delighted to have found another Englishman, spoke of England's superiority in sport. "Cricket, for example. Been to Lords?" he asked, then rushed on, not waiting for an answer. "Two centuries in the same match. Well, it goes without saying, doesn't it? Now you take…"

Hart stopped listening to his mixed metaphors and non sequiturs. He murmured a reply, but his thoughts were on the chamber upstairs where his bride waited. Impatient, and fearing he'd lose his manners if the fellow didn't stop rambling, he excused himself and left the room. He smoked a cheroot outside in the cold air, something he rarely did. Odd how he felt nervous. Finally, he stubbed it out beneath the heel of his boot and went up to the room.

He knocked on their chamber door. Bid entry, he found Maddie waiting in a frilly white nightgown. A waterfall of lustrous hair fell down around her shoulders and hung in loose curls down her back. A sight he'd longed to see and touch. "How pretty you look," he said, his voice husky.

He glimpsed something in her eyes. Not fear, he was sure. A game girl like Maddie wasn't easily frightened. Dear lord, she'd just shot a man who tried to kill her. That took a cool head. He cursed himself again for the mistake he made phrasing his proposal in such unromantic terms. But they had drawn closer during the past weeks, and he'd hoped by tonight...

All such thoughts fled at the alluring sight she made, her breasts with their deep pink areolas jutting from the filmy cloth, and the dark shadow at the juncture of her thighs. He had done and said little to show her he desired her, wishing to take it slow. Well, he would now.

He stepped forward and framed her waist with his hands, drawing her to him. His mouth covered hers. She murmured something he didn't quite catch, but reluctant to spoil the moment, he didn't ask. She leaned into him, and her sweet lips softened against his. Blood rushed through his body, along with a fierce desire to make her his.

Still unsure of her feelings, Hart drew back and gazed into her eyes. "Remember I said our marriage could be anything you wanted it to be? Do you want this, Maddie? If you wish, we can spend the night playing cards. We'll be seen to have spent the night together." It cost him a lot to say it, and for a moment, he feared she might agree.

Her eyes widened, and her tongue licked her bottom lip, which did nothing for the state of his body. "No, Hart, you know I'm not good at cards."

Hart grinned at her cheeky rejoinder, and his spirits soared as a rush of pleasure and rampant need consumed him. He had wanted this since the first moment he saw her, he realized now. Had he subconsciously planned for it? Hart gathered her up in his arms, and breathing in her light, fresh perfume, carried her to the bed. Easing her down, he rested his hands on either side of her on the coverlet. Their gazes collided, her brown eyes dark as satin. His breath caught at the passionate desire he found there. He eased himself down, cradled her face, and claimed her mouth, the touch of her lips and warm soft body against his, electric. Her response delighted him. She murmured softly in his ear, her fingers threading through the hair at his nape. His kisses deepened as he stroked the curve of her waist and hip, eager to discover all of her, his beautiful, mysterious Maddie.

After a moment, Hart reluctantly pushed himself away. He left the bed to undress, pulling off his boots and tossing his clothes onto a chair. When he returned, he lay naked beside her and she turned to him, passion darkening her eyes.

He kissed her and fondled a nipple, which firmed through the cloth. "I've longed for this."

Her lips parted in surprise. "You have?"

"But the need to keep you safe was uppermost in my mind," he said, a smile in his voice. Not entirely true, as he'd thought of this many times, but still... "It made me a poor excuse for a lover, Maddie."

"Hush." Her finger traced along his jaw. "That was then. This is now."

His hand skimmed her thighs, drawing up her nightgown. "Yes, this is now."

WHEN HART UNDRESSED, Maddie caught her breath. If you could call a naked man beautiful, Hart certainly was. She marveled at his satiny, smooth skin, strongly delineated muscles, and that fascinating part of him which he urged her to touch and moaned when she did. His body fascinated her, hard and yet soft, and when he entered her it brought her such pleasure that she lost all sense of herself.

As their breaths slowed, she lay quiet and sated, her leg resting partly over his in the soft glow of the candles while she considered their future together. Hart seemed to have withdrawn from her, his eyes closed, and that nagging worry entered her mind she could not keep at bay. Although he was an unselfish and considerate lover, he had not told her he loved her, or allowed her a glimpse into his heart. It made her reluctant to be honest with him, and left a hollow feeling of unfulfillment, which, had she voiced it, would only make her sound unreasonable. And she was afraid of his answer.

Why was Hart reluctant to reveal much about his life before he met her? She yearned to know everything about him, and was impatient to tell him all about hers, the good and the heartrending. To hear him say how meeting her had changed his life, and how he loved her. But he had not invited such intimacies. And then, in the throes of passion, when her confession of love hovered on her lips, she bit down on it, fearing Hart would not wish to hear it.

While he murmured endearments as his body and skillful fingers brought her to climax, he never spoke those words she longed to hear. This marriage was not a love match, she told herself sternly, and she must not allow herself to forget it, or want more, for that would lead to dissatisfaction. But what might this mean when they returned to London? His friends would believe their marriage to be one of convenience, and some would wonder at the reason for it. She stiffened. She had her pride. If Hart took a mistress, it would humiliate her.

Hart turned his head to look at her. "You seem tense, Maddie. Have I fallen short as a lover?"

She laughed and leaned over to stroke his muscled chest, curling her fingers in the tufts of dark hair. "Don't be silly."

He rolled on his side and propped his head with an elbow, his eyes roaming over her. "I can always remedy that. You have only to ask."

Maddie felt his gaze like a stroke from his warm hand, but her fears had cooled her ardor. "That would be most unreasonable of me. I am a little sleepy." She stretched, suddenly irritated with herself. Why did she let these thoughts spoil the most wonderful moments of her life?

"Sleep then, sweetheart. We must head home tomorrow."

"Yes," she murmured, closing her eyes. *Home.* But the thought failed to lull her to sleep.

Chapter Fifteen

HART WOKE WITH a start, but it was not yet dawn. Beside him, Maddie slept deeply, her legs curled within his. How well her body fit. It began to rain, and a flash of lightning lit the sky, brightening the room for a moment. Heavy drops pattering against the window, Maddie sighed in her sleep and rolled onto her side. When her hand found his, Hart smiled and pulled the covers over her shoulders. Warm and dry and completely content, he fell asleep.

When he woke again, bright sun shone through the gap in the curtains. It must be late. He had instructed the servants not to disturb them this morning. He watched his bride sleep, wanting to wake her and make love to her again. But he should allow her to rest. He considered himself the most fortunate of fellows. As a lover, Maddie was not only beautiful, she was sensual and giving.

A knock at the door interrupted his pleasant reverie. Expecting the maid with their coffee and chocolate, he pulled the sheet over his sleeping wife's creamy breasts and rose to don his dressing gown.

"Come."

Henry stuck his head in the door. "Sorry to interrupt, milord."

"You should be, Henry. This had better be important."

"You said you wished to leave at ten and it's gone eleven-thirty."

"That late, eh? I hadn't noticed." Henry looked at his feet and shuffled them. "We shall be down shortly for breakfast. Send Jane to attend to her mistress."

He would prefer to allow Maddie to sleep a little longer. But they must cover some ground before nightfall. He leaned over and kissed her lips.

She opened her eyes and sleepily smiled at him.

"Good morning, my sweet."

"Have I overslept?" She sat up and stretched. "What time is it?"

Admiring her naked body, he wished he could join her in the bed. "Late. I've sent for Jane."

Gathering up his clothes, he left her to wash and dress in the adjoining chamber. Cursing the absence of his valet, he got himself ready to leave. He looked dubiously at his crumpled waistcoat, then donned it and buttoned it up. His coat had fared better. He tied his cravat before the mirror. Having pulled on his boots, he returned to Maddie's room. Jane had not arrived, and Maddie was out of bed, her peignoir in her hands. A glimpse of her naked body gave him an inconvenient cock stand. He retreated to the door before tempted to act on it. "I'll see you in the dining room for breakfast, my sweet, after which we must depart."

She turned to him with a smile as she slipped her arms into the sleeves, remarkably unselfconscious about her nakedness. And why would she be? He watched the elegant play of her muscles, her slender thighs, her rounded belly, dark hair over her sex. Years of riding had fashioned a lissome beauty. He turned away from the beguiling sight, smiled, and opened the door. Stepping out into the corridor, he closed the door behind him with a chuckle and a shake of his head. He foresaw the journey home would be frustrating and pleasurable in equal measure.

MY SWEET! MADDIE frowned at the closed door. Hart's lovemaking had swept her away. She'd been in a fog of bliss until he'd used that name for her. As if she was his mistress. She moaned softly. Did it matter so much if he didn't love her? He desired and liked her. Did she expect too much too soon? She supposed he'd used that endearment before. Had those women yearned like her to hear him declare his love for them? She narrowed her eyes. Perhaps he said that to all his mistresses? Could someone have broken his heart? Such sentimental nonsense. She laughed at herself.

"I won't allow this to spoil my happiness," she said firmly to her reflection in the mirror. She imagined she looked different. A more mature expression in her eyes. Well, she was a married lady and no longer a girl. And she must hurry to ready herself for the journey ahead. But where was Jane? The maid usually came immediately after she was summoned.

Maddie poured water into the bowl on the washstand and took up a washer and soap for a quick but thorough wash. Then in her peignoir, sorted through her poor selection of clothes. The scent of their lovemaking lingered in the air, and despite her misgivings, she wished he was here with her.

There was a knock at the door and Jane opened it. "I'm sorry I've kept you waiting, milady."

Maddie gave up her musings. "I'll wear the carriage dress, Jane."

Not her usual neat self. Her maid's hair looked hastily arranged and her cheeks had a heightened color. She had been slow to come to attend her. Might something be amiss? If it was, it couldn't be a bad thing, for Jane smiled as she went to the wardrobe, looking as happy as a lark. Henry, Maddie supposed. "Did you and Henry enjoy dinner last night?"

Jane turned to Maddie, the dress in her hands, and her smile fell away. "We did, ever so much, milady."

Maddie gazed at her, perplexed, then hurriedly dressed.

When she entered the dining room, Hart rose, smiling, from his chair. Her heart did a strange little flip. One day, he would tell her he loved her. Even if it was after a long marriage and several children before he realized it. She would wait patiently. *Ha!* She didn't believe it. She knew herself too well.

While the coach ate up the miles to the next coaching inn on the Great North Road, Maddie leaned against her husband's shoulder, their night together lingering in her mind. It still made her blush. While she understood what occurred between a couple when they made love, she had not known the many ways a man might pleasure a woman. She snuck a glance at Hart. His eyes were closed, his body relaxed. He had a noble profile, and she itched to trace it with her finger. Did he enjoy their night together as much as she did? She must learn how to please him. Become more skillful in the bedchamber than any mistress if she was to keep him from looking elsewhere. *That is the way to keep a rake, Aunt Gabby.* That made her smile, thinking of what her aunt's response might be if she were still above ground.

"Why the smile?" Hart's voice drew her out of her thoughts. She hid her fiery face, wanting to say, *thinking of you, my love.* But she made some reference to the dog that chased after them farther back on the road. She searched for a suitable topic of conversation to hide her embarrassment. "Do you have a dog you favor above the others, Hart?"

"Yes. He is called Rasputin."

"Rasputin?" She laughed.

"He's a devil. Funnily enough, the one dog I've failed to train, and I have grown most fond of him."

"You admire his spirit."

"Yes, I suppose I do. I'll introduce you to him when we arrive at Pembury."

Pembury. A shabby old Elizabethan house in a riot of gardens. She'd noticed cobwebs in the corners of the hall and a smell of dust when she and her uncle called on Hart. Something else to get her teeth into. And Lilybrook cottage, she would miss it. Would they ever go back there? Just for a holiday, perhaps. Would Hart laugh at her if she suggested it?

But now, she must concentrate on what lay ahead in London. *London!* Everything she feared and was reluctant to face seemed to suddenly gallop toward her with each mile they passed.

Hart's arm came around her as if he sensed her thoughts. But he couldn't, could he?

Still tired, she snuggled against him, and closed her eyes, directing her mind to more pleasurable things. Diane's company. The two of them shopping together. With that, she slept.

When she woke still resting against Hart, the coach had pulled into the inn forecourt, the ostler darting out to grab the horses, the innkeeper on the doorstep, eager to welcome them into the ivy-covered brick building. The footman put down the step and opened the door. Jane edged forward, ready to disembark directly after Maddie and Hart. As the maid followed her out, Henry jumped down from the box with a big grin. Glancing at her maid thoughtfully, Maddie realized she'd been so caught up in her own affairs she'd barely noticed the change in Jane. Not until this morning. It seemed as if Jane kept a secret from her. Maddie would endeavor to find out what it was when she had time to address it. Right now, she looked ahead to the evening spent with Hart. And their time alone.

Chapter Sixteen

Montford Court, Mayfair

I N THE LATE afternoon, their long journey ended. Hart introduced Maddie to his butler, Crispin, in the black-and-white marble tiled hall and requested a footman escort her to the marchioness suite. As Maddie and Jane followed the footman upstairs, Hart went to the library, where his secretary awaited him.

An hour later, Maddie came into the library where Hart sat alone reading his post. She wore the green gown he liked. She smiled and came to rest her hand on his shoulder.

"Diane has replied to my letter." Hart gazed up at her. "By return post. She is keen to come and stay. But she must first make arrangements for the children." He held up the letter. "Two crossed pages. I'll leave it for you to read. I doubt I'm mentioned once."

"Oh, she's coming! What good news." Maddie took the letter from him and scanned it. "Diane has recommended a dressmaker. I'll go to see her tomorrow." She looked up and smiled. "She mentions the Bond Street Bazaar, and Harding Howell & Co in Pall Mall, where I might purchase lace and fans." Maddie sighed. "I have missed shopping so much."

Hart turned with a laugh and drew her down onto his lap. His arms around her, he said, "It would be entirely unnatural should you not have. Something all women seem to enjoy."

She brushed his dark hair back from his brow. "You don't like to shop?" She shook her head. "Men and women are so different."

"Vive la différence." He kissed her. In his arms, her soft body stirred his passion. He deliberated on disturbing the intricate arrangement of her hair, but before he could act, Maddie, who might have suspected his intentions, climbed off his lap and went to sit on the sofa.

"I shall visit the Bond Street shops tomorrow after I've seen the modiste," she declared.

Hart sighed. Rising, he walked to the drinks table. "A glass of wine?"

"Please."

He poured two glasses from the carafe. "Are you pleased with your bedchamber?" he asked as he handed her the wineglass. He joined her on the sofa. "If you require anything, send for Mrs. Hatton."

A footman knocked and brought in a plate of biscuits, placing it before them on the occasional table. Maddie reached over and took one. "The suite is perfect. Elegant yet comfortable. Your housekeeper has been meticulous." She took a bite. "Mm. These are delicious. I must consult the cook about the menus."

"And you might give them your recipe for beef and onion pie."

She laughed and shook her head. "I think not."

"You'll wish to make changes here. The house has been empty since before my father fell ill. He preferred country life and never came here again."

"Wasn't this your home?"

"No. I had rooms in Piccadilly."

"Surely this would have been more comfortable?"

Maddie's practical nature, he thought, although she'd chosen her words carefully. She didn't wish to pry, but was understandably curious. He didn't wish to speak of the past. "My father thought it an unnecessary expense to keep the house open for me alone. He preferred to lease it."

"I see."

She didn't, of course, but said no more. One more thing about her he was grateful for. Her sensitive nature. She would learn the family secrets eventually, some of which he was not proud of. He liked to think that he was a better man now and would have handled his father differently. When he thought back, he realized that despite his history of a string of mistresses, his father seemed unloved and alone in his declining years.

Somehow, in the past weeks, it had become important for Maddie to think well of him. He thought of the night ahead when they would be together. Just sitting close beside her on the sofa made him want her in his arms. This unruly passion surprised him. Ordinarily, it would worry him. He'd always kept a cool head where women were concerned. But since Maddie, his former life of excitement and change seemed to lose its hold on him. "You must be tired after the journey."

She glanced up at him, a smile in her eyes. "My bath refreshed me."

Hart wanted to kiss her, but never seemed able to stop at one. Fearing a kiss would lead to him taking his wife on the library desk, he returned to sort through the rest of the mail his secretary had left for him. Invitations he would decline until Maddie had the right clothes. He looked over at her. She had grown silent. "I'll visit my bank for the engagement and wedding rings in the morning. They have been in the family for generations. But if you would prefer new rings, we can go to the family jewelers in Ludgate Hill. They will have a fine collection."

"Oh, no. Were they your mother's?"

"Yes, my mother's and my grandmother's before her, but it is your choice, Maddie."

"Then I shall love them, Hart," she said firmly.

"I'll arrange an appointment with your solicitor."

Her forehead creased. "I imagine he will advise my uncle of our marriage and our London address." She sighed. "Uncle Arthur will be furious to learn you were involved, Hart. He will hate to be outwitted."

Seeing how nervous she was about him, Hart left the desk and sat beside her. "That's his prerogative." He brushed a finger over her soft cheek. "I have plans for him he will hate more."

"I wish you wouldn't get involved," she said with a worried frown. "My uncle is dangerous. He intended to kill me without a second thought."

Hart raised his eyebrows. "I am not afraid of your uncle or his henchmen."

"I remember how well you can handle yourself." She smiled. "I saw what you did to his men when you rescued me. But you are an honorable man, and my uncle is not."

"I hope to deal with him without breaking the law, Maddie." He shrugged. "But if he sics his men onto me, they'll get what they deserve."

She opened her mouth to protest, but he framed her face with his hands and stopped her with a kiss, forgetting his intention not to. Fresh from her bath, her skin was warm and scented. He drank the last of his wine and put down his glass, wanting to hold her and reassure her, and make endless love to her. "We have an hour or two before dinner. Shall we go upstairs?"

"Let's." The smile in her eyes told him she'd expected this. He feared he was becoming predictable as Maddie took his hand and rose.

⫸⫷

HART HAD SPENT the night with her, but left early to visit his bank. Maddie rose late, and after breakfast, sat at the dainty desk in her sitting room. She wrote a letter to Aunt Libby on the crested writing paper she found in a drawer. She invited them to call on her at

Montford Court tomorrow afternoon after two o'clock if they were not otherwise engaged. Her marriage would shock them, but they would be happy for her, she was sure. But explaining how it came to be to her aunt would not be easy. Maddie expected the news of her and Hart being seen together would have reached her aunt from Bath, which would not be favorable. A whirlwind love affair, she would say. Aunt Libby was a lover of romance and visited the Bath lending library often for novels. Gazing out onto the plane trees in Berkeley Square, Maddie wished that were true. That Hart had fallen in love with her instantly. Still, no words of love passed his lips, even in the throes of passion. But what they felt for each other was explosive. She grew warm thinking of it and urged herself to be content and not wish for more.

Maddie rang for a footman to deliver her letter to the address where her aunt and cousin stayed, then she consulted the housekeeper about the week's menus. Mrs. Hatton was obliging, and Maddie suspected glad to have a mistress at last. But Maddie knew Hart's preferences, and because he wasn't often here, Cook might not. After the housekeeper left, Maddie considered how to fill the hour and a half before her appointment with the modiste.

The door opened and Hart walked in. "I have something to show you." He removed a jeweler's box from his pocket. "Do you have a moment?"

"Of course." She rose from the chair, curious and excited. "You've fetched the rings from the bank?"

"I have." He flipped the lid open, revealing two rings nestling in a bed of satin. A plain gold wedding band and an engagement ring with a large diamond surrounded by smaller stones in an intricate gold setting, which was heavy and ornate, but quite glorious.

"It's old fashioned," he said, removing the rings. "We can have it reset in a modern design when you have time to visit the jeweler." He snapped the lid shut and put it down on her desk. "They may need some adjustment."

Her heart beating fast, Maddie gave him her hand, and he slipped the rings on her finger. For a long moment, their eyes met. Something special passed between them. Dare she hope he was falling in love with her?

The rings fit perfectly. With a murmur of delight, she held up her hand. The big center diamond flashed a myriad of colors. "Beautiful," she murmured. "No, I shan't change it."

"You like them then?" Hart pulled her close and nuzzled her neck, and she slipped her arms around his slim waist.

"I do, very much."

"When is your appointment with the dressmaker?" he murmured in her ear, his voice husky.

"One o'clock."

"Then we have time?"

She reached up to touch his face, wanting him. "You'll make me late."

Hart's smile held intent. His hands at her waist, he walked backwards, taking her with him. He hefted her up in his arms, then slowly laid her down while Maddie helplessly gazed at his adored face, thrilling to see the flare of passion in his eyes. Just his touch made her stomach throb with need. While she wished not to be late for her first visit to the new modiste, when he kissed her, it ceased to matter. With a moan, she gave in to his demanding kisses. She could never say no to him.

When Hart left her bedchamber, Maddie gathered up the handful of pins scattered over the coverlet and languidly rose. With a smile, she touched her lips, slightly swollen with his kisses, then donned her dressing gown. She would have to send for Jane to do her hair again, but she didn't care. She felt carefree, her limbs loose. Seated before the dressing table, she admired her rings. How calm she'd become, as if all her worries were vanquished. But they would emerge to plague her soon enough. She smiled into the mirror, her eyes bright and her skin glowing. This was what it meant to be blissfully in love. A word of caution nagged at her. Her stern commonsense warned her of the trials ahead. But so free and joyful, she laughed and pushed the thought away as she brushed her hair.

Jane came in. She looked unsettled and distracted. "His lordship said you wanted me, milady?"

"Yes. I must dress quickly, Jane. I have an appointment with the dressmaker in half an hour." Maddie rose. "I shall have to wear the carriage gown."

When Jane brought it from the wardrobe, Maddie groaned as she gazed at the sad state of it. Jane tried valiantly to care for her clothes, but the gown had seen too much wear. What would the dressmaker think of her?

"Shall I run the hot iron over it, milady? To remove the wrinkles. It will only take a moment."

"Oh, yes, Jane, do." She would hate to confront the woman, looking like she'd been dragged through a bush.

Jane picked it up and went to the dressing room, where a fire had been lit earlier. Maddie sank back on the stool and took up the brush. After a moment, something about Jane's demeanor broke into her thoughts. She called to her maid, who was removing Maddie's shoes, hat, and gloves from the wardrobe while waiting for the iron to heat. "You appear to be wrestling with a problem, Jane. Would you care to tell me about it? Perhaps I can help."

Jane reappeared, looking uncomfortable. "Oh no, milady. It's nothing, really."

"If you're sure." Unconvinced, Maddie let it go. When Jane brought in the gown, which the ironing had improved, she didn't persist. Aware of the time, she quickly dressed. As Jane's deft fingers arranged her hair, Maddie tried not to smile. Hart would insist on removing all the pins with no care to the work required to restore it.

Jane flittered about the room with a light step as she tidied things away. Intrigued, Maddie, while closing the clasp on her locket, watched her maid in the mirror. In time, she would learn the truth. Henry would be the cause, she knew. Was Jane in love? And might they have quarreled? That didn't seem likely with what she'd seen of the two of them together. Dressed, Maddie rose and turned her mind to what she would ask for from Madam Benoit.

Full length gilt-edged mirrors and crimson velvet drapes decorated Madam Benoit's elegant establishment. The French woman had a reasonable command of English, although she lapsed into French when overly exuberant. She draped fabrics over Maddie's body and stood back to study her, a finger tapping her chin. Maddie agreed with her choice for the evening gown. In the mirror, the glowing, greenish-bronze-colored satin for the underdress suited her coloring.

Maddie drank coffee while she studied the latest fashion plates and material samples laid out on the table before her. Two hours passed before she and Madam came to an agreement. And Maddie left with the dressmaker's promise of delivering a morning gown, a promenade dress, a carriage gown, and a filmy nightgown, as well as the evening gown, the following week. The ballgown would require another fitting. "To ensure it is perfection," Madam said. White gauze over white satin was decided as white was still all the rage. Maddie agreed, although the dress would not make the statement she wished for.

Maddie and Jane spent another hour roaming the fascinating shops Diane had mentioned in her letter. The footman followed, his arms full of packages. When he could carry no more, Maddie reluctantly thought it best to return home. He deposited the parcels in the carriage and stood at the open door for them to enter. Before Maddie put a foot on the step, a man loomed up beside her. She turned.

Her uncle stood before her, his legs planted as he looked her up and down, an array of expressions from shock to anger and disgust crossing his face. "It appears you have found a gentleman to keep you.

What quick work, Madeline."

Her throat tightened. His voice carried, and his insinuation was embarrassing. For Hart's sake, as much as hers, she would hate the shoppers walking by to hear it. "I am married, Uncle Arthur."

He looked incredulous. "Married? Don't be ridiculous. You are not yet twenty-one and neither have you sought my permission."

Maddie's hands trembled. She hated how he could still make her feel like the helpless young girl she'd been when he first appeared in her life. Annoyed with herself, she moved back from his disturbing presence. Pulling off her glove, she held out her hand, displaying her ringed fingers. The large diamond flashed in the sunlight. "Have you not noticed the crest on the carriage door? I am Marchioness Lady Montford."

Her uncle's eyes widened as realization dawned. "So, the marquess was behind this. I might have known. He has snatched you up. Looking for a mistress, was he? Your reputation is now in shreds, my girl. You shall come home with me now." He swung around to Jane. "But not you, Miss Frost. You left my employment without a word and encouraged my ward to do this. I shall make sure you do not find a position as lady's maid again. You will work on your back in some brothel!"

The tall, well-built footman cleared his throat and took a step closer, causing her uncle to fall back a pace.

"Lord Montford and I were married in Scotland," Maddie said stiffly.

Her uncle's laugh grated. "A wedding over an anvil? Hardly legal, my dear Madeline."

"Should you wish it, my husband will show you the document."

He scoffed. "No such legal document exists. You are underage and I shall prove he's taken advantage of you. Foolish girl, he is after the money your father left you, and by doing so has ravished you and ruined your reputation. It is common knowledge his father's death left his finances in disarray. I am your guardian. If you won't come with me now, I shall seek the assistance of the law."

"I wouldn't advise it, Uncle." Maddie turned before she mounted the carriage steps, her hand on the footman's arm. She didn't want to say it here, but could not resist anger at his betrayal of her trust twisting in her stomach. "That would only draw attention to your attempts to murder me."

"Murder you? What nonsense. As if I would hurt a member of my family," he blustered, but the expression in his eyes told her she'd rocked him.

"I know you were behind it, uncle. The man you sent to kidnap me and who later tried to kill me I saw first at your house. He visited you often, and I believe Lord Montford saw him there, too."

"Lord Montford was prowling about my property?"

"He came to take my mare before you took out your revenge on her."

"That is theft! I shall have the law on him!"

"He did not steal her, uncle. The horse belongs to me."

He stared at her, then wordlessly turned on his heel, disappearing into the gathering crowd who, having sensed something interesting afoot, had stopped to watch.

Maddie, on shaky legs but with her chin held high nodded to the footman to assist her into the carriage. Jane, looking shaken, followed. "Uncle Arthur believes I've never seen his men," she gasped, able to breathe again now the carriage door had closed. "He thought it safe to dispose of me without fear of discovery."

"He can't hurt you now, milady." There were tears in Jane's eyes, and her voice shook.

"Don't be afraid, Jane," Maddie said firmly. "His threats were horrid, I grant you, but empty, for he has no hold on you. Hart would never allow him to hurt you. You are in our employ now, not my uncle's. Nor can he do anything more to me," Maddie added as the carriage took them back to Montford Court.

As if she found no comfort in Maddie's assurances, Jane miserably dropped her chin and, clutching her reticule, stared at her trembling fingers.

More shaken than she wished Jane to see, Maddie tried to convince herself that her uncle's threats were merely bluster. Tomorrow, Hart would accompany her to the solicitor and learn the truth of her father's will, which she hoped would reveal the reason behind her uncle's actions. But that wasn't her biggest fear. Would this urge Hart to deal with her uncle and place himself in danger? Hart had gotten the better of them so far, but next time, who knew what might happen? What those murderous henchmen of her uncle's might do to Hart gripped her and made her slightly ill.

Chapter Seventeen

MADDIE RUSHED INTO the library where Hart sat reading his post. Alarmed at her flustered appearance, he rose to his feet. "What is it, Maddie?"

"My uncle accosted me on the street," she said in a rush. "People stopped to listen. It was awful. If the footman hadn't been there, I don't know what he would have done."

"Curse that man!"

Hart held her, battling to control his anger while his thoughts turned murderous. "That was most unwise of him," he said, his jaw tight. "And he will live to regret it."

"You'll have the law deal with him, Hart?" she said, leaning back, her eyes questioning his. "Surely, as soon as that villain in jail confesses and tells the truth about him, he will be arrested, won't he?"

Hart couldn't be sure of it, but didn't say so. Maddie had grown in confidence since they married. Now she wilted, hurt and confused, and he hated Wakeham more for that than anything. What he had done to his young ward placed in his protection was unspeakable. And right now, Hart wished for an equally unspeakable ending for him. But he smiled and drew her down onto his lap, moderating his voice. "He can talk all he likes, but can do nothing, Maddie."

She leaned against him, tears in her eyes. "That document, Hart. Is it legal?"

Dash it all. That certificate was just meant to reassure her. "It was unnecessary, Maddie. I could tear it up now and we will still be married. No court in the land will rule otherwise."

"But would he try to get the law to overturn it?"

"He's hardly likely to. Not with his man in jail who could start spilling all, as a heavy sentence in Newgate awaits him."

She fiddled with a gilt button on his coat. "So, I am safe from him?"

Hart watched her pretty face, her dark lashes fluttering over her teary brown eyes. He swallowed, overcome with emotion. "You are, darling. No one would dare attack a marchioness. My footmen guard this house better than any jail. Should you wish to go out, I'll instruct my footman to be armed. Should he try, Wakeham will find you've become as unapproachable as a star."

She nodded silently and rested her head against his shoulder.

He felt her heart beating hard and his arms tightened around her. "Now kiss me, sweetheart, and tell me you feel more reassured. Or I shan't like to leave you tomorrow."

"My uncle has always had a disturbing effect on me. I'd feared he'd become my jailer, and I'd never escape him.

"My brave darling," Hart said. And she might have been right, had she not been courageous enough to escape him.

Maddie kissed him, then escaped his lap. She straightened her shoulders. "I hate how I become a marshmallow when my uncle is near."

"Not difficult to understand, is it?" He was sorry she'd left his lap so promptly. "The man is unpredictable and cruel."

"I'll go up and open my packages. There are so many! I confess to getting a little carried away! Such a wonderful display of goods. Bath shops are excellent but do not compare to London. And I approve of my new dressmaker. Her gowns are magnifique! I can't wait for you to see them," she said over her shoulder and laughingly crossed the room.

He stared after her until she shut the door behind her. Maddie rarely let him see how troubled she was. He was pleased she'd allowed him even a glimpse so that he might assuage her concerns. But had he convinced her? None of this would matter, because he planned to go after Wakeham and bring him down with whatever means were available to him. Armed with what they may learn from Maddie's solicitor tomorrow.

The solicitor, Mr. Cosgrove, a round-faced, balding man in his fifties, welcomed them effusively into his office. He shook hands with Hart and offered his felicitations. "A wonderful surprise," he said, gesturing to two chairs placed facing the desk. After removing a folder from the drawer, he tossed up his coattails and sat down. "May I offer you a libation? No? Then we shall proceed." He placed both hands atop the folder. "Perhaps we could begin by you telling me what you wished to know."

"They did not permit me to attend my parents' funeral, nor was I present at the reading of the will, Mr. Cosgrove," Maddie began. "So I know very little. Only that my uncle was the sole guardian. He handled everything for me. I have a dowry of twenty-five thousand pounds, is that not right? And the bulk of my father's fortune he left to my Aunt Elizabeth? My uncle said he received a modest amount."

Cosgrove frowned. "No, that's quite incorrect, Lady Montford. I am upset to think you have had this misconception." He took papers from the folder, searched for the one he wished to view, and cleared his throat. "We wrote to you to explain the contents of your father's will. And sent two further letters. These are your replies." He slid them across the desk to her.

Maddie picked them up and read them. She turned to Hart, confused. "I did not write these."

Hart took them from her and scanned them. "Could they be written in Wakeham's hand?" he asked the solicitor.

Cosgrove raised his graying eyebrows, his eyes wide behind his spectacles. "I never imagined for a moment..." He took the letters from Hart and compared them with other documents he drew from the folder. It was clear by his expression that he thought it was Wakeham's hand. "It is possible," he said carefully. "But then, I imagine as he was handling matters for you..." His voice died away.

"I'd like you to explain the will to us in its entirety," Hart said sternly, sitting back with his arms crossed.

"Certainly," Cosgrove said. He cleared his throat. "I will summarize the main provisions for you. My lady, your father, the earl, left your Aunt Elizabeth a hundred pounds a month annuity for the rest of her life, plus a small gift to her daughter Catherine. A sum of five thousand pounds went to your uncle, along with smaller sums to your father's servants. The estate consists of the proceeds of the sale of the earl's home, Green Oaks, including the livestock, together with a valuable art collection which is currently in storage. Your father also held shares in a number of prominent companies and owned three other properties in London, which are leased. We have obtained a valuation of your father's estate of some eight hundred thousand pounds. The entire estate has been bequeathed to you, apart from the matters I have mentioned."

Maddie gasped and turned to Hart. "I knew none of this."

"The scoundrel," Hart said.

"My uncle told me he sold the paintings," Maddie said. "Even my parents' portraits by Gainsborough." Her voice hitched. "And the painting of me as a young child with my mother."

Cosgrove shook his head. "Rest assured, my lady. No paintings have been sold, nor the statues, china collection, furniture, or rugs. A further provision in the will states that in the event of your death, Mr. Arthur Wakeham becomes the beneficiary. But now that you are married, this particular provision no longer applies." He closed the folder. "If you have questions, I would be pleased to answer them."

An hour later, they left the office, Maddie holding Hart's arm. "I can't believe it," she said again.

"I can believe it of Wakeham," Hart said curtly.

"To think I am the recipient of my father's fortune." She gazed at Hart. "On my death, he inherits everything!"

"I suspected as much," Hart said through his teeth.

She turned to look at him in horror. "That is why he wanted to see me dead." She shivered. "I only wonder why he waited so long."

Hart took her elbow and escorted her down the stairs. "It would have been too obvious if anything happened as soon as you took up residence with him. You have had a dreadful shock, Maddie. We don't have to talk about this now."

She shook her head. "No, we must. The time will come when we can put it all behind us. But not yet."

Hart nodded. "It appears Wakeham intended to make it look like an accident. But he needed time. There was the cut strap, which failed because of your skill on a horse. He had to be careful because of this business he's mixed up in. He wouldn't want to bring the law to his door."

"I wish we knew what that was. It must be something illegal. We could have him arrested," she said.

"I will find out. Perhaps the Bow Street Runner has discovered something." Hart gazed into her eyes. "Are you all right, sweetheart? Even though we suspected something badly amiss, it is horrible to hear the truth."

She nodded, fire in her eyes, more like the Maddie he knew. "His cruel betrayal has shocked me, certainly. I disliked him from the first. I found it difficult to believe anything he told me. But this?" She put a hand on her chest. "His hatred of me and his cunning makes my blood run cold."

Hart slipped his arm around her. "We shall be free of all of this soon."

"I hope so." She looked up at him. "What happens now, Hart?"

"I'll return to Pembury tomorrow. To speak to the Bow Street Runner. He's putting up at an inn near Tunbridge Wells."

"You won't search my uncle's property? Not alone," Maddie cautioned.

"No. I doubt that would be helpful."

"I wish I could come with you."

Hart laughed. "To keep an eye on me?"

"Yes," she said firmly. She reached up to touch his face with a smile.

"A pity, but with Diane coming to stay, I'm afraid I must go without you."

She narrowed her eyes at him. "You are far too eager to leave me behind."

He laughed. "I am having the house painted. Some rooms were completely refurbished. The house still reeks of turpentine and paint."

"Must I face the *ton* alone with only Diane to introduce me?"

"I'll be back in a week. In plenty of time for our first appearance, which I wouldn't miss for the world." He grinned. "It will be the Duke of and Duchess of Lindsey's spring ball. Tate and Ianthe are good friends of mine. If your ballgown is ready by then."

"I hope so. There will be one more fitting."

"I wish you could come with me to Pembury. I will miss you." He cupped her chin and gazed into her eyes. "Very much."

"Well, Lord Montford, how nice to find you back in London," came a woman's voice behind them.

He turned, already aware of who it was. "Mrs. Spencer, allow me to introduce you to my wife, Lady Montford."

Maddie smiled and held out her hand. "How do you do, Mrs. Spencer?"

For a moment, Vivian looked shocked. Recovering herself, she took Maddie's hand. "Well! This is a surprise! The news of your marriage has not yet reached our ears. My felicitations, Lady Montford."

"Thank you, Mrs. Spencer."

Vivian turned to Hart. "Congratulations, Lord Montford! What a dark horse you are." Her smile was strained. "You have married under the noses of the society matrons, hoping you would choose their daughter. Where was the wedding held?"

"A country ceremony," Hart said pleasantly.

Vivian shifted her gaze to Maddie. "I look forward to learning all about it when next we meet, Lady Montford. Shall we see more of you this Season?"

"We have accepted a few invitations, haven't we, darling?" Maddie said, taking his arm. "But not yet. We have only just returned from a short honeymoon."

"Indeed! Where did you spend your honeymoon?"

"Touring in the north," Maddie said, the tone of her voice not inviting any further comment.

Hart thought it wise to keep silent. His bride could well take care of herself.

"How pleasant." Vivian curtsied and hurried away down the street.

"Is Mrs. Spencer a friend of long standing?" Maddie asked him as they approached the carriage. "Do you know her husband?"

"Mm? No. She is a widow and a recent acquaintance. Here we are. Allow me to assist you."

They settled in the carriage and the horses pulled away into the street.

"How odd," Maddie remarked. "She seemed so much more like an old friend."

Hart fought not to sigh. The look Vivian gave him could have set him on fire. And the road ahead seemed to be filled with potholes.

As THE CARRIAGE took them to Montford Court, Maddie glanced at her contemplative husband. He'd become annoyingly evasive. There must be more to his association with Mrs. Spencer. Maddie didn't miss the proprietorial look the woman gave him. Their marriage had surprised her, but there was more to it than that. Had she expected something else from Hart? A commitment? Had she been his mistress? Maddie had no energy to give to it. The astonishing news they had learned from the solicitor overwhelmed her. Her father had left her his fortune. It brought tears to her eyes. She brushed them away with her gloved fingers before Hart saw them. Maddie didn't want to always appear to be a watering pot. But she would honor her father's memory and manage her inheritance wisely. She was now in control of her life. The revelation came to her like a heady rush of energy. Hart would never stand in her way in whatever she chose to do. Her avaricious uncle, who sought to destroy her happiness, could no longer have any hold over her.

She wished she could go with Hart to Pembury. She admitted she wanted to put off the day she'd appear in society, but most particularly because she feared for Hart. He could take care of himself, as he said, but her uncle was clearly a very dangerous and unscrupulous man. While Diane's visit prevented her from leaving London, Maddie looked forward to having an experienced woman to advise her. With a new wardrobe, there was no reason to delay accepting some invitations, which arrived daily. Enough to attend at least two events each evening until the end of the Season. Would the *ton* warm to her? People would naturally be curious about their hasty marriage. Might they consider an elopement romantic? Or find it a disgrace? Or even, as her uncle had, question its legality? News of their marriage was sure to be plastered over all the newspapers and gossip sheets. It was a miracle they'd avoided scrutiny thus far. Hart had told his friends at his club, but relied upon them to be discreet. He wanted her fully prepared to face the avalanche of interest their marriage would cause.

"Are you sure you'll be back in time to escort me to my first engagement?" she asked, smiling. "Or might I have to find another gentleman?"

Hart chuckled. "We can't have that. I promise I'll return within a few days." An arm around her, he drew her close. "Don't look so threatened. You will like my friends. And they will love you." She sank against him. For a moment, being close to him reassured her. But Mrs. Spencer slipped back into her thoughts. Maddie saw beneath the woman's good manners that she didn't like her. Did she look on her as a rival? Because she was once Hart's mistress? Maddie glanced at him. Was Mrs. Spencer to become a threat to their happiness?

She moved out of Hart's arms.

He glanced at her with a questioning look.

"I can't allow this gown to be crumpled," she explained. "I haven't another yet."

"Nothing can dim your beauty, Maddie." Sympathetic, he took her hand in his, but she could see his mind was elsewhere.

Did he consider her beautiful? As beautiful as Mrs. Spencer?

Mrs. Spencer had roused Maddie's fear Hart would take a mistress. And this was before they even entered society.

Chapter Eighteen

I N MADDIE'S BEDCHAMBER, Hart kissed her goodbye.

"I hope it all goes well." Her eyes widened. "Your trustees must surely agree you have done all your uncle wished for."

"One would think so." He lifted her chin and smiled into her eyes. She was rumpled and warm from the bed, the air scented with their lovemaking, and he was reluctant to leave her.

"I hope the runner has news for you."

Hart nodded. "Enjoy your visitors this afternoon. And give Diane my love when she arrives tomorrow."

"I will."

Hart kissed her briefly again and left the room, going downstairs to where his curricle awaited. The nights would be cold and lonely without Maddie, and he would stay at Pembury no longer than he had to.

He climbed into the curricle and drove from the quieter streets of Mayfair into busy Piccadilly. He hoped to reach the inn where Mr. Boyle, the Bow Street Runner stayed, before nightfall.

Some hours later, Hart pulled his horses up before the white painted inn, The Red Cockerel. Pulling off his gloves, he strode inside. "Mr. Boyle, is he here?" The innkeeper looked hopeful Hart might stop for the night, but was soon disappointed.

"Hasn't been here for two days, milord."

Hart stroked the prickles on the back of his neck. "Are you sure you didn't miss him?"

He shook his head. "Left in the morning the day before yesterday. Said he'd be in for supper, but never showed up. I have his baggage here when he wants to claim it."

Climbing into the curricle, Hart took up the reins, then considered what best to do. The situation had become dire. Boyle would never have left for London without his baggage. Hart hoped to learn something at Pembury. But the worrying thought persisted. Had Wakeham spotted Boyle on his land and ordered his men to deal with him?

It was late afternoon when Hart drove through the gates and onto Pembury drive bordered by aged elm trees. Emerging into the gardens in the soft light of the setting sun, the old mansion sat above freshly scythed lawns, the timbers enhanced by a fresh coat of paint.

At the stables, one of his older grooms took the reins. "Nothing untoward happened while I was away, Bevan?" Hart asked.

Bevan blinked, surprised at the possibility that anything might disturb his peace. "No, milord."

At the house, Hart ordered a footman to bring him a light meal, then sent for his steward. In the library, he poured brandy from the crystal decanter and took it to his desk.

Albert came swiftly in response to his summons.

"Have my uncle's solicitors returned to inspect the property?"

"A few days ago, milord. Said they would contact you in writing. They appeared to be impressed with the work." Albert paused. "I heard you have married, milord."

"I have, Albert," Hart said with a smile.

He hurried over and offered his hand. "Allow me to congratulate you. Is the marchioness here with you?"

Hart rose to shake it. "Thank you. Lady Montford remains in London, but is eager to view the house. I wasn't sure it would be ready for her."

"They've completed the work. I believe Lady Montford will find her suite to her liking. The painters and decorators have done a magnificent job."

"Excellent." Hart paused as a knock at the door brought a maid with his luncheon. She placed it on a low table, and after Hart requested coffee, bobbed and left the room. Hart left the desk. "I shall ride out this afternoon and see what's been done. Will I like what I find?"

"I believe you will, milord. The last few weeks have brought good rain. The farmers are cautiously positive."

"No one has called for me? Not a Mr. Boyle?"

Albert raised his eyebrows. "Boyle? No. And I've heard nothing from the footmen at the door."

"Very well, Albert. We'll speak again later."

When the door closed behind his steward, Hart reached for a slice of bread and slapped a piece of meat and cheese on it. Having not eaten since early morning, he was hungry, and he took a large bite. He would ride over the estate on Blaze tomorrow. And tonight, when it got dark, would go in search of Mr. Boyle with little hope of finding him, and if he did, what condition would he be in?

Some hours later, when the moon rose above the long stand of pines on the far hill, Hart rode Blaze over his land and continued onto his neighbor's. He left his horse tied up a distance from the Wakeham stables, ran across the ground, and vaulted a fence. Keeping low, he crept toward the three outbuildings near the stables. All was quiet. No lantern light showed in the stables or the staff quarters. They appeared to have all retired for the night. Hart skirted the stables and chose the nearest of the buildings used for storage. Inside, he struck his tinderbox and lit a rushlight. Its feeble glow enabled him to see that apart from brushes, hoes, spades, and bags of manure, the shed was empty. He pinched the rushlight out between his fingers then slipped from the building. Keeping to the shadows, he entered the next. That, too, was empty. Losing heart, he eyed the last one, situated a distance from the stables, its roof groaning under the weight of pine needles. It was much older, the boards falling into disrepair. Hart listened at the door. Nothing, just the creak of the timbers as the wind picked up.

Then he heard it. A faint moan. Or was it the wind?

He found the door barred. Hart removed the bar and opened the door. It gave a loud creak. He paused to listen, but when no one challenged him, he shut the door behind him. The interior turned black as pitch, except for a sliver of moonlight shining on the floor from a high window. Something moved within it. At first he thought it was a rat, but as his eyesight adjusted to the dark, he discovered a foot.

"Boyle?" With a hissed curse, Hart was at the man's side in a moment. He risked lighting the rushlight again. In its faint light, the runner's bloodied face became clear as he peered woozily up at Hart. "Is that you, Lord Montford? Or am I dreaming?"

"Not dreaming, Boyle." Hart squatted beside him, but couldn't find evidence of a wound. "Quietly, man. How badly are you hurt?"

Boyle struggled, his hands tied behind his back with twine. When he moved his head, he groaned. "Wakeham's men crept up on me, knocked me out. My head aches, and I'll have a lump to rival Scafell Pike, but apart from that, I'm remarkably unhurt."

Hart moved over behind Boyle and wrestled with the tightly tied twine. "Will you be able to walk?"

"My legs will probably cramp something fierce, but I'll crawl out of here if I have to."

"Hopefully, that won't be necessary. Did you discover anything before they found you?"

"Wakeham runs some sort of smuggling racket. Didn't get a chance to learn more. I took a risk and moved closer, and they caught me. Stupid of me. That's how we runners get killed."

"Did you hear what they planned for you? Will it happen tonight?"

"No. Tomorrow. They made no bones about it. They plan to make me disappear somewhere, miles from here."

"Then they are about to suffer a bitter disappointment."

The twine fell away, and Boyle gingerly rubbed his wrists.

"I'll have to douse this light," Hart said. "Go carefully."

Once Boyle was on his feet, he limped after Hart to the door. Another loud noise as the door creaked open. Outside, it remained quiet, apart from the hoot of an owl from a nearby tree. At the house, lights shone from several windows.

"We need to get closer. Are you up for it? Or do you want to wait here?"

"I'll come, milord."

"Move slowly and stay within the trees, and we'll see if we can find out what's going on there."

It was slow going through the underbrush. Nettles caught at Hart's breeches, and Boyle stumbled over a rock. He would have fallen had Hart not grabbed his arm.

They came level with the front windows, where candlelight shone behind the curtains. On the drive, braziers burned.

"Looks like Wakeham expects a visitor," Hart said.

Ten minutes later, the jiggle of harnesses and the clatter of wheels broke the silence. A large coach lit by carriage lamps lumbered along the drive driven by six horses. Hart moved farther back into the shadows with Boyle.

The black vehicle loomed out of the darkness and stopped before the house. The front door opened and Wakeham and his two men emerged.

A big bruiser of a man jumped from the box to put down the steps, opening the coach door. A man bent his head in his tall beaver hat and stepped down. He wore an evening cape, the lining glowing red in the lantern light. Another big, broad-shouldered lackey followed him.

"Do come inside, milord. Warm yourself on this cool night."

Wakeham sounded obsequious, and Hart detected an underlying note of fear.

"What have you to tell me?" The peer had a strange, whispering voice. He shrugged up a shoulder and made no move to follow Wakeham inside.

"The last shipment has gone to London," Wakeham said in an anxious voice, tripping over his words. "Won't you come in and partake of some French brandy? I have a few bottles kept for you."

The lord shrugged his shoulder up against his neck again, as if it hurt him. "I intend to have words with you first, Wakeham. You've foolishly put us all at risk by your reckless intention to kill your niece. One of your men sits in a jail cell ready to spill his guts and take us all down with him."

"You can blame Montford's interference, milord. It would have all gone smoothly but for him taking a fancy to my niece. The marquess, a neighbor of mine, stole my niece's horse from under my nose, and sent a Bow Street Runner to prowl around my grounds."

"A Bow Street Runner was here?" the lord hissed.

"No need to worry about him. We've dealt with him." Wakeham gave a strained chuckle. "And Johns won't talk. I've already made arrangements to have him silenced. I can get at him, and he knows it. But let us discuss the business. I have done what you requested and shifted all the goods. This is the last payment, milord. Just give me the agreed share of the bounty. And then we are done."

The peer took a step forward. "Very well."

When Wakeham turned away to enter the house with his henchmen, the lord gestured to his men. They drew their pistols. Three explosions rent the air, causing a shrieking flock of birds to fly from the woods. Wakeham and his tallow-faced thieves fell down like puppets with their strings cut.

The lord stepped up onto the porch and nudged each of them with his shoe. "Dead as doornails," he said with a huff of satisfaction. "Bury the bodies in the woods. And don't let the servants catch you at it. Make it fast. I am expected at a ball in Tunbridge Wells."

Hart and Boyle backed away then turned and moved stealthily through the trees to hide.

"Wait here until they leave. I must search the house," Hart murmured. Now that this murderous lord knew of him, Hart needed to learn who he was.

The men had taken shovels from the shed and buried Wakeham and his men. Then the coach trundled away down the drive.

Hart knocked on the front door. A terrified servant answered it. "What has happened, milord?" he cried, peering into the dark.

"Your master has been killed. I'll send the constable tomorrow. In the meantime, I wish to retrieve Lady Madeline's possessions. Please direct me to her bedchamber."

"Yes, milord."

A group of frightened servants hovered in the corridor. Hart followed the servant upstairs. Maddie's trunk sat in the middle of her bedchamber floor. He doubted Wakeham intended to send it to her.

"Have the trunk brought down. I'll collect it tomorrow." He gazed around and spied Maddie's impressive riding cups and blue ribbons displayed on a shelf. "Don't forget those. Make sure the maids check the wardrobe and drawers."

Hart descended the stairs and went to Wakeham's bookroom. Taking the chair at the desk, he searched through the stack of papers. He found nothing that gave him even a clue to the lord's identity. On his way out, a box filled with bottles of French brandy sat by the front door, perhaps waiting to appease Wakeham's visitor. Hart picked up a bottle. "Mr. Wakeham won't be needing this," he said to the worried servant who held open the front door. "I require more servants at Pembury. Any in need of work should apply to my steward, Mr. Carver."

The distress on the man's face ebbed away. "Thank you, milord," he said with a bow.

Hart walked with Boyle past the stables. The coachman and grooms had emerged dazed from their beds and were talking in loud whispers. They stared at Hart as he passed. "What has happened?" one asked him.

"The servants will tell you," Hart said.

On reaching Blaze, Hart gave Boyle a leg up behind him, and they rode back to Pembury.

After Boyle's head injury was attended to, they sat together in the library, drinking the purloined French brandy before the fire.

"Well, that went well, milord," Boyle said with a sigh of satisfaction. "But who is this lord? Did you discover anything?"

"No. I only saw him in profile. The light wasn't good. But I doubt I've met him. I hope to recognize him should I see him again." Hart took a deep sip of the excellent brandy. "I wonder if he has any plans in mind for me?"

"I hope not, milord."

"And I. He's a ruthless man."

He must spend one more day here with Boyle to consult the magistrate, Sir Joshua Fleming. After a ride over his estate with Rasputin to check on the work done, which need no longer appease Wakeham, or apparently Hart's uncle's trustees, he would return home to Maddie.

⟫⟫⟫⟪⟪⟪

WHEN MADDIE AND Jane returned from a morning walk in the park, Crispin met them at the door. "A note has arrived for you, my lady."

"Thank you, Crispin." Surprised, Maddie took it from him, wondering who it might be. She knew of no one in London except her aunt and her cousin, and they were to call in the afternoon.

She went upstairs to her sitting room to read it. At her desk, she sliced it open, finding it to be one of those gossip pamphlets she'd heard about. Much of it would put a lady to the blush. A scandalous piece about Lord W. who had been discovered in flagrante delicto with his maid by Lady W., whose scream could be heard throughout the house. A kerfuffle erupted after she poured the contents of the chamber pot over them both.

Maddie scanned farther down the page. She paused at the mention of a Lord M. and as she read on, grew more horrified.

Ladies will wear black at the news that the rakish Lord M. has married. It appears to have been hastily done, and taken everyone by surprise, including those ladies who have enjoyed his attentions in the past. And that is quite a number! Yours truly has found out little about his new bride, except the lady is young and not yet out, and is the daughter of an earl. Has love smitten the rake no one thought would marry? Or is this marriage one of convenience for them both? Or another reason entirely for the hurried nuptials? We wait with bated breath for her ladyship's appearance in society! Keen to learn the juicy details.

Maddie gasped and pushed it from her as if it would combust. She rested her head in her hands. It had to be about Hart and herself. How could she face people after this? With a few deep breaths, another thought occurred to her: Who had wished her to see it?

Seething, she went in search of Crispin, the paper still clutched in her hand. When informed by the footman that the butler was in his rooms, Maddie descended the servants' stairs.

Startled, Crispin put down his knife and fork, his luncheon on the table before him, and leaped to his feet, looking concerned. "My lady?"

"Forgive me for interrupting your meal, Crispin." Maddie waved the paper as if it scalded her hands. "Do you know who sent this to me this morning?"

"I'm afraid I don't, my lady. A footman took delivery of it. A delivery boy, apparently."

Maddie nodded. "Thank you. Please continue with your meal."

She hurried back upstairs. Aunt Libby and Catherine would be here in a few hours. She could hardly mention this to her aunt, but if she had time to speak to Catherine alone, she would be glad of her opinion. Failing that, Diane arrived tomorrow. Maddie desperately needed advice, but she suspected Hart would prefer her to rise above such gossip and toss it into the fireplace. She held it in her fingers by its edge, approaching the small fire smoldering in the grate. She should destroy it. But someone had wished to hurt her. She found that difficult to take lightly and would attempt to discover who sent it. Maddie sank back in the chair. Many in society would discuss her and Hart after reading this scandal rag. But it only made her more determined to get the better of the one who wished her harm. Mrs. Spencer came to mind. But it was unfair to jump to conclusions. News traveled fast, and it could be anyone.

Seated around the tea table, when Maddie gently informed Aunt Libby of her uncle's malice, her aunt paled. She still looked unwell, and it worried Maddie. She deeply regretted upsetting her.

Her aunt played with the pearls at her neck. "I trusted him. Arthur wrote explaining you were not well, but your illness was mild and not overly concerning, I took him at his word." Her blue eyes grew wide. "We had not received a letter from you for over a month. Should I have questioned him further? If he'd said you were very ill, I would have come straight away."

"I wasn't ill at all. He made that up. He also destroyed our letters," Maddie said.

Cathy moaned. "How deceitful of him."

Maddie would not reveal his attempt on her life. She leaned over and placed her hand on her aunt's, where she sat with her tea growing cold. "But there is nothing to concern you, Aunt, for my uncle can do no more to hurt me. Now I am married to a kind, decent man."

"I remain a little hazy on the details of your betrothal," her aunt said with a faint smile. "But I gather you met him again in Bath when you came to see me." She looked relieved as she gazed around the room. "I couldn't be happier for you, my dear."

When her aunt left the room, Maddie took the newssheet from a bureau drawer. She came and sat down next to Cathy. "What do you make of this? It arrived this morning. Should I show Hart? Or relegate it to the fire?"

Cathy read it. "It's a dreadful scandal sheet. I've heard about it." She looked up with a questioning frown. "But who sent it? And why would they send it to you?"

"I don't know, but suspect it was to hurt me. To make my first appearance in society more of a trial."

"Then destroy it. And just forget about it, Maddie dear."

"Then I shouldn't show it to Hart?"

"I wouldn't. He would tell you the same thing. There are always those who seek to hurt those they envy. Pay no attention. Shall I destroy this for you?"

Hart didn't need to see it. While she doubted he'd take much notice, he would feel bad for her. "Yes. Burn it." Cathy went to the fireplace. She tore the newssheet into pieces and dropped it among the coals. "There, think no more about it."

Maddie stared at the flames eating up the last of the paper. "Now, please tell me what has happened since you came to London, Cathy. Do you have a beau?"

Cathy's cheeks grew pink, and she pushed a fair curl behind her ear. "Not exactly, but I danced twice with Mr. Blackburn at the Smiths' ball." Cathy sighed. "He has beautiful manners, and has made me promise him a dance at our next ball."

"Does Aunt Libby like him?"

"Yes. I think so."

Maddie said, delighted to see her cousin so happy, "Come upstairs and see my new gowns. They've only just arrived."

They climbed the stairs while Cathy chatted about fashion. Maddie merely nodded. She had an awful feeling the distress the newssheet brought was only the beginning.

Chapter Nineteen

THE MAGISTRATE, SIR Joshua Fleming, was a stout man with a ring of white hair circling his bald head, and a round face which made him appear amiable. But his gray eyes were sharp with a clear intelligence, and a man would be a fool to underestimate him. Hart explained how he and Boyle came to witness Wakeham's demise. He added a sketchy description of their association with Maddie's uncle.

The magistrate confirmed he had ordered the bodies to be exhumed and Wakeham's closest relative, a female cousin, be informed. He selected a muffin from the tea tray and raised his white eyebrows. "You saw this peer of the realm order the killings?"

"I did. The runner and I witnessed it from the trees."

"You didn't recognize him?"

"No. The light was poor. But I'm quite certain I've never met him."

"But might you still identify him? Should you see him again."

Hart thought back to the scene where Wakeham breathed his last. The most distinguishing feature of the lord was his voice. A hoarse, chilling whisper. The callous voice of someone familiar with violence, which had made the hairs stand up on Hart's neck. "I am not sure, Sir Joshua. But I might. The thing is, that before he died, Wakeham told him I was to blame for what happened to one of his henchmen now in jail. I have an interest in this, as his niece is now my wife. Wakeham also threatened to kill the man in jail before he can talk to the authorities. I suggest, Sir Joshua, the man be questioned as soon as possible."

With a nod, Fleming leaned back in his chair, causing a shriek of complaint. "That we will do. Parliament is to sit for Lord Sidmouth, the Home Secretary, to approve the bill to suspend the Habeas Corpus Suspense Act. Magistrates will then have the power to send anyone to prison who might be likely to commit an act prejudicial to public order. This lord might appear in the House," Sir Joshua said. "Might you be there, my lord?"

"Yes, I will."

Hart did not agree with it. He saw it as an overreaction, which would allow magistrates to throw a man into jail for the paltriest of reasons, even if the magistrate didn't like the cut of his jib. But Hart did not voice those sentiments before Fleming.

"Good. A man of mine has infiltrated the smugglers on the Kentish coast. Some turn their backs on smugglers, believing it to be justified to smuggle high taxed goods over the Channel, but these cutthroats are responsible for many murders of innocent people. When my man advises me about their operation, we will round them up and put them behind bars. But you, Lord Montford, could be of invaluable help to me if you could identify this lord. Then we'll have the lot of them. After all," he sat back again, "a fish rots from the head down, you know."

Hart left with the firm conviction that he must find this man. He didn't want to chance more violence coming into Maddie's life.

The following day, Hart returned to London. When he walked into the blue salon, he found Maddie on the sofa, poring over fashion magazines with his sister.

"Hart!" Maddie jumped up and came over to him.

"Sweetheart." Hart kissed her.

His sister greeted him from the sofa. He found her much changed with a lift of her shoulders and interest in her eyes. More as he remembered when Edgar lived. "Diane, I'm glad you could come. I hope you had an unremarkable journey?"

"Tedious, at best, uncomfortable at worst," Diane said as he bent to kiss her cheek. "You look a little weary, Hart."

"A hot drink and a bite to eat shall restore me."

Maddie pulled the bell. "Any news, Hart?"

"A lot has happened." He sank into the chair opposite the sofa. He sat forward, his hands resting on his knees, and related his experiences of the last few days while Diane expressed her horror and Maddie's eyes grew wide. When he'd said as much as he was prepared to, filtering out the bloodthirsty bits, they fell silent.

"My uncle is really dead?" Maddie looked stunned.

"He is. Along with his two henchmen."

"Shot by some lord of the realm? I thought they were good men."

"Not always, Maddie," Hart said dryly.

"What is his name?"

"We don't know that yet."

"We?" She pounced on the word, and he swore under his breath. Maddie would not want him to have any further involvement in this.

"The magistrate investigating him," he said calmly.

"I can't say I'm sorry for the man," Diane said. "It's hard to believe he could treat the niece in his care so cruelly." She turned to Maddie. "I am surprised your father chose him for your guardian."

"There simply was no one else. And Papa didn't know what my uncle was capable of," Maddie said quickly, eager to defend her father. "My Aunt Elizabeth was ill and there was some talk at the time that she might not live." She smiled. "Thankfully, Aunt Libby has rallied since, and is here in London for her daughter's debut."

"The work on the estate is finished." Hart attempted to lighten the atmosphere after the distressing conversation about Maddie's uncle. He wanted to move on and put this affair with Wakeham behind them, so that when he carried out the magistrate's wishes, Maddie would not be involved. "I expect a letter from Uncle William's solicitors advising me they are to proceed with probate of the estate."

Maddie came to sit on the arm of his chair. "Oh, that is such good news, Hart. I can't wait to see the changes to Pembury."

He searched her face, finding strain in her brown eyes. He wanted to pull her down to him and hold her close when she'd been through so much. To tell her this nightmare was at an end.

Two footmen carried trays in loaded with the tea things and plates of small pies, sandwiches, and cake. While Maddie served the tea, Hart took a pork pie and bit into it, enjoying the crisp pastry and meaty flavor. He nodded his thanks as she placed the teacup before him. He studied his wife, who looked like a breath of spring in a new gown. "Your gowns have arrived?"

"Yes." She smoothed the frilly sleeve of the muslin gown patterned with spring green leaves. A matching ribbon sat snug beneath her bosom, and another was woven through her red hair. "My gown is to be finished in time for the ball." She chewed her bottom lip. Something he noticed she did when she was worried. He would ask her what troubled her later.

As the footmen removed the trays, Hart stood. "I will leave you ladies to your discussion." He gestured to the books stacked on a small occasional table, none of which, he suspected, came from the library.

"I'll come with you, Hart," Maddie said. "There is something I must tell you." She turned back to Diane. "I'll be only a moment, Diane."

Diane's eyes sparkled. She picked up a book. "There's no rush. But I shall read all the best scenes while you are gone."

Laughing, Maddie left the room. In the corridor, Hart bent and kissed her. A footman appeared, and he took her hand and walked with her to the library.

As soon as the door closed, he pulled her into his arms. "I've missed you."

She traced her fingers along his jaw. "I missed you, too."

"Do you enjoy having Diane to stay?"

"Very much."

"Something is troubling you. What is it?"

She raised her eyebrows. "No, there's nothing. Why would there be? I had another fitting, and I think you'll approve of my ball gown."

Hart thought she protested too much, but he let it lie. "Come and sit by me for a moment."

"I shouldn't stay long," she said as she sat close to him. "It will be rude to keep Diane waiting."

"Diane was a married lady. She will understand. And I suspect *The Mysteries of Udolpho* will hold her attention."

Maddie grinned. She spoke of her aunt and cousin's visit, but Hart wasn't in the mood for talk. He framed her face with his hands and kissed her with increasing passion.

"Oh, Hart..." Maddie sighed against his lips. "I've missed you so, but I should..."

"No," he said, his voice husky. "You should not."

She wriggled. "A footman might come in. Or heavens! Crispin!"

"They know better than to do that." His fingers threaded through her hair as he bent to smell its lavender scent.

"Don't you dare unravel my chignon, it took Jane ages to... Oh, Hart! What will Diane think?"

⟫⟩⟨⟨

MADDIE FORGOT ABOUT Diane. She forgot everything. She had missed him so much. To have him here with her, revealing how much he'd missed her. She gave in to him, and leaned back with a soft moan as he drew her gown up over her legs.

Hart adjusted his breeches and pulled her astride him. Her urgent breath matched his with a moan of pleasure as she rose and fell in a hasty coupling which ended with them both gasping.

Twenty minutes later, flushed, her heart beating rapidly and her hair escaping the pins, she ignored Hart's entreaty to stay and hurried from the room, mounting the stairs to restore her appearance.

When she came back into the salon, Diane smiled with a knowing look. "It's good to have him home, isn't it?" She held up the book. "I have marked a passage you might enjoy reading, but I suspect life far exceeds anything on the written page."

Maddie flushed and took the book from her. "Yes, it does."

"It warms my heart to see you both so tender with each other," Diane said. "I sorely miss that."

"Oh, you would miss it, Diane," Maddie said, her embarrassment forgotten. "But you might meet someone special this Season. Perhaps it will never equal what you and your husband shared, but to be alone is not a good choice for anyone."

Diane smiled. "It doesn't happen just because you wish it, Maddie. There's something magical in meeting someone you could love."

Maddie nodded. Hart certainly desired her, and he was a caring husband. But he never really told her what was in his heart, so was that any different from the other relationships he had before her? But she would not let such thoughts destroy her happiness, now with her uncle gone from her life. Her monthly courses were late, and her breasts tender when Hart touched them. Might she be pregnant? It was far too soon to tell, and she probably imagined it. After the horrid scandal sheet which suggested theirs was a forced marriage, would a pregnancy bring more gossip? She didn't care. She wanted Hart's baby. They would become a family.

On the evening of the ball, dressed in her gown, Maddie added a touch of rouge to her pale cheeks. Then she rose to view herself in the long mirror.

"The color suits you, milady," Jane said with approval. "You look ever so lovely."

"Thank you, Jane."

Butterflies batting about in her stomach, Maddie left the room. In the hall at the bottom of the stairs, Hart stood waiting. Maddie descended in her claret red ballgown. She wore diamond earrings and bracelets, but nothing at her throat except the locket with her parents' likenesses inside, because she wished they could be here with her. A dainty diamond tiara Hart had brought from the bank graced her hair.

Hart's eyes told her all she wanted to know. "There will be many ladies wearing that red after tonight. You look lovely, Maddie."

He gave her the courage to face the inquisitive *ton* and those among them who might be critical of her. Diane, after Maddie told her about the scandal sheet, thoroughly agreed with her choice. It was nothing like the understated white gown Maddie had planned to wear. But after receiving that vicious newssheet, she returned to the dressmaker and had this one made. She wanted to make a statement. To show those who might not approve of her that she was not a woman to be intimidated. The French woman chose the red fabric, and Maddie thought it perfect. The color alone was enough, the low scooped neck trimmed with red satin understated, yet the dress would stand out among the many white and pale hues women chose in the spring. Madam Benoit, as good as her word, delivered it a day before the ball. Maddie had tried it on and almost faltered and changed her mind. The other gown hung in her bedchamber, the safer choice. But having gained Diane's support, she would wear it. If she was to become the subject of gossip, she did not intend to fade into the background and scurry away like a mouse, but face them head on with her head held high.

In nervous anticipation, she glanced in the mirror in the entry as Hart slipped her evening cloak over her shoulders. She pulled on her long white gloves and took up her fan and black beaded reticule. With a deep breath, she took Hart's arm as a footman opened the door.

"Ready?" Hart murmured.

She gave a decisive nod.

The three went out into a fine moonlit night to the coach waiting outside the front door, the carriage lamps throwing a soft glow over the pavement.

In the great hall of their mansion, the Duke and Duchess of Lindsey warmly welcomed them. Maddie knew that Tate and Ianthe, a beautiful blonde lady, were good friends of Hart's. They quickly put her at her ease.

Once they were announced at the ballroom door, the chatter and laughter ebbed away. Faces turned to watch Maddie as she descended the stairs, a gloved hand on Hart's arm, with Diane behind them. When they reached the ballroom floor and moved among the guests, the hubbub resumed. Some ladies curtsied before Maddie and gentlemen came to speak to Hart and ask to be introduced. A few looked at them with disapproval, but none turned away.

It was unmistakable how popular Hart was, but the chatter on everyone's lips would mostly be about her.

"What a wonderful color," a lady remarked to her companion as Maddie passed within earshot. "I shall demand my modiste find that fabric and make me a gown."

"I never thought it would suit auburn hair," the other lady replied. "But it does, doesn't it?" She patted her frizzy orange hair. "I shall wear it myself."

Hart put his hand over Maddie's. She looked up to see him smile. He had heard them too.

Mrs. Spencer stood within Hart's circle of friends. When first Hart and then Maddie greeted her, she sank into a curtsey. The tight smile in which she returned Maddie's greeting carried a sense of foreboding. Was it Mrs. Spencer who sent her that horrid gossip sheet? Maddie could believe it of her. Then it was forgotten as she was presented to His Grace, Charles, Duke of Shrewsbury and his wife, Lady Nellie.

Maddie met Lady Ianthe, Tate's wife. They warmly drew her into their conversation. Maddie felt shielded, protected. She met the Earl of Redcliffe, Dominic, and his wife, Olivia, a warm and very natural lady with a decided lack of airs. And then, as if by magic, any whispers about her seemed to die down as the *ton* turned their attentions to other matters.

Maddie needed to sit down. She feared her legs wouldn't carry her another step, but then the orchestra struck up for a quadrille, and Tate asked her to dance.

Strange how soothing music could be. Maddie was soon laughing at the duke's witty remarks. Hart danced by with Ianthe. Their eyes met his with a message of reassurance. She may not have proved an instant success. Some on the dance floor treated her with cool indifference, and perhaps some would only ever tolerate her because of Hart and his friends, but Maddie felt her spirits soar. She's always loved to dance and smiled as she performed the steps.

When the waltz was called, Maddie looked for Hart, hoping he would dance with her. But as another gentleman friend she'd been introduced to earlier came to claim her hand, she accepted him. Hart entered the dance floor with the dainty Mrs. Spencer on his arm.

Shocked, Maddie tried to wrestle her surging emotions under control. From Diane she learned that husbands were discouraged from dancing with their wives. The men she'd met tonight had several different partners. Why did she feel this woman was a danger to her? Just then, Mrs. Spencer glanced over Hart's shoulder at her, and Maddie saw something in her eyes akin to ownership. She almost gasped aloud. Were her worst fears about to come true?

When the next dance was called, a foppish gentleman crossed the floor to ask her to dance. Diane leaned over. "Lord Pickering is an outrageous rake. Best to avoid him and accept Lord Benning, who approaches behind him."

"I don't see why," Maddie said. "He looks harmless enough."

She rose and accepted Pickering's request, giving him her arm.

"You are quite the most striking woman here tonight, Lady Montford," Pickering said as they joined the others on the dance floor while the orchestra began its preparations for the Sir Roger de Coverley.

"Thank you, sir." He was undeniably handsome, but his self-satisfied smile made her wonder what any woman would see in him. She employed the fan at her wrist, sweeping it in front of her face. "It is entirely too warm tonight, is it not?"

"Indeed," he said huskily. "London society has seen too little of you, Lady Montford. I should like to discover more about you."

The music began. Maddie spied Hart frowning at her as he danced with Olivia. She smiled at Pickering. "I am flattered by your interest, sir. But really, there isn't much to tell."

"I can't believe that," he said throatily as his hand moved lower on her waist in an attempt to draw her closer.

She ignored it, but suddenly hated being here with him. Suddenly, the dance floor seemed too crowded and the ballroom airless. When the dance ended, she coolly thanked him.

Diane was back in her chair, having danced twice with Lord Peter Wallace. "You should avoid Pickering. He has a bad reputation."

"So I gather. I shan't dance with him again." Maddie turned to Diane. "But Lord Peter has claimed you twice. Do you approve of him?"

Diane made a vague gesture with her fan. "Lord Peter is pleasant company."

Maddie suspected there could be more to it, but she let the matter drop.

Later, when Hart joined her in her bedchamber in his dressing gown, Maddie was at last able to talk to him. "I was surprised to see you waltz with Mrs. Spencer."

"The waltz was promised to the lady before you and I met," Hart said. "It would be ungentlemanly not to honor it."

Maddie thought that a fine excuse. "I expected you to waltz with me."

"Did you? It is not usually done."

"Does that mean you and I will never waltz?"

"You have done marvelously tonight, Maddie. I can see you will become very popular. But I thought it was your intention not to cause controversy. We shall waltz at our next ball."

She tied up the strings of her nightgown as if shutting herself away from him. "I should like that."

The gesture didn't go unnoticed. He leaned back against the pillows to study her face. "You need to avoid John Porter."

"Oh? Who is he?"

"Baron Pickering."

"Oh," she asked airily. "I found him charming."

"Nevertheless, I should prefer you to avoid him."

"Are you ordering me to do so?"

"No, of course not, but…"

"And shall you avoid Mrs. Spencer?"

He frowned. "You make too much of one dance with a lady I knew before you."

Maddie wondered if they had slept together. Was she Hart's inamorata before Maddie met him? Surely a man of his passions would not sleep alone in London.

"We are discussing Pickering. And my warning comes from a genuine concern. Much scandal is attached to him. He has ruined more than one young debutante."

"I am hardly a gullible young debutante."

"No. But you are unfamiliar with the ways of society, Maddie. You should look to Diane and me for advice."

She sighed. "Very well, Hart. I won't dance with Baron Pickering again." She actually had no intention of it.

She took note that he offered no such promise about Mrs. Spencer.

Her heart throbbed with distress. Was she being foolish? She put her hand to her mouth and yawned. "I'm sorry I am so cross. It's just that I am most dreadfully tired."

Hart rose from the bed. "Yes, you must be, sweetheart. I shall sleep in my bed tonight."

Maddie watched him leave the room. How lonely it was without him.

She should not have mentioned Mrs. Spencer. Most wives would have kept it to themselves. She chewed her bottom lip. But she knew she was not like most wives. She wanted a marriage filled with loyalty and love. Not the shabby substitute Lord Pickering might offer a lonely wife.

The next morning, Maddie rose early and dressed. She sought Hart in his suite, where his valet shaved him. "Good morning." Hart rose and wiped his face with a towel. "Leonard, we are finished here. Go down and eat your breakfast. I shan't need you for the rest of the day."

Hart wore a navy banyan with gold braid over his trousers. "You're up early, sweetheart."

"I...I missed you."

He drew her into his arms, his hand stroking her back. "I missed you too." He kissed her neck beneath her ear, sending a thrill rushing through her. "Come and lie down. We need to talk."

Talk? There would be little talk involved, Maddie suspected. But she was so pleased to be with him, she took his hand and walked with him into his adjoining bedchamber, decorated in the somber tones of gray and black except for the crimson bedhangings on the enormous carved-oak bed.

Apart from a brief look in through the door, Maddie had never been into this male domain. Until last night, Hart had never slept here. Maddie glanced at the door between the dressing room and the bedchamber. Might Leonard return? "Someone might come in."

"Most unlikely. But I shall remedy that." Hart drew her over to the bed. He untied the silken cords which held the curtains back against the posts. They fell free, leaving him and Maddie cocooned inside among the rumpled sheets in the rosy-tinged space. She leaned her head back on the pillows. "This seems entirely too wicked."

Hart leaned over her, and a corner of his mouth quirked. "Does it? Shall we make it so then?"

Maddie giggled breathlessly. She would use all her newfound skills to make him remember this moment. She must be cleverer than she had been. Smarter certainly than Mrs. Spencer, whom she was now sure intended to claim Hart as her lover.

Chapter Twenty

THE SUN WARMED the room. Through the drawn open curtains, Hart glanced out of Maddie's bedchamber window at a gray-blue sky buffeted by clouds. Not the azure blue of country skies, but at least not gray with soot. That would come soon enough. As the second ball they had attended ended close to dawn, they'd slept later than usual. Summer was only a few weeks away, and Hart wished to return to Pembury. A letter had arrived from Uncle William's trustees to say that the monies and property in the will would soon be handed over to him.

It meant that money was no longer a concern. He did not wish to use any of Maddie's inheritance and would advise her to talk to the trustees, as she should be made aware of how her money was invested. She expressed an interest in charity work, and he wanted her free to pursue it.

The last few weeks had been busy, the Season in full swing. Thankfully, Vivian had kept her distance since that first ball, which suited him. He had no wish to pursue her.

Parliament would go into recess on the 12th of July, and would not meet again until late January. If they were to go to Pembury as soon as the hot weather arrived, it gave Hart little time to discover the identity of this peer at the head of the smuggling ring.

As the House of Lords sat later today, Hart intended to search for the lord. A letter from Sir Joshua despaired how his contacts failed to discover anything about him. It appeared the lord was cautious and kept his association with the smuggling ring secret from the smugglers themselves.

Yesterday, as he left the house, Hart caught sight of a man loitering in the square. It might mean nothing at all, but he wanted this lord arrested in case he proved a danger to them. He intended to single him out, but with little idea of the man's appearance, he had little to go by.

Maddie yawned. "We weren't home 'til dawn." Propped up by pillows, she drank the last of her chocolate and nibbled on a slice of toast. "We haven't had a moment to spare since we came to London. Out every night, then breakfasts and card parties or riding in Rotten Row. I feel as if I could sleep for a week."

"Your looks belie your words, Maddie. You are positively radiant," he observed while drinking his coffee.

She laughed. "Before I brush my hair?"

He reached over and gave a soft tug to a lock curling beguilingly over her breast. "I like your hair in a tangle."

"You should, as you are responsible for it."

She was different since her uncle died. More sassy and confident. She'd become the girl he sensed she could be when he first met her. He never tired of her company, or making love to her.

"Diane and I are to visit a mantua-maker at midday. We dine at home tonight before we attend the opera house. There's a new musical drama called *The Slave* we'll watch with Ianthe in her box."

"Mm?"

She poked him in the chest, breaking into his pleasant thoughts of them earlier. "You must be sorry to miss it."

"I am," he said with a grin.

"And I believe you," she said with a lift of her eyebrows.

"Maddie, already you know far too much about me," he murmured with a shake of his head. He slid a hand across the smooth skin of her belly and breathed in the heady mixture of her perfume and arousing feminine scent.

She giggled and pushed his hand away. "Stop that. I don't like to be tickled."

"If I had time, I might pursue that challenge," he said. "But unfortunately, I haven't."

"I am shopping for suitable hats, as we are to spend the summer months at Pembury." She sighed. "And new clothes. I've put on a little weight. One is so much more active in the country. A ride in Rotten Row is not nearly enough. I can't wait to ride Pearl again. We used to travel for miles."

"I once watched you galloping Pearl. You looked as though you might ride on until you disappeared. For a moment, I thought you wouldn't come back."

"Perhaps I might have one day." Her eyes darkened.

He cursed himself for mentioning those desperate times when it was his intention to put the experience behind them. He smiled and rested a hand on her thigh. "I like you a little plumper."

She looked indignant. "I am not plump!"

"In all the right places," he said, grinning. "I have the House of Lords later, which will probably go late into the evening." He kissed her nose and rose from the bed. "Afterward I'm to meet Tate at White's."

"Then I shan't see you until late tonight?"

"You'll probably be asleep. I won't disturb you; I'll sleep next door."

"I'll be awake," she called as he tied the sash on his dressing gown and made for the door. Hart blew her a kiss and went through to his suite.

While he bathed and dressed, he considered how he might handle this lord if they were to meet face to face. Should he be lucky enough to recognize him? He could hardly wander the halls of Parliament on the off chance of coming across him. Hart had a sense the lord was tall, but as he wore a tall beaver, it was difficult to gain an idea of his height. Only his voice lingered in his memory. A voice to send the chills down the back of any man who had reason to fear him. Hart wanted to find this criminal as much as Fleming did. The violence perpetrated on Wakeham was a little too close to home. Fleming's letter mentioned boxes of smuggled goods they'd uncovered in the basement of Wakeham's house. As well as a stash of money hidden in a cupboard. Would the thieves come back for it? And might this lord's interest have been aroused after Wakeham mentioned Hart's involvement?

After an early luncheon, Hart left the house. He searched the Square again for someone who might seem out of place. In the fenced-off gardens in the center of the Square, a gardener weeded the beds. A footman walked a pampered pet. Two ladies strolled with a gentleman along the path and a housemaid sat watching a young child. Satisfied he found no one suspicious, Hart climbed into his carriage and went to Parliament House.

EAGER TO BEGIN her day, once Hart had removed his distracting presence from the bedchamber, Maddie scampered out of bed and rang for Jane.

A few moments later, her maid entered. "Shall I ring for hot water for your bath, milady?"

"Yes, thank you, Jane." As Maddie searched her drawers for a clean handkerchief, she watched her maid in the mirror, moving about the room, tidying up. She supposed she'd been too distracted as of late to take much notice. It was clear her maid was quite unlike herself. Her actions were not as quick and efficient as they normally were. She looked drawn, and by the expression in her eyes, Maddie was sure something worried her. Jane had sighed too, several times. Maddie had let this go long enough. Diane wouldn't care if she was late.

"I should like a moment to talk to you, Jane."

Jane turned to look at Maddie, and her face blanched. "Is anything wrong, milady? Has my work not been up to scratch?"

"It is not about your work," Maddie said. "Come and sit by me on the sofa."

Jane slowly crossed the room. "It doesn't seem right to sit with you. When I have so much to be getting on with."

"Don't be foolish. We have been together through thick and thin, Jane. Now is not the time to become so…so maidish," Maddie said for want of a word. She patted the sofa beside her.

Jane sat ramrod straight on the sofa. She swallowed. "What is wrong, Lady Madeline?" she asked again.

"I was about to ask you the same thing, Jane."

"Me? I…I am not sure…"

"Yes. You are very sure. What worries you?"

Suddenly, Jane covered her face with her hands. "You will be shocked."

"I'll survive. Goodness, how much we have faced together? There is nothing you could say to shock me now."

Jane's shoulders heaved. She dropped her hands and turned her teary face to Maddie. "I am with child."

Maddie gaped at her. This was the last thing she expected. "You have lain with Henry? Oh, Jane, how foolish. It is a grim life for an unmarried woman with a child in this world." She firmed her lips. "Henry must marry you."

"That's just it, milady. We are married."

Maddie stared at her. "What? You're married? When?"

"The same day as you and his lordship. We went back to the Marriage House for the handfast ceremony."

"And all this time you've kept it from us? How difficult that must have been for you." Amusement twitched Maddie's lips. "But somehow you have overcome it. But why on earth didn't you tell me?"

Jane wrung her hands. "His lordship will put us off. We wanted to wait until there was somewhere else we might go where we could be together."

"Lord Montford would let you go? What made you think such a thing?"

"It happens in all the big houses, milady. Staff are not supposed to marry."

"What nonsense. You shall remain in our employ as long as you wish." Maddie patted the maid's shoulder. "Now dry your tears and let's see what can be done. You need to be settled before you have your baby." She paused. "I shall have to tell his lordship today, you understand."

"Oh, milady, are you sure he won't dismiss us?"

"Perfectly sure." Maddie rose from the sofa. "Come, we'll talk about it as you help me bathe and dress. I don't want to keep Lady Diane waiting."

Jane was already pulling the bell rope for hot water to be sent in. "Which gown will you wear today?"

"The lavender and gray stripes with the cream bonnet. And Jane?"

"Yes, milady."

"Smile."

Jane broke into a relieved smile and sniffed. "Henry will be ever so glad to hear we can stay."

"Then you must tell him as soon as you have finished here." Maddie thought for a moment. "I shall arrange a larger chamber for you both. I'm sure the single bed you have now is most uncomfortable."

Jane flushed and ducked her head before disappearing into the dressing room.

Chapter Twenty-One

H ART'S HACKNEY PUT him down outside the Palace of Westminster in front of the row of crenellated arches on the north bank of the River Thames. He tipped his hat to the doorkeeper and made his way to the House of Lords among peers who crammed the halls summoned by the bell. Entering through the solid brass gates into the luxurious chamber where the Spiritual and Lords Temporal gathered for the presentation of Sidmouth's bill.

Not all peers would make an appearance, but Hart hoped the man he wished to find would be here.

Voices rose in the long room already filled along the red benches of the Lords Temporal and the green of the Commons end. Beneath the ornate ceiling, the walls decorated with statues and allegorical frescoes, overlooked by the magnificent stained-glass window by Pugin. Hart searched the seats occupied by the Tories and Whigs, unsure of what he looked for. The mannerisms of a killer? He remembered the man shrugged one shoulder, as if it pained him. But none in the rows of peers sparked any recognition. On a dais, the Prince of Wales waited, seated on his gilded throne. In front of him, the Lord Speaker sat on his woolsack.

After Sidmouth's impassioned speech, the Whigs spoke out against it, demanding better reform, but within the hour, the quorum accepted it and passed it back to the House of Commons with few changes.

When Tate joined the other members to file out of the chamber, he was still none the wiser as to the identity of the lord. Tate came to join him and agreed with Hart's opinion on the bill. They made their way to the door, planning their evening at White's.

Two gentlemen walked a little ahead of them in the corridor. Something about the taller of them caught Hart's eye. He was speaking to his companion.

Gesturing to Tate to silence him, Hart moved closer to listen. Then he froze. Tate laid a hand on his arm, his eyes questioning, then turned at Hart's instigation to the gray-haired man talking in a hoarse, whispering voice.

Hart slowed to allow the lord and his companion to get well ahead. "Know who he is?" he asked Tate.

"Lord Buchanan," Tate replied.

"Has his voice always been that way?"

"For many years. Kicked in the throat by a horse when he was a lad."

"What sort of man is he?"

"Don't know him personally, but it's said he's well respected. But from what you told me about Wakeham's death, it would seem that respect is ill deserved."

Hart tried picturing the man giving the cold-blooded order to shoot Wakeham. It was difficult. His doubts remained until they approached the door, where Buchanan stopped to put on his tall beaver. Then, as they left the building, and as Buchanan said goodbye and walked away, he turned to look at Hart, then hitched up one shoulder beneath his ear. And Hart knew. "He's the man I want," he said after Buchanan disappeared. "I must inform Sir Joshua Fleming."

They left Parliament walking away through Westminster to hail a hackney, and partly to escape the river at low tide, the rotten smells rising from the mud.

It had grown dark when the jarvie put them down outside White's club in St James's Street. The famous bow window once occupied by the infamous Beau Brummel was empty now, reserved for the Duke of Wellington. In the foyer, men gathered around White's betting book.

Freddie Holgrove, always keen on a wager, turned to them to explain the latest bet which had piqued their interest. "Mills has bet Captain Fielding ten guineas to five that a certain gentleman understood between them marries a certain lady also understood within six months."

"Sounds like a good way to lose money," Tate said.

Refusing an invitation to a game of vingt-et-un, and another for billiards, they entered the library, where Hart ordered a bottle of whiskey from the waiter.

Seated in a leather armchair, his booted foot resting on his knee, Hart sipped his whiskey. "Is there anything more you can add about Lord Buchanan?"

"Not much. His estate lies southeast of Canterbury, and he has a townhouse in Mayfair. A wife, but no children. I've seen him here at White's."

"Perhaps he'll appear tonight." Hart shifted to gain a view of the busy hallway beyond the door.

"You'll just advise the magistrate?" Tate asked with a worried frown. "Not wise to take on the fellow. Should he be the man you want, he'll have a dangerous gang at his beck and call."

"It's him. But I won't act unless provoked. I'd be happy to leave well enough alone, but for this feeling that I'm being followed. I take umbrage at being drawn into Buchanan's criminal world. If the ruffian lurking in the square has anything to do with Buchanan, I won't hesitate." He cursed. "I refuse to place Maddie in any more danger."

"Send me a note. I'll bring a couple of sturdy footmen to help."

"Good of you, Tate." He chuckled. "I can't imagine the young men in livery taking on the smugglers. But I appreciate the offer. I hope not to need it. Shall we go into dinner? Freddie said the salmon is excellent."

Tate rose. "What do you fancy after dinner? Faro?"

"Sounds good." Hart tightened his jaw, furious at the thought of thieves threatening his peace again. "Tomorrow, I'll visit Jackson's rooms in Bond Street. I fancy a bout."

Tate laughed. "In this murderous frame of mind, I wouldn't advise it. You might do some damage, and not to yourself."

"Then I'll settle for Manton's, and some pistol practice." He joked, but the possibility of being followed worried him. He had not missed the look Buchanan gave him, staring back at Hart before walking away. In that moment, Wakeham's trembling complaint before he died came back to him: *you can blame Montford.*

Buchanan's ice-gray eyes were as chilling as his voice. Hart didn't trust his sort not to go after a man's family to knock the fight out of him. He wondered if he could persuade Maddie to go to Pembury without him. While the lord was here in London, so would Hart be, until they arrested Buchanan. It was only a matter of time before Fleming brought him in. But before the magistrate could accuse a peer, he'd need to produce some sound evidence. Buchanan would engage the best firm of solicitors in town. Hart wondered if the ruffian who broke into Lilybrook cottage, who he'd thrown in jail, survived Wakeham's attempt to silence him. If so, he might make a credible witness.

Seated in the busy dining room, Hart studied the menu, his thoughts on Maddie. Persuading her to leave London during the Season would be difficult. She wouldn't want to go to the country without him.

THE NIGHT AT the Tivoli had been entertaining, although the noisy audience below in the pit shouted over the actor's lines. When the final curtain went down, Ianthe, not only beautiful but gracious, ordered her carriage to drive them home.

It was still relatively early when Maddie and Diane took coffee in the salon.

Maddie smiled. "Fancy, Lord Peter Wallace appearing tonight."

"We would not have seen him, but for Ianthe inviting him into her box," Diane said airily.

But her attempt to dissuade Maddie from this conversation failed. "Peter seemed delighted, didn't he? Surprising when his box had a better view of the stage. I daresay he enjoyed our company."

"Stop fishing, Maddie," Diane said, but her lips curled up in a reluctant smile.

"Very well, my dear. But you must know Lord Peter is smitten."

Diane flushed. "I wouldn't go so far as that."

"I would." Maddie studied her sister-in-law. "You like him too, don't you?"

"I...I don't know. Yes, I like him, but what is that? I am hardly a debutante. And I have children."

"Isn't he aware of your children?"

"Yes, but still..."

"You are hardly in your dotage, Diane. You're a very attractive woman, not yet thirty. Quite a prize. And I think Lord Peter knows it."

Diane laughed. "A prize? You have a way with words, Maddie."

"Just promise me you won't dismiss him out of hand. Of course, you need time to get to know him, but please, give this a chance."

Diane held up a hand. "I cannot argue with you, Maddie. I promise, if he continues to show an interest in me, I'll endeavor to learn more about him and see if we suit one another."

A little too cold-blooded for Maddie, but a beginning of sorts. She nodded her head approvingly. "You can begin on Saturday."

"Saturday? Aren't we to attend a ball?"

"Yes. But I have invited him to dine before the ball."

Diane widened her eyes. "When did you do that?"

"At interval when the box became crowded."

Diane shook her head and laughed. "You would make a good spy!"

Maddie's eyes searched Diane's. "You are pleased?"

"Yes. I'd like to see him."

Maddie grinned. "Good."

"What time do you expect Hart home?"

"Very late, he said." Maddie rose and went to the window to look out on the square. "That's odd. There's a man near the park railing. He's just standing there. Doesn't seem the sort one might find here."

Diane came over. "Where? Oh, I see him. He must be waiting for someone."

"I don't like the look of him," Maddie decided.

"It's hard to tell what he's like from here. Best check later and see if he's gone."

Maddie let the curtain drop. "I will."

Diane yawned. "I'm for bed. It was fun tonight, wasn't it?"

Maddie kissed her cheek. "It was. More for some of us than others."

"Oh you!" Diane laughed and crossed to the door. "See you at breakfast."

Maddie selected a periodical from the shelf and curled up on the sofa. She hoped Hart wouldn't be too late, for she intended to be awake when he arrived.

The grandfather clock in the hall chimed two. Maddie stirred and raised her head from the arm of the sofa, rubbing her stiff neck. The fire had gone out. She was cold, and with a shiver rose to cross the carpet to the window. Pulling aside a narrow gap of curtain, she peered out. It was very dark in the Square. The large houses were in almost total darkness. The street lamps, too, were out. But there was enough light to see movement across the street. Was it the man she spied earlier? She couldn't be sure, but a chill ran down her back, and she shivered.

The wheels of a carriage sounded on the cobbles. Maddie watched Hart pay off the jarvie and run up the steps.

Maddie went out into the hall, where the footman on duty opened the door.

Coming in, Hart smiled at her. "Still up?"

"I fell asleep on the sofa waiting for you," she said as they climbed the stairs.

"But why, sweetheart?"

"There was a man loitering in the square. I don't know why he alarmed me. Is he there now?"

"No. He's gone. Come to bed, we'll talk there."

As Maddie snuggled into bed beside Hart, she felt drowsy and had to fight to concentrate to keep awake as he described his evening.

"And I found the man who killed your uncle."

Her eyes flew open, and she sat up. "You did? Who is he?"

"There's no doubt it's this Lord Buchanan. I will inform the magistrate tomorrow. But with this man hanging about and frightening you, I'd like you to go to the Pembury."

She frowned. "Shall we go together?"

"I wish I could, but I must remain here."

"For how long?"

He pulled her down against his bare chest and stroked her hair. "Not for long, sweetheart. I'll come as soon as I can."

She pushed away from him, indignant. "You're going to confront this lord, and you want me out of the way."

"No, it's not that, Maddie. I just want you safe."

"I am not going anywhere without you, Hart."

Hart raked his hands through his hair. "But Maddie…"

"No buts. I shall stay in London."

He sighed. "Very well. I'll instruct the footmen to be armed when-ever you leave the house."

"If you must, darling." Maddie lay down again and stroked his satiny skin. "You would miss me if I left, wouldn't you?"

She could feel the rumble of his laugh in his chest and raised her head. "Lord, Maddie, you know how to wind me around your finger." He pulled her atop him, his hands cupping her bottom. "I would miss you very much," he murmured against her ear.

Chapter Twenty-Two

I N THE MORNING, Hart sent a footman to deliver the message to Fleming. When he left the house, there was no sign of the fellow who had been loitering in the square, obviously watching his home. A neighbor emerged and was about to climb into his waiting carriage when Hart approached him and asked whether he had noticed the man.

"Thought he might be a beggar," Lord Telford said. "I didn't give it much thought, but now, thinking back on it, a beggar wouldn't still be there late at night. I've not seen him since. Do you think he had a nefarious purpose for being there, my lord?"

"I don't know," Hart said, "but he appeared to watch my house. If you see him again, it might be a good idea to notify the constabulary. I will do the same."

As he made his way to Manton's shooting gallery for some prac-tice, his neck prickled, but it was hard to see if anyone followed, as the streets were busy this time of the morning. The question remained, why would anyone want to tail him? Could it be Buchanan's doing?

Some familiar faces greeted Hart when he walked into Manton's, including Lord Yarmouth, one of Prinny's set. Yarmouth, a known wastrel, invited Hart to join them in a contest. Hart tossed down his coins, adding them to the pile. When his turn came, he aimed and fired, hitting the wafer dead center. Yarmouth and the other men clapped him on the back and cheerfully paid up. While pleased with the accuracy of his gun, Hart declined to take part again when the bet rose to a ridiculous sum.

He tucked his gun into the waistband of his trousers beneath his coat and took a hackney to Bow Street, intent on speaking to the Magistrate about Buchanan. He also wanted to ask about the man he'd put in jail near Gilford.

According to their records, the man had died after a fall. Cursing, he wondered if Buchanan was behind this as well. Hart went in search of the Bow Street Runner, Boyle, hoping he was here and not away on a case.

He was in luck, finding Boyle kicking his heels at the courts, waiting for his next mission. Hart hired him to watch Montford Court to see if they could discover this man's intentions should he turn up again.

"Buchanan eh?" Boyle said. "A pity Wakeham had to open his mouth about you, milord."

Hart frowned. "You've heard something since we last met?"

"On the magistrate's orders, as Fleming told us, a runner, a friend of mine, Colin Croft, infiltrated the smuggling ring. But he must have made a mistake because his body turned up near Folkestone. On his last trip to Bow Street before he died, Colin said he had an idea the leader of the gang was Lord Buchanan, because the smugglers knew him. Colin went back to find proof and never returned."

Hart wondered if it was possible to get this man. It appeared Buchanan had the remarkable ability to evade the law even when coming under suspicion.

"If the man turns up in the square, I want you to get a message to me immediately and not approach him yourself," Hart said. But he wished he had persuaded Maddie to leave London.

THE NIGHT OF the ball, a dozen guests dined at Montford Court. It was a handsome room, with fine furniture, paintings, an Axminster rug, and a sweep of damask at the tall windows. Tate and Ianthe, Charles and Nellie, Dominic and Olivia, and Peter Wallace, seated opposite Diane, his eyes only for her. Hart sat at the head of the long table, Maddie at the opposite end. She considered it a success for her first dinner party. Cook had outdone herself with a twelve-course meal. Crispin served the best wines from the cellar, and the footmen served the dishes. To Maddie, it seemed as if this house was a home again, and the servants seemed as eager as she to make the evening perfect.

Later, when they entered Beauchamp's ballroom, Maddie, for the first time, felt part of this exciting, beautifully dressed throng of guests. The musicians on the dais played Mozart, the dancers already on the floor performing a cotillion. The perfumed scents and candle smoke drifting from the chandeliers overhead and the buzz of conversation and laughter added to the ambiance.

Maddie danced the next two dances, then sat watching Diane dance with Peter. They already looked like a couple falling madly in love. While Maddie was glad for them, she felt a little dispirited. She'd hoped to be pregnant, but found earlier tonight to her disappointment she wasn't. The baby represented something special, apart from the fierce love she would give it. It meant she and Hart would be a family. As it was, she struggled to believe that's what they were. His life in London so often took him away from her. And she felt his absence keenly because she didn't feel secure. Especially now watching Mrs. Spencer enter the circle of friends around Hart. She said something amusing, and they all laughed. Her gaze had rested on Hart longer than Maddie thought acceptable. Did not Hart notice? Or didn't he mind?

Earlier, Maddie had danced with a gentleman who a friend had introduced to her. He offered her fulsome compliments and made no secret of his attraction to her.

When she lightly chastised him, he looked surprised and said he would be available whenever she might wish to pursue an affair. Maddie had wanted to rebuke him, but she held her tongue, longing for the end of the dance. This was the way society had proved to be. Ladies passing notes to gentlemen who were not their husbands. And those husbands looking the other way, or dancing with their mistresses, but Maddie knew that was not for her. Not everyone was that way. There were good marriages among their friends. It was up to Hart to decide what sort of marriage he wanted.

Maddie excused herself from her group of friends, fearing they would discover the reason for her sudden change of mood. Walking to the room allocated for the ladies, she didn't look back. She didn't want to see if Mrs. Spencer still flirted with her husband.

In the ladies' retiring room, Maddie smiled at the attendant. She dampened her handkerchief and cooled her hot cheeks while she tried to calm herself. She must not let her imagination run away from her. Hart had done nothing to upset her.

She went behind the screen to adjust the tight bodice of her evening gown. Her breasts seemed to have grown since she had it made.

Outside, in the room, two ladies came in. "Mrs. Spencer is making her play for you know who," one of them said. "She has him laughing and eating out of her hand."

"Well, his reputation with the ladies is no secret. I doubt that will change, even though he has married a pretty girl."

"They never change. Lord Montford never stays long with any-one."

The other lady giggled. "Hush."

"Come on. Best we go back and watch the drama unfold."

When the door closed, Maddie felt very much alone. She nodded to the attendant on her way out, who glanced at her sympathetically, then chin held high, Maddie returned to her chair. Her friends danced a gavotte, and she sat alone.

Hart noticed and walked over to her. "Why aren't you dancing?"

"I find it a little too hot."

His gaze roamed over her. "You look flushed. I hope you're not ill, my sweet."

"No, I've grown tired of London. The pace is exhausting."

"I thought you were enjoying it," he said with a worried frown.

"I think I will go to the country, as you suggested."

He sat beside her. "I am glad, Maddie. Although I'll miss you, I will breathe easier when the magistrate has dealt with Buchanan."

"I will be relieved when all that is behind us."

Hart searched her eyes for a moment then nodded. "When will you leave?"

"Diane returns home tomorrow. I'll leave the day after."

"Good."

"Can we go home soon?"

He raised his eyebrows. "If you wish. We'll thank our host and hostess, and I'll send for the carriage."

She nodded. "There's no reason for Diane to cut her evening short. Peter will bring her home."

They spent the brief journey home talking about inanities.

Later, when they climbed the stairs to bed, Hart put his arm around her. "You're very quiet."

"I just need a good night's sleep. I've been nervous since I saw the man watching us from beside the park railing."

On the landing, Hart turned her to face him. In the candlelight from the wall sconces, he lifted her chin with his palm. "Why didn't you mention this to me?"

"I didn't want you to worry. After all, I am perfectly well. I'm looking forward to riding Pearl in the fresh air."

He smiled as they entered her bedchamber. "I will join you at Pembury as soon as I can."

She turned to him. "Would you mind if I sleep alone? My head throbs and I might disturb you."

He frowned. "Disturb me? This is something new, Maddie. You say you're not ill, but you are most unlike yourself."

"I'll take some Feverfew. But you must understand, Hart, I have been through much," she said earnestly. "The recent event has stirred all that business up with my uncle's henchmen again."

He studied her. "Yes, of course. I'm sorry, sweetheart. Rest well and I'll see you in the morning."

Maddie stood watching the door close, tears in her eyes. Was she wrong to go away? Should she stay and fight? But how can a wife fight when it all happened behind her back? Would all the *ton* know if a liaison occurs between Vivian Spencer and Hart? Would they laugh behind their hands, or worse, pity her?

When Jane came and helped to prepare her for bed, she asked if Maddie had told Hart about their betrothal. It had completely slipped Maddie's mind. "I haven't, Jane, but I will tomorrow. We travel to Pembury on Tuesday. As Henry comes with us, I'll make arrangements for the proper accommodation for you."

"Oh, milady, you are very kind. I shall sleep better tonight," Jane said before she left the room.

But Maddie knew she would not sleep at all.

Maddie farewelled Diane the next day. "You must come to Pembury," she called before the carriage took her away.

"As soon as I can," Diane said at the window.

"I could invite Peter down with a few guests. We'll hold a house party once summer is upon us."

Diane nodded, her answer lost in the noise of the horses' hooves striking the cobbles as the coachman cracked the whip.

Maddie saw Diane throw her a kiss and smiled as she turned and walked up the steps. "Well, Crispin, it was nice to have Lady Diane here, wasn't it?"

Crispin shut the door. "It was, indeed, my lady. Almost like old times."

She smiled at the graying butler. "They must have been good times."

"Many years ago, when Hart's mother was alive, there were always guests in the house. She liked to entertain." He looked sorrowful. "But then his lordship decided her health would improve in the fresh air of the country."

"That was probably wise." Maddie nodded and climbed the stairs to see Jane about her packing. Hart must have been a young boy at the time. He had not been forthcoming about his early life, and she wondered why.

The next day, Maddie left with Jane for the country. Hart kissed her and wished her a safe journey. An armed footman sat on the box beside Henry and the coachman.

She gazed through the window as the coach began its journey. Hart stood gazing after her. He was worried about her, she knew. But she'd seemed unable to say anything to put his mind at rest.

The coach had been traveling for a couple of hours when it suddenly lurched to a stop at a loud bang.

"I heard a gunshot." Heart pounding, Maddie stared at Jane and then peered out the window.

"Please God. I hope Henry is all right," Jane cried.

"We have an armed footman. I can't see how..."

The coach door flew open. At first she thought the well-dressed man who came up the steps was offering assistance, but then she saw the pistol in his hand. He frowned. "Where is your husband, my lady? Is he not traveling to Pembury?"

He spoke in an odd whispery voice which chilled her. "No, sir. What do you want?" Maddie hated how her voice wobbled.

"I must ask you to leave the coach, Lady Montford."

"Why? Who are you?"

"My name is Buchanan. You will come with me, please."

"Not until you explain why," Maddie said, refusing to budge.

But he leaned in and took a tight hold of her arm, hurting her, and pulled her roughly down from the coach.

"How dare you!" Maddie cried, trying to break away from him.

"Milady," Jane wailed.

"Stay where you are or you'll regret it," Buchanan shouted at Jane.

He thrust Maddie into the arms of a ruffian who manhandled her while he tied her wrists with twine. "My husband will see you on the gallows," Maddie said in a fierce hiss, her throat closing in horror. But the man just laughed, showing a wide gap in his teeth. When he finished tying her, Maddie stared up at the box. Another armed man held a gun on Henry and the coachman. The footman lay still on the ground. He was bleeding. *Please God, may he be still alive.* Maddie drew in a sharp trembling breath, appalled. "What do you want with me?"

Buchanan wrote something on a piece of paper. "It's not you I want, Lady Montford. It's your husband, and you will help me get him."

He stepped up to the open door of the coach and thrust the paper into Jane's shaking hands. "I'm sending you back. Make sure Lord Montford gets this note."

Jane just stared at him, her fingers closing tight over the paper.

He reached in and took her arm, shaking her hard. "Did you hear what I said, woman?"

Her eyes wild, Jane nodded.

Buchanan jumped down. He signaled to his man, who stepped forward and gestured with his gun to the coachman. "Return to Montford Court." While Henry stared worryingly back at her, the coach with Jane inside took off down the road.

Maddie felt abandoned and afraid. The foul-smelling man who had tied her hands hoisted her up onto his horse and settled her before him. He turned his horse's head and rode in the opposite direction from the coach, the other man and Buchanan following. Maddie gasped at the pain from his rough handling. "Where are you taking me?"

"You'll find out soon enough." He pinched her thigh, hard. "So shut your trap."

His eyes stared into hers, cruel and uncaring. His breath was so foul she turned her head away and looked at the road through a blur of tears, praying someone would come along who would help her.

Chapter Twenty-Three

HART SAT IN his study, holding a letter which arrived in this morning's post. He read the same line several times without taking it in and, in the end, put it down. His unsettled thoughts focused on Maddie, her face at the coach window as it pulled away. She reminded him of a wild bird you might tame for a time and then wished to be set free. And no matter how much he wanted it, he could never penetrate that part of herself which she kept from him. Would it have been this way if the circumstances of their first meeting had been different? While he did not know the reason, there had been a definite change in her. She had slowly withdrawn from him since they came to London. He feared she was content to leave him, and his heart yearned for her. He had never known such love. It made him vulnerable, and he wasn't sure he could live without her. In such a short space of time, Maddie had become everything to him.

As soon as he was able, he would go to Pembury and try to regain those heady earlier days of their marriage. Had she been in love with him then? Fool that he was when he failed to realize the depth of his feelings for her. And now, when he wanted to be the best he could be for her, and earn her love and trust, was that even possible?

The knocker banged and Crispin went to open the door. Hart heard a man's voice and went out into the corridor.

Lord Telford stood in the hall. "Sorry to disturb you, milord. I wanted to alert you. I saw that fellow again when I went to the stables for my early morning ride. He talked to your staff. When he saw me, he ran off. There was no sign of him when I returned later from Rotten Row. But I considered it prudent to advise you of it."

"I am grateful you have, sir," Hart said. "I will question my stable boy. Thank you for alerting me."

Telford turned away at the door. "Just as well to investigate," he said. "I hope it's nothing to concern you."

Hart went immediately to the stables in the lane behind the house where the stable boy swept out the stalls. When he questioned him, the boy shrugged. "I didn't 'ear what e' said, milord, e' spoke to old Pratchett. But the coachman didn't see fit to tell the likes of me."

Returning to the house, Hart deliberated whether to ride after the coach. Was he making too much of it? Devil take it. He couldn't risk ignoring it, not with Maddie involved. He called for his valet and ran upstairs to change into his riding clothes.

When he came down, Crispin had admitted Boyle, who waited in the hall. He hurried across to Hart. "I saw the fellow this morning, milord. I gave chase but lost him in the crowds in Piccadilly."

Hart cursed. "The coach is on its way to Pembury with Lady Montford. I'm about to ride after it. I'd like you to come with me."

"Happy to, if you'll just lend me a horse, milord. I have my gun."

"Good man."

A short time later, they rode through the busy London streets and out on the road to Tunbridge Wells. Not long afterward, they rode through green fields. If they pushed their horses, Hart expected to catch up with the coach not far along the road well before they reached Tunbridge Wells.

He had not expected to see his coach rounding a bend driving furiously toward him, the coachman, Pratchett, cracking the whip with Henry beside him on the box. Pratchett saw Hart riding toward him and pulled on the reins. The horses, snorting and sweating, came to a stop.

Hart dismounted and ran over to the coach. His heart pounding in his ears, a distressed Jane was inside tending to his wounded footman. But no Maddie.

Fear ripped through him as he pulled open the coach door. "Where the devil is Lady Montford? And what's happened to William?"

"They shot poor William, milord. And one of them took milady away on his horse. They told me to give you this." Jane held a note out to him in a trembling hand.

Hart read it. "Buchanan has my wife." Hart bit back a frustrated growl. "He wants me to come to his hunting box in Godden Green, a mile from Seven Oaks. Alone. If I don't, he will kill her."

"We'd best get after him, milord," Boyle said.

Henry looked grim. "They rode out of nowhere and took us by surprise. Shot William, milord, before he could raise his shotgun."

"Take him to Montford Court, and have my butler call a surgeon."

"Yes, milord."

"How many men were with Buchanan?"

"Two as well as he."

"Not such bad odds," Boyle said.

"My lord, please save Lady Montford," Jane cried, crushing a bunched handkerchief in her hand.

"I will, Jane."

Life wouldn't be worth living if he lost Maddie. So this was love, the kind the poets spoke of. Had it come too late for him to tell her how much he loved her? "We have the element of surprise," he said to Boyle. "Buchanan would expect me to come alone, and we'll arrive sooner than he anticipates."

As he and Boyle pushed their mounts into a gallop, Hart calmed himself with the thought that Buchanan wouldn't kill Maddie while she was useful to him. He would find her and bring her safely home.

Close to an hour later, they reined in atop a hill. He and Boyle looked down on the roof of the hunting lodge. Trees, which would provide handy cover as they approached, bordered three sides of the lodge. Green painted shutters were closed over all but a few windows.

Hart directed Boyle to the trees on the east side of the house while he made his way warily to a copse near the front. When he settled into position, a man walked close to where Boyle hid. As he passed, Boyle crept up behind him. Hart saw the man fall. Boyle then dragged him into the bushes.

Hart stepped out and gestured to Boyle to follow him. He had seen an unshuttered window and hoped to gain entry to the house that way.

Boyle nodded and moved stealthily across to him.

Hart edged closer and peered through the window, finding the dining room empty. "It's locked, curse it. Can you jimmy up the window with your knife?"

Boyle had it open within minutes.

"I'll go in. You stay out of sight near the front door," Hart said. He climbed over the windowsill into the room. A thick rug muffled his footsteps as he ran over to the door. He could hear Maddie's and Buchanan's voices in the next room, but not what was said. Murderous anger tightened his chest, and he took a deep breath to steady himself. Then he opened the door a crack.

They were in the parlor before the unlit fire. On a straight-backed chair, Maddie twisted her hands tied behind her, fighting to free them, while Buchanan, seated on the sofa opposite, smoked a cheroot.

"You'll only chaff your wrists doing that, Lady Montford. And your husband won't be here for an hour or more."

"And when he comes, he will kill you," Maddie said fiercely.

"My men will cut him down before he reaches the house. After which, I'm not sure it would be wise to let you go."

Maddie dropped her head and grew still.

His other henchman stood at the window. "I don't see Charlie out there on the drive, Lord Buchanan."

"He must be there, Tom. Charlie might be beetle-headed, but he wouldn't wander off. He'll be hiding in the trees. Find him. Tell him to stay hidden until Montford turns up. Then he knows what to do."

Tom opened the front door and called to Charlie. He turned around. "He doesn't answer, my lord."

"Get out there. What are you afraid of, you lily-livered fool?"

Tom ventured cautiously from the house.

Once he had gone outside, Hart entered the room. He leveled his gun at Buchanan. "Get up, Buchanan, and be careful about it."

Buchanan swung round in surprise. He threw down his cheroot. "How did you…"

Maddie's eyes, stark with fear, begged him to be careful.

"Untie her," Hart ordered, his voice an angry growl. "Do it fast, if you don't wish to see your brains splattered over the sofa."

Buchanan slowly rose. "I have two men outside, Montford, and several more on the way here."

They heard the rush of footsteps on the drive and panicked breathing. A scuffle, then silence.

"There's no way you can escape," Buchanan said. "Charlie! Tom!" he yelled. "My men are coming. You can't kill us all."

"I'm afraid you've misplaced those who do your dirty work, Buchanan. You are on your own." He glanced at the door. Where in God's name was Boyle?

As Buchanan untied Maddie's hands, he pulled a knife from inside his coat and shoved her in front of him, pressing the blade against her throat. "I'm walking out of here. If you want her ladyship to live, you won't stop me." His hideous whisper struck fear through Hart as he watched him walk backwards toward the door, using Maddie as a shield.

Hart's heart almost stopped beating as Hart watched Maddie, her eyes desperate, edge closer to the door. Where was Boyle? Hart wondered who survived that fight. If it was Boyle, why wasn't he here? Ice threaded through Hart's veins. He had to stop Buchanan from taking Maddie outside.

Buchanan stood by the door. "Drop your gun, Montford. I won't hesitate to kill your wife if you cross me."

He was a tall man. Maddie's head barely came up to his chin. Hart had only one chance. Steadying his hand with a deep breath, Hart raised the gun and fired.

Buchanan's knife slid away over the carpet as he crumpled to the ground, shot through the forehead.

"Hart!" Maddie rushed into his arms. She collapsed against him, clinging to his coat. "I knew you would come. It was the one thing that kept me from breaking down."

"He can't hurt us anymore, Maddie." He eased her away and gazed into her face. "Are you all right? Stay here. I must go out and see what's happened to Boyle."

"No. I'm not leaving you."

"Keep behind me."

The man Buchanan called Charlie lay on the ground outside the house. He was dead, a knife in his chest. Boyle lay slumped half under him.

Hart ran over to them. He rolled Charlie's body off Boyle and knelt down. The runner was unconscious, but Hart could find no evidence of a wound. He shook him. "Boyle!"

Boyle opened his eyes and his bleary expression cleared. "Milord?"

Hart helped him sit up. "What happened?"

Boyle gave a weak chuckle and rubbed his head. "As he fell, he pulled me down with him. I must have hit my head on the step."

Rubbing his head, Boyle climbed to his feet.

"Maddie," Hart said, "I'd like you to meet Mr. Boyle. The first-rate Bow Street Runner I engaged."

Maddie held out her hand. "I am glad you were here, Mr. Boyle."

Boyle shook it. "I'm mighty pleased to find you unharmed, Lady Montford."

"Buchanan is dead," Hart said. Oddly, he felt no remorse at taking a life. Not after the man threatened Maddie. "We'll have to advise the magistrate in Seven Oaks before we return to London."

When Boyle went to retrieve their horses, Hart turned to Maddie and pulled her into his arms. His hand on the back of her head, he murmured, "My love. I couldn't have borne it if I'd lost you." With a moan, he crushed his lips to hers.

Maddie threw her arms around him, and for several minutes, they kissed as if they couldn't bear to part.

"I love you, Hart," she said. When they finally drew apart, her eyes filled with tears.

"I adore you, Maddie. You are my life."

Hart hugged her to his side as they walked to the stables to find a mount and a suitable saddle for her. "I'd give anything for you not to have gone through that."

"I'm perfectly all right, Hart. Now that you are here."

With a sharp intake of breath, Hart kissed her again, pulling her hard against him. "Maddie, my brave love," he murmured against her lips.

A discreet cough drew them apart as Boyle rode up, leading the other horse by the rein. "I'll see you in Seven Oaks, milord."

Boyle turned his horse's head and rode away.

"He's a good man," Maddie said, watching him disappear at the top of the drive.

"A splendid fellow."

Hart saddled a horse and assisted Maddie to mount. "We can hire a vehicle in Seven Oaks to take us to London. I know you are tired. We could stay at an inn for the night."

"With no baggage? What will the innkeeper think?"

Hart laughed. "That you are a fallen woman."

"Let's stay the night then, Hart," Maddie said with a grin. "I rather fancy that."

AT THE MAGISTRATE'S rooms on the London Road, Hart, Maddie, and Boyle told Mr. Grosvenor of their kidnapping and their escape, which left two men dead. Grosvenor agreed to send a constable to the hunting lodge and write to Sir Joshua Fleming.

Hart then handed over the smuggler's horse and left his mount in the local stables.

Boyle joined them for a meal at the old whitewashed inn, The Oak Tavern, on the high street. Then he departed to ride back to London, intending to join in the hunt for the remaining members of Buchanan's gang still at large.

Hart engaged a bedchamber, explaining that they had no luggage because their carriage met with an accident. When it was accepted without question, they retired early.

As he shut the door, Maddie laughed. "You made us sound too respectable. Like an old married couple."

He took her in his arms. "Well, aren't we?

Her eyes gazed into his. "One day, if God wills it, we shall be. What memories we will have to tell our children."

"What indeed." He took her hand and drew Maddie over to the bed. When she sat beside him, he kept a hold of her hand. "Will you tell me what has been troubling you, my love?"

Emotion made it difficult for her to speak. "I have always feared that because of the way we began this marriage, you might…"

He looked puzzled. "Might what?"

Disarmed by his loving manner, she told him all of it. She began with the scandal sheet, which Hart merely dismissed as rubbish few read. "While in the ladies' retiring room at the Beauchamps' ball," she continued, "I overheard two women speaking of Mrs. Spencer. One of them said the widow intended to become your mistress."

"Mrs. Spencer?" Hart's eyebrows rose. "That's nonsense."

Maddie felt foolish. Aware she sounded like a jealous woman, she persisted. "You and Mrs. Spender might have been lovers before we met. I am not prudish, Hart, a man like you would have lovers, it's just that I couldn't bear it if you continued to do so." Her words, so long held inside, tumbled out. "Men do, I understand that, but I am not like those women who look the other way." She glanced up at him to gauge his reaction. He was smiling and shaking his head. "I cannot live like that, Hart," she rushed on. "I need to love and respect my husband and to know he feels the same." She brushed back her hair, aware of how untidy she must look. "Am I being unreasonable? Because if I am, I shall retire somewhere and live alone."

Hart laughed and put his arm around her, squeezing her tight. Then he sobered. "Maddie. I have no intention of taking a mistress."

"Never?"

"Never."

"But because of that scandal sheet, most of society is aware our marriage was not a love match, and they expect to see us live as many of the *ton* do, seeking pleasure elsewhere."

"Then we shall show them otherwise."

"How?" she asked as hope rose in her breast.

"At the very next ball, we shall waltz together."

"I haven't seen a husband dancing with his wife," she said. "Do they? Isn't it bad *ton* to show too much affection for your spouse?"

"It is my intention to waltz with you. I want them all to know how much I love you. And I want to tell you about my life when my mother was alive. Then you will understand why I have no intention of ever straying from your side."

"I'd love to hear it. Although it will tug at my heart."

"Then I shall tell you all of it. But later," he said, passion in his eyes as he drew Maddie down on the bed and kissed her.

She nuzzled her face against his, then kissed his chin and his eyelids, her hand sliding into his hair and tugging it.

He laughed as he kissed her. She closed her eyes and for a while there were only the murmurs they made.

Hart stroked her hair. He pressed kisses over her neck, telling her how much he loved her, how essential she was to his happiness.

Maddie's body was on fire with yearning for him. She undid the buttons on his breeches, and when his erection leaped free, she ran her hand over it, marveling at its strength and softness. Hart groaned and took her hand, guiding her, showing her how to pleasure him.

The longing to have him inside her became so urgent she hitched up her skirts and climbed on top of him on the bed. Hart groaned and helped her settle her thighs over his hips. Maddie sank down on him. She moaned at the intense pleasure as Hart pulled down her bodice to free her breasts and shaped them with his hands, thumbing her nipples.

Joining with him was so utterly perfect she could only gaze into his slumberous eyes as she moved until passion swept her away. Her movements quickened as she sought her release. With Hart's loud moan, they came together.

As their breaths slowed, they lay with their arms and legs entangled, unwilling to part. "Do you think we were overheard?" she breathlessly asked Hart.

"If we were, they will only have expected it," Hart said with a grin. "The innkeeper winked at me when you turned away to climb the stairs."

"Oh!" Maddie giggled. "You beast!" She attempted to move away.

Hart held her in his arms. "You, my lady wife, are going nowhere."

She smiled and rested her head against his chest. She closed her eyes. Then they flew open. She still had her shoes on. She sighed. She couldn't fight sleep any longer.

Maddie had no notion of how long she slept. They had woken during the night to undress and climb between the sheets. As their naked bodies came together, Hart made exquisitely slow and gentle love to her before they slept again.

She gazed into the dark, aware of her body, which seemed light, as if her bones and flesh had little weight and barely pressed into the mattress. Amazingly free, she stretched out her spine, careful not to wake him, then prodded her mind like one might a sore tooth to be sure she had overlooked nothing. Did something dire lurk there she might have missed? But there was nothing, only an all-encompassing happiness which spread through her like a ray of sunshine. Hart loved her. The source of her happiness lay with his back to her. The blankets had fallen away, and she studied his naked back, his light olive-toned skin warm and smooth over his muscles, his ribs, his hip bones, his rounded backside. She curled her fingers, wanting to trace them down his spine, but resisted. Then, snuggling close to him, she nestled into his warmth and slept again.

Chapter Twenty-Four

THE SHERRINGHAMS' SPRING ball was the last of the Season before the heat of summer made London intolerable and sent the *ton* to their country retreats.

Hart thought Maddie looked especially lovely in a white gown with lavish pink embroidery on the hem and sleeves. A circlet of pink roses dressed her hair.

They made their way through the crowded ballroom. Guests greeted them, while others merely observed them, and Hart felt Maddie's hand tense on his arm.

Hart met Vivian Spencer's flirtatious smile with a cool nod. As they moved farther into the ballroom, their circle of friends closed around them, and Maddie relaxed. She danced the quadrille with Tate while Hart partnered Ianthe.

When the waltz was called, Hart escorted Maddie onto the floor. She lifted her head closer to his. "Are we about to shock the *ton?*"

"Impossible. The scandals they've seen have made them inured to most things. A husband dancing with his wife? Not worthy of the scandal sheets."

"I'm relieved. I never wanted to be seen as outrageous."

"Are you sure? What about that red gown?"

"It was claret-colored." Maddie laughed. "Well, perhaps a little."

The music rose as Hayden's exquisite music filled the ballroom.

Hart swept her out onto the floor as their eyes met.

"I longed for this," Maddie said. "The second time I met you."

He cocked an eyebrow. "Not the first time?"

"No. You were stuffy and condemning. You suggested I was a poor rider who had recklessly put Pearl over that hedge."

"I quickly realized how wrong I was when I saw how skillful you were on Pearl. But the first time for me was when you wore those breeches."

Maddie laughed. "I noticed you were a little distracted."

"Shameless. You had little idea of the effect they had on me." He shook his head with a grin. "Will you promise to wear them at Pembury?"

Her eyes danced. "I might if you behave yourself."

Hart's eyes smoldered. "I might."

He smiled as he settled her closer. "I fell madly in love when I found you sitting on the ground having fallen off Pearl. It took me too long to realize it. But learning of that cut strap and the urgency to rescue you from your uncle clouded my mind, and I never realized my true intention. While I worked to save you, I didn't realize the extent of my feelings. I wanted so much to marry you, I was afraid you might refuse me after I put the proposal in less than romantic terms. Forgive me?"

"I did long ago." She touched the hair at his nape with her gloved fingers. "I can't remember when I didn't love you. I think I must have always."

They suddenly became aware the music had stopped, and the dancers left the floor. Those around the edge of the dance floor watched with amusement.

Hart leaned down to press a brief kiss on Maddie's lips then took her hand to lead her from the floor.

"Bravo!" came a cry from an elderly man in the crowd. Even the old dowagers who were sticklers for convention smiled their approval.

"A love match," another man said in fake disgust as they passed. "I hope it doesn't become too fashionable. Society will become very dull indeed."

>>>≫≪<<<

MADDIE FELT SUCH joy tonight, surrounded by their good friends. Before she'd given much thought to it, she'd promised to hold a house party at Pembury before Christmas. She then panicked, thinking of the state of the old mansion, but she'd come to realize how strong and capable she was.

When at the end of the week, they arrived at Pembury, Maddie looked around in amazement at the freshly painted reception rooms and the fashionably decorated bedchambers. The drawing room was almost unrecognizable from when she'd visited here with her uncle. The exquisite old furniture buffed to a high shine, the air scented with beeswax.

Maddie met the staff and was pleased to see some of her uncle's servants had been hired.

Hart had to deal with estate matters, but came to find her where she examined the glorious crimson damask curtains at the dining room windows. "Are you pleased with the improvements?"

"It has been done in the very best taste. Remarkable, when there was no lady in the house to advise them."

"Many letters passed between my steward and Diane. I think it's a triumph."

"It is. I must write to Diane and ask her down."

"Yes, she will be eager to see it. Will you join me for a ride this afternoon?"

"I am going to see Pearl in a moment." She put a hand on his arm. "Before you go, I forgot to tell you about Jane and Henry."

"What about them?"

"They are married."

"What? When?"

"The same as us at the Marriage House."

Hart's eyebrows rose. "They kept that a close secret."

"I have known for a little while, but yes, they did. Jane is pregnant, Hart. I would like to find suitable accommodation for them."

Hart thought for a moment. "I can offer them a small cottage on the grounds. But it would be impossible for Jane to remain your maid."

"I shall have to advertise for another lady's maid. Jane will want to be with her baby."

"Old Pritchett will be retiring soon, and I'll need a new coachman. I'll ask Henry to take over the running of the stables. He has proved he is capable and loyal."

She kissed him. "Thank you, darling."

"I must go. I'll see you at three o'clock at the stables."

Maddie watched him cross the room. He had told her about his childhood. It had made her cry. To think of him as a young boy having lost his mother he dearly loved and tried to protect from his father's bad temper, then to be sent away to school. That would never happen to their son. Hart wouldn't allow it, and neither would she. They would employ a tutor for him until he was of an age to wish for the companionship of other boys.

She went in search of Jane to tell her. The maid was in her dressing room, unpacking Maddie's trunk. Her round stomach was obvious to Maddie, probably because she knew. She told Jane about her and Hart's plans for them. Her maid's gratitude warmed her. "I will miss you, Jane. You weren't just a wonderful maid, we went through so much together. I think of you as a friend."

Jane's eyes widened. "I will miss looking after you, milady." She fought a smile, and then gave in to it. "A cottage of our very own? I can grow vegetables and have chickens, and even a pig. It will be like living on the farm again."

"Yes, but this farm is yours, Jane. No one will ever take it away from you."

Jane burst into tears and searched frantically for her handkerchief. "I can't wait to speak to Henry."

"Go now, the clothes will wait."

"May I, milady?"

"Yes, go."

Alone in the grand bedchamber, Maddie went to the window. She looked out over the gardens, restored to their former beauty. In the distance, she could see Hart riding out with the estate manager, a hound, which could only be Rasputin, running behind. Life here would be perfect, especially if they had a baby to make it complete. That hadn't happened, but she remained hopeful. When she was blessed with so much, she shouldn't wish for more. But the desire for a child remained as strong as ever.

Epilogue

Lilybrook Cottage, September

THE EARLY FOG had cleared, the sky now a clear blue-gray arch overhead as the coach turned into the driveway, now devoid of potholes. Their coachman pulled the horses up outside the small cottage. The leaves of the graceful chestnut tree had turned golden brown, and the air was crisp.

Hart opened the door and jumped to the ground, beating the footman by a whisker. He put down the steps and offered Maddie his hand.

"Well, what do you think, sweetheart?"

Maddie stepped down carefully, always aware of the precious baby she carried in these first vulnerable months. She stood back, shading her eyes with a hand, and looked at the freshly whitewashed dwelling. "It looks like a storybook house with its rustic charm."

Hart planned to lease it, but she secretly wished to one day bring their son here. Maddie put a hand to her stomach. She knew she carried a boy. She could see him riding over those hills on his pony. Strangely, it wasn't the frightening experience she and Jane had suffered here that stayed with her. It was how her short time here had restored her confidence after her uncle had made her doubt herself. Performing the simple tasks of cooking and growing vegetables, she learned she could manage well with very little and be content.

"The caretaker I hired must be here somewhere," Hart said, looking around.

A red-haired man walked toward them with a smile.

Maddie cried his name and hurried to him. "Jack! Is it really you?"

Her parents' former groom who had saved Pearl and brought the mare to her smiled and nodded. "It is me, my lady."

"But how…"

"You told me you wanted to find Jack, Maddie," Hart said. "So I had my steward look for him."

Jack grinned. "He found me working for Lord Summerton. But as he was about to let some of his staff go, here I am."

"Jack is to become a groom at Pembury," Hart said.

"I can't be more pleased," Maddie said, casting a warm, grateful smile at her thoughtful husband. "Father would be pleased too."

Jack frowned. "About that, my lady. Didn't like to tell you at the time because you'd suffered the loss of your parents. But now that his lordship tells me your uncle is dead, I feel I can speak up."

"What is it, Jack?" Maddie's heart thumped wildly.

"Your uncle came to see your father some weeks before their carriage accident, did he not?"

Maddie nodded. "Yes, he did."

"I went back later and examined the carriage. It confirmed my suspicions. That drive shaft was tampered with."

Maddie put a hand to her chest. "You think my parents were murdered?"

"Perhaps it isn't wise to speak of this now…" Hart began.

"I want to hear it, Hart," Maddie said.

Jack glanced at Hart, who nodded. "I think there's little doubt of it," he continued. "I wanted to tell the parish constable, but I had to leave the area to search for work and keep body and soul together. And I didn't have any proof, so I doubted they'd believe the likes of me against your uncle."

Maddie gasped. "I believe it to be true, Jack. My uncle was an evil man. I am glad you told me." She had long wondered about the accident. She could make little sense of it because her father was a stickler for keeping his vehicles in top order.

As Jack walked away, Maddie gazed up at Hart. "Thank you, darling. This means a lot to me."

"Then I'm glad, Maddie. I wasn't sure I should dredge up the past. I wondered if it should remain buried."

"No, I am glad you did, Hart."

They wandered hand in hand through the gardens, which had become a colorful autumn display. Returning to the house, Mrs. Fletcher hurried down the drive, carrying a bunch of lilies.

Maddie went to meet her with Hart following. "How good to see you, Mrs. Fletcher."

"And I you, Miss Burrell." She held out the flowers. "I suppose you stayed away while they completed the renovations. It is nice to see you here again."

Maddie took the lilies with a nod of thanks. "I am Lady Montford now, Mrs. Burrell. I'd like to introduce you to my husband, Lord Montford."

"Oh, my goodness." The farmer's wife sank into a low curtsey.

Hart took her hand with a smile. "No need for that, Mrs. Fletcher. I want to take this opportunity to thank you for your assistance to my wife."

"It was nothing, my lord," the flustered lady said. "I mustn't keep you. Shall you be living here then?"

"No," Maddie answered her. "But we shall keep the cottage and visit it sometimes. It means a lot to me."

Mrs. Fletcher looked at her keenly, scenting a romantic interlude. "Yes, of course. Then we might see you here again."

She turned and walked away up the drive.

"I'm afraid I have flummoxed her," Maddie said.

"No, I think you have made her day. I foresee some tasty gossip in the church group."

Maddie laughed. "You are unkind. I'll go up and inspect the bedchambers. Then we must return to Pembury. Diane and Peter and the children arrive tomorrow and there's much to be done."

"That's what we have a housekeeper for." Hart slipped an arm around her. "Those steps are steep. I'll come with you."

She reached up and touched his cheek. "Don't fuss."

Hart gave her an exasperated yet indulgent look. "Maddie, I know you like to remain as independent as possible, but you must allow me to care for you now that you carry our precious daughter."

"Daughter?" Maddie put a hand to her stomach. "This is our son. And I know he will be as handsome and strong as his father."

Hart smiled. "We shall see, my love." He took her hand and kissed it then followed her up the stairs.

ABOUT THE AUTHOR

A USA TODAY bestselling author of Regency romances, with over 35 books published, Maggi's Regency series are International bestsellers. Stay tuned for Maggi's latest Regency series out next year. Her novels include Victorian mysteries, contemporary romantic suspense and young adult. Maggi holds a BA in English and Master of Arts Degree in Creative Writing. She supports the RSPCA and animals often feature in her books.

Like to keep abreast of my latest news? Join my newsletter.
http://bit.ly/1m70lJJ

Blog: http://bit.ly/1t7B5dx
Find excerpts and reviews on my website: http://bit.ly/1m70lJJ
Twitter: @maggiandersen: http://bit.ly/1Aq8eHg
Facebook: Maggi Andersen Author: http://on.fb.me/1KiyP9g
Goodreads: http://bit.ly/1TApe0A
Pinterest: https://www.pinterest.com.au/maggiandersen

Maggi's Amazon page for her books with Dragonblade Publishing.
https://tinyurl.com/y34dmquj

Printed in Great Britain
by Amazon

25590064R00136